Soren

Vampire's Mate Book Two

Grae Bryan

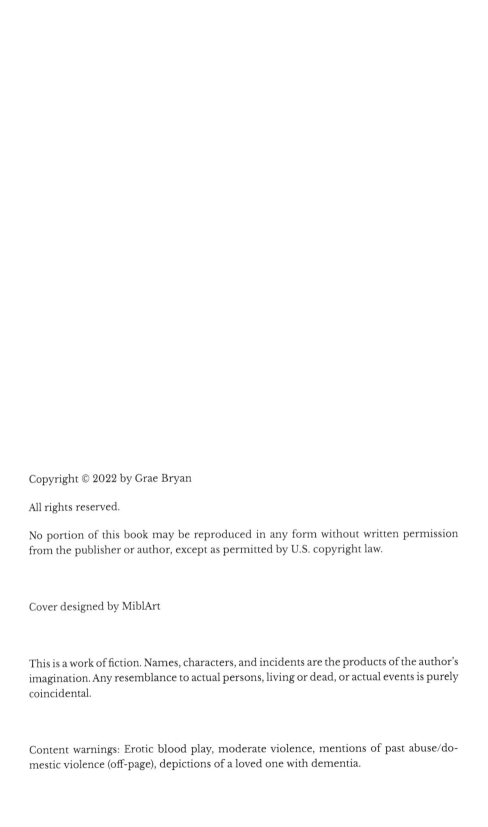

Contents

Prologue

Gabe

There were a lot of things Gabe found awkward—witnessing other people's PDA, being forced to mediate the family drama of his patients, spotting for strangers at the gym—but morning-afters had to be some of his least favorites.

"So"—Jessie leaned against her car door, seemingly in no rush to actually use it, her green eyes sparkling with mischief—"we gonna do this again sometime?"

"Um..." Gabe ran a hand through his dark-brown curls. Fuck. He hated this part. He hadn't wanted to do breakfast at all, but she'd been there, at his apartment, and he'd felt like an asshole just kicking her out, so he'd suggested grabbing something to eat. He'd asked to take separate cars, claiming he had something to do afterward. He supposed he could make that a true statement by stopping by Danny's on the way back home.

His little brother had been acting strangely lately. And that guy Roman he'd been hanging around with... Gabe didn't like it. Didn't like *him*.

Jessie smirked at his hesitation. "Uh-oh. Don't tell me. One-time thing?"

Gabe bit his lip, giving her a sheepish smile. "It's not you, it's me?"

He shouldn't have slept with her. She was nice enough, sure. They'd had classes together in high school, and he'd always thought she was cool—funny, smart, totally hot. But really he'd just been looking for some stress relief, and she'd been in the right place at the right time to provide it.

Jessie laughed at him, her good humor proving she was too good for him in the first place. "No worries, King. I know your reputation."

"Uh. Reputation?"

But Gabe didn't get a chance to find out what his reputation might be because the next thing he knew, he was facedown on the pavement, Jessie was screaming, and his arm was being held behind his back at a painful angle.

"Hello, Gabriel." Gabe didn't recognize the voice—deep and raspy, with a hint of an accent.

He tried to struggle out of the man's hold, but his grip was like iron. Gabe didn't manage even an inch of leeway.

"Do I know you?" Gabe finally grunted, giving up his efforts.

The man holding him down chuckled. It wasn't a nice sound. "I wanted to send my regards to Roman and his little human toy. Be a good big brother and pass along the message, won't you?"

That was...what? Gabe had questions, so many questions, but before he could voice them, he heard a crack and then...

Pain. Searing pain.

Gabe screamed. His arm. The man had *broken his fucking arm.*

He was flipped onto his back before he could even attempt to catch his breath. He stared up at—at what?

The stranger looked like a man, more or less—one with a handsome face, his dark hair grayed slightly at the temples. But his eyes were terrifying—fully black, not even a hint of white around the edges.

A monster's eyes.

He smiled down at Gabe, and a pair of honest-to-God fangs glistened in the morning light.

Gabe whimpered. He hadn't even known he *could* whimper. "What—what the fuck?"

In answer, the man bent his head down, and the pain in Gabe's arm was forgotten in favor of the sharp, unbearable burning at his neck. The man was *biting* him. And it fucking *hurt.*

Gabe didn't have a chance to scream again. As soon as it had started, it was over. He heard a growl, snarling sounds, and then the monster was gone, Gabe's injured body dropped unceremoniously on the pavement.

He blinked up at the cloudless sky.

What the fuck had just happened?

He flinched as a shadow loomed over him. But it wasn't the terrifying man from a moment ago. Gabe knew this man. Blond hair, pale-blue eyes. A face so beautiful it almost hurt to look at.

Roman's little friend. *Soren.*

For once, the fucker wasn't smiling that disconcerting smile; instead, Soren's golden brows were drawn together in concern as he knelt on the ground beside him.

Gabe didn't know why, when Soren usually left him feeling so unsettled, the man's presence now felt like a soothing balm.

Still, he couldn't help but cry out as Soren picked him up by the shoulders, gently placing Gabe's upper half in his lap. Fuck. For a man who looked so delicate, he certainly was strong.

"Don't freak out," Soren murmured.

And then he...*changed.*

Soren's pupils expanded, the black covering first the pale blue and then the whites of his eyes. His incisors sharpened, lengthening into fangs that poked out from full pink lips.

Gabe held back a scream, trying to struggle out of Soren's hold, but the attempt at movement sent searing pain shooting down his arm.

What the fuck was happening?

He found himself whimpering again, to his mortification.

"Shh." Soren used both hands to hold Gabe's head still, forcing him to meet his unnatural-looking eyes. "You're okay," Soren said firmly. "You're safe. I won't hurt you. You're not afraid of me."

And, looking into that endless black, Gabe suddenly...wasn't.

He knew somewhere in the back of his mind that he should be. But that rush of fear was replaced with an unnatural calm.

Soren wouldn't harm him. Still...

"I hurt," Gabe whispered. "Everything hurts."

"No," Soren said, his thumbs rubbing soft circles onto Gabe's cheeks. "You don't hurt anymore. You're not feeling any pain. None at all."

And just like that, the pain faded. Gabe sighed in relief, staring up at the face looking down at him, his brain skipping right over the more alarming details. He saw delicate features, sharp cheekbones, soft-looking pale skin.

Soren was...

"So beautiful," Gabe murmured, reaching up a hand to touch the pretty man.

Soren's eyes widened in surprise, his lips twitching. "None of that." He pushed Gabe's hand down. "We need to heal you."

He bent over Gabe and started...licking Gabe's face? He seemed to be aiming for all the injured spots, his tongue softly touching all the abrasions Gabe had received from the pavement.

Gabe laughed when Soren reached the bite on his neck. "Tickles."

Soren ignored Gabe's protest, continuing his ministrations. Gabe wasn't sure, but he thought he heard Soren mumble something like, "Why do you taste so good?"

But that couldn't be right. Gabe's neck was covered in blood. And blood had to taste...gross. Right?

Gabe wasn't sure how many minutes passed like that, his mind a blissful haze while Soren lapped at his injured skin. Eventually, Soren lifted his head, looking down at him with an inscrutable expression. "I fixed what I can, but the arm is beyond me."

Gabe had forgotten his arm was even broken. How strange.

"We have to get you to the hospital," Soren told him.

"Maybe they'll give me an employee discount." Gabe laughed again. He knew the situation wasn't actually funny, but he was having a hard time accessing the fear and anxiety he knew he should be feeling.

He let Soren half carry, half drag him to his car and drive him to the hospital.

Hours later, the nurse pushed pain medication through Gabe's IV, and everything changed again. The calm he'd been feeling fled, and the fear from before returned tenfold.

Gabe's heart raced, his palms growing damp with sweat. He turned his head slowly to the blond man next to him—Soren hadn't left his side, not for a moment—who was holding himself with an unnatural stillness, his pale gaze meeting Gabe's.

Soren's eyes were blue again, his teeth their normal size. But his expression was wary, as if he was waiting on Gabe's reaction, and Gabe knew he hadn't imagined what he'd seen earlier.

"What— Who—" Gabe had trouble finding the words.

"Gabe—" Soren started.

But Gabe knew this trick. If Soren started talking, he was going to fool Gabe again. Convince him everything was okay. Trick him into believing whatever he wanted.

"Monster," Gabe accused, not caring that his voice was too loud. "You... That guy. You're fucking *monsters*. Get out."

"Gabe," Soren said again.

"Get. The fuck. Out of here." Gabe couldn't think. He couldn't breathe. What the fuck was going on? "Get out!" he shouted again.

He saw the nurse talking to a security guard. Gabe didn't care. He just needed the other man gone. He needed to get rid of this new, unknowable threat.

Soren wasn't safe.

Then why had Gabe felt that way in his arms? Even before Soren had used his weird voodoo on him, Gabe had felt...soothed. Secure. Was that all a lie?

It didn't matter. Soren left soon after, the hospital staff kicking him out for agitating their patient. Gabe didn't miss the hurt look on the blond man's face. But what did that look even mean?

The man wasn't even a man. He wasn't human.

Soren couldn't really care.

One

Gabe

One year later

"Dearest, darlingest, most bestest brother of mine."

Gabe looked up from his plate, narrowing his eyes at his younger brother across the table. Danny had many nicknames for him. "Golden boy." "Jerk." "Asshole." But "dearest, darlingest, most bestest brother of mine" definitely wasn't one of them.

"I have a favor to ask you," Danny said, his big brown eyes all wide and hopeful.

Gabe swallowed his bite of chicken carefully, unease growing in his gut. "Okay..."

"See, Roman and I have decided to have a proper honeymoon."

Gabe's eyes darted reflexively to their other dinner companion, Danny's husband, whose bright-blue eyes were focused on Gabe in a way that was definitely intended to say, "Don't fuck this up for me."

Gabe ignored him easily enough. He was used to Roman glaring at him.

He turned back to his brother with a smile. "That's great, Danny Boy."

Danny nodded, grinning wide, his freckled cheeks pink. "It is. Super great. We're, um, spending three weeks in Bali."

"*Three weeks?*" Gabe's brows lifted. A little over a year ago, his brother would barely take a full weekend off, working way too many nights in a row as a nurse in their town's ER. Gabe worked as a doctor in the same hospital, and he'd hardly ever had a shift without his brother's face popping up at some point. Danny had reduced to two shifts a week since settling down with Roman, but he'd still never taken any sort of significant vacation.

"Three weeks," Roman confirmed in a tone that just begged Gabe to make a fuss over it.

Gabe would never. Not anymore. He was done getting in Danny's way. He wanted his brother to have...well, whatever the fuck he wanted. "Okay. That's still...great? Good for you, kiddo."

Gabe couldn't even be jealous of their vacation. Not really. Danny deserved it. Gabe hadn't realized until he'd finally seen his brother happy just how *unhappy* he'd been before.

And how much of that was your fault? Gabe pushed the thought aside. Guilt was such a familiar feeling for him he barely recognized it anymore.

Danny was still looking at Gabe as if this had anything to do with him. "Yes. But the thing is—I was hoping—"

"We need you to watch the mutt." Trust Roman to make a request sound more like a command.

"The mutt," Gabe repeated.

The mutt in question, a six-month-old blue heeler mix, was currently lying under the kitchen table, nosing at Gabe's feet, clearly hoping for some dinner scraps to drop down from above.

Gabe would have been offended on the puppy's behalf if he didn't know for a fact that Roman had chosen the dog himself, gifted it to his pet-starved husband, and could often be caught looking at it with a fondness he usually reserved for Danny alone.

"Ferdy's just so young," his brother pleaded. "I don't want him with a sitter. He needs someone he *knows*."

Gabe cleared his throat. "What about your, uh...roommate?"

"Soren?" Danny laughed at the idea.

Gabe controlled his flinch but only barely. He found himself glancing around furtively, as if speaking the name out loud was enough to summon the little monster.

Gabe wouldn't even be surprised if that were true.

"He could help out," Danny offered cautiously. "But I'm not so sure he could be trusted to remember that mortal puppies need to be fed twice a day. Or that they need water. Or bathroom breaks."

Gabe looked over to Roman to see if he was offended by this assessment of his friend, but he was nodding along sagely to Danny's words.

It wasn't really a big ask. Gabe had no problem watching his brother's adorable puppy for a few weeks. "Okay. Yeah. I can take him. I'm sure he won't be able to manage too much destruction in my apartment."

Danny shook his head, shifting in his seat. "Um, but not at your apartment? We were hoping you could stay here, instead."

Gabe raised a brow at his brother.

Danny blushed but stood his ground. "He needs familiar surroundings, Gabe. He's just a—just a *baby*."

Gabe couldn't help but laugh at his brother's overprotectiveness, but it wasn't an unreasonable request. Danny's house was their childhood home. Gabe had grown up there—still had a room that could be considered "his"—it wouldn't exactly be a hardship.

But...

"And Soren will be here too?" he made himself ask.

"Yep." Danny had the grace to look a little nervous at the idea. "Like I said, he can help out. And with Mom too. So you can still visit her while I'm gone?"

Gabe's throat went dry at the thought. He tried to restrain any bitter feelings, but this felt an awful lot like *he* was getting a babysitter, not the puppy. Someone tasked to make sure Gabe wouldn't shirk his...family duties...with Danny away.

"Roman promises Soren will behave."

Gabe looked again at Danny's husband. Tall, imposing, not a strand of his jet-black hair out of place. Roman's expression was neutral enough, but there was a set to his jaw when he looked at Gabe that Gabe didn't love. He knew he wasn't Roman's favorite person. Roman cared fiercely for Gabe's brother, and Gabe had been letting his brother down for far too long.

Then again, Roman wasn't Gabe's favorite either.

The man was a monster. A *literal* monster.

Because Roman was a vampire. A fact Gabe had found out last winter when Roman's ex-friend, Lucien, had attacked him viciously one sunny winter morning.

Of course, Danny was a vampire now too.

But that just wasn't the same, Gabe reasoned. Danny was...Danny. He was still Gabe's little brother, only now with a new...*particular* diet.

And Danny would still be human if Roman hadn't come waltzing into the picture. Roman and his other little vampire friend.

Soren.

Gabe wanted nothing more than to stay far away from that particular monster, but Danny never asked Gabe for anything beyond the bare minimum of brotherly duty.

Gabe couldn't let him down now.

"Sure, Danny Boy," Gabe agreed, ignoring the new twisting in his stomach. "Of course I'll do it."

He even got a small smile from Roman for that before the vampire turned his face to Danny, and the smile grew so big and sappy that Gabe was embarrassed to witness it.

The sound of the front door opening cut through the moment.

Gabe's muscles tensed. There was only one other person who would walk into this house without knocking.

A moment later and there he was. The little monster. Svelte, blond, and unbearably beautiful.

At least that was what Gabe used to think. But Gabe knew what lay under that beauty now. He didn't care how his body reacted to Soren's presence.

He wouldn't be fooled again.

"How cozy," Soren purred, leaning a shoulder against the kitchen doorway, his pale gaze landing immediately on Gabe. "A family dinner."

Gabe's fingers flexed around his fork. Soren was always doing that. Always *looking* at him.

"Want some?" Danny offered, smiling genuinely at the other vampire. Gabe's brother had a fondness for Soren Gabe couldn't even begin to understand. Of course, Soren treated Danny with rare sweetness, whereas he seemed to love nothing more than tormenting Gabe, so that might have something to do with it.

Gabe didn't know why Danny bothered offering. Gabe was the only person at this table who *needed* to eat. The others only did it for—well, for *funsies*, as Danny put it.

"No, thanks, cutie pie. Just ate." Soren ran his tongue over his incisors suggestively.

But that didn't stop him from sauntering over and perching on a seat at the table anyway. "So did His Highness agree?" Soren asked.

Gabe's jaw clenched at the nickname, but Danny answered for him before he could object. "He did. And"—his brother gave Soren a pointed look—"we promised you'd be on your best behavior."

Soren's lips widened into his familiar grin, a manic smile that always managed to send a shiver down Gabe's spine. "When am I not?" the vampire asked innocently.

There was a glint in Soren's eyes that told Gabe he was in major trouble.

Fuck.

Gabe rushed through the rest of his dinner, despite the fact that his appetite had long since disappeared. He needed to get out of that house.

The drive back to his apartment was a blur. For too long, he sat in his car in its parking space, trying to will his stomach into settling. He forced himself to take deep, even breaths.

So...living with a vampire who thrived on torturing him, who could mess with his mind just by looking him in the eyes. With no Danny or even Roman to protect him.

This would be an interesting three weeks.

Gabe could only hope he'd survive them.

Two

Soren

"Stop nosing at that." Soren pulled his yarn away from Ferdy's snout, glaring at the puppy. The little mutt kept thinking Soren's crochet supplies were some sort of dog toy in disguise. Soren was almost done with this top, and if Danny's pet ruined it, Soren was going to be forced to commit doggy murder, and then Danny would be mad at him, and then Roman would murder *Soren* for upsetting Danny, and it would all just be one terrible mess.

He considered flashing his fangs for additional deterrence, but he'd already learned the puppy was completely unfazed by any of them going full vamp in front of him.

It turned out humans were much easier to intimidate than dogs.

"Shoo." Soren motioned with his free hand. "Go find your daddy."

"Am I the mutt's daddy?" Soren glanced up to see Roman leaning against the doorway, looking much too amused at the scene in front of him for Soren's taste.

"No," Soren replied, narrowing his eyes at his longtime friend. "Danny's Daddy. You're Papa. Much more suitable for your advanced age." He grinned broadly at the annoyed look on Roman's face.

"You are older than I," Roman argued.

"Yes, but I *look* younger, and that's what counts."

"Ridiculous," Roman sighed, his expression pinched—a familiar sight where Soren was concerned.

"You two heading out soon?" Soren asked cheerily, ignoring his friend's displeasure. Roman would get over it in two seconds. He was used to Soren's ways.

"When Danny returns from the care home," Roman answered, tucking his hands into his pants pockets. Soren eyed the other vampire's outfit skeptically. Why anyone would want to wear a full suit for an entire day on an airplane was anyone's guess.

He shrugged internally. To each his own. "Well, have a blast. Bring me back lots of souvenirs. I want something pretty. Or delicious. I'll accept either. Or both."

Roman hummed noncommittally, eyeing Soren with a weirdly intense look. It made Soren's skin itch.

"Three weeks with my mate all to myself," Roman finally said after another long minute of staring.

Soren hummed, clacking his crochet needles. He wasn't entirely sure whether Roman's words were meant to be a pointed statement. Soren had been living in the same house as the two lovebirds for over a year now. He did his best to stay out of their way, and neither gave any indication they wanted him to leave, but maybe Roman was trying to casually meander his way into a verbal eviction.

"All right...," Soren drawled when Roman didn't elaborate. "Are you about to start telling me your horny honeymoon daydreams? Because I'd rather not. No offense."

Soren had already overheard enough of those two going at it to last a million lifetimes.

Roman shook his head. "I would be very...upset...if a lack of control over things at home were to distract Danny from this honeymoon," he said, his voice staying deceptively mild. "I want his full...*attention*."

Christ. Roman really was a possessive beast.

Although Soren couldn't really blame him. Roman had been lonely for a very, very long time, and Danny had been his surprise salvation. Not to mention his destined mate, the tether to his humanity.

Lucky bastard.

Not every vampire found their fated mate, the one whose soul would bond to theirs, preventing them from devolving into a feral state. And what if the one they *did* find didn't like them one bit? That was a dilemma Soren was very...invested in...at the moment.

Soren put down his crochet, folding his hands in his lap, giving Roman his most sincere look. "I promise we'll take good care of the little doggie."

"And you will ensure Gabe visits their mother." Roman made it an order, not a question.

Easier said than done, but Soren nodded anyway. "I'll make sure of it."

There was another long silence, Roman searching Soren's face for something.

"What?" Soren finally snapped, his patience wearing thin.

Roman cleared his throat. "This fascination you have with the brother. It will not be a problem?"

Soren supposed he should have been expecting this, but that didn't mean he had to play along. "What fascination?" he asked innocently, batting his lashes. "The man's boring as dirt."

Roman's lips pressed flat. "I know you still follow him sometimes."

Soren didn't deign to reply to that particular statement. Honestly, it was more than just sometimes, but what was this, an intervention?

Roman gave a heavy sigh at his silence. "Just... Keep your distance."

Soren arched a brow. "You know the two of us are living together for three weeks, right?"

"You know what I mean..."

Soren was saved a response by the sounds of Danny returning home. "I'm here!" Roman's mate called across the house. "I'm ready! Let's go, let's go, let's go!"

The look on Roman's face changed so quickly it was almost amusing. Gone was the harsh skepticism he'd been directing at Soren, replaced by a softness that Soren had never thought to see on his friend's face.

"I have our bags in the car already, little king," Roman said, reaching an arm out to his mate. "Your mother was well?"

Danny joined Roman in the doorway, greeting Soren sweetly before answering, "She was as well as can be expected these days." He turned to Soren again, his doe eyes pleading. "You'll take Gabe tomorrow morning to see her?"

"She'll be in good hands," Soren promised. He meant it. Even if Doctor Muscles was a stubborn dick about it, Soren would make sure their mother had regular visits. He wouldn't tease Danny about something like that.

Other things though...

"You two have fun fucking each other's brains out." Soren grinned in delight as Danny blushed immediately. The baby vampire really was too cute for words.

The pair left for the airport shortly after, leaving Soren alone in the little house. He stared at his crochet, unable to muster up his earlier enthusiasm for it.

What was the point? What was the point of any of this?

Soren had been in Hyde Park, Colorado, now for over a year, the longest he'd stayed in any one place in almost two centuries. He was a sitting duck.

Roman didn't need him there, even if he and Danny acted happy enough to have a permanent roommate. Ostensibly, Soren had stayed to be there as backup if Lucien decided to return, at least at first. But that psycho vampire had clearly moved on. Soren should too. He couldn't lie to himself and say he was staying just for friendship's sake anymore. Danny and Roman were clearly safe.

He sighed dramatically, sprawling onto his back on the couch.

Denial was so *dull*.

He knew why he was staying—why he couldn't make himself drive out of this town and never look back. It was just incredibly embarrassing to be so captivated by one boring human man.

One boring human man who'd made it clear he thought Soren was an annoyance at best and a monster at worst.

One boring human man who'd been doing his best to avoid Soren for over a year now.

One boring human man who happened to smell and taste like the most delicious thing Soren had ever encountered.

And as much as Soren knew it was pointless—that three weeks in close proximity to Gabe wouldn't be enough to change the stubborn human's mind about him—he couldn't help that his inner vamp perked up at the thought of having the human so close.

It was very much interested in getting closer to Gabe.

In fact... Soren sat up, a wide grin stretching his lips.

He knew exactly what he was in the mood for.

Soren waltzed into Death by Coffee, stopping briefly to wipe his heeled boots off on the entrance mat. Spring was finally showing its face in Hyde Park, and while the warmer weather was nice enough, it meant the last round of winter snow was melting, leaving slushy puddles all over town.

Another thing to be grumpy about, if Soren was feeling inclined to be grumpy.

Spoiler alert: he was.

He waited impatiently in the admittedly short line at the counter. The barista at the register, a short redhead with amazing taste in jewelry, was one Soren knew by name. *Alicia.*

How pathetic—Soren was an actual regular somewhere in this Podunk town.

"Soren," she greeted when he arrived at the front of the line, her brown eyes twinkling under her purple eyeshadow. "Your usual?"

"Sure thing." Apparently Soren was worse than a regular; he was a regular with a "usual."

It was true enough he came here for one particular tooth-decaying concoction. Not that Soren, stunning, ageless vampire that he was, had to worry about tooth decay...

"I don't know how you do it," Alicia said, drizzling caramel into a cup of ice. "This much sugar and caffeine and I would be up all night."

What a bitchy thing to say. It was almost enough to make Soren like her.

He was tempted to tell her he was an immortal predator who sucked the blood out of humans for sustenance and thus his metabolism worked a little differently than hers, but it wasn't worth the effort. She'd think he was kidding anyway.

He paid for his drink and took a seat at a table facing out toward the street. He kept his gaze firmly out that window, humming quietly to himself.

There was another reason Soren liked this particular coffee shop—besides the silly goth name and the caramel, chocolate, and whipped cream coffee creation he'd become addicted to—and that was the view.

The big front window looked out to the gym across the way. And while Soren liked to tell himself it was worth it just to ogle the various gym bros coming in and out of the place, the truth lay closer to the fact that it was the same gym a certain someone visited before his shifts at the hospital.

That certain someone, regular as fucking clockwork, exited the building just as the barista was placing Soren's order on the table.

Ugh, the human was so predictable. It almost took the fun out of stalking him.

Soren smirked to himself. Almost but not quite. Because sweet Jesus, the man was unfairly good-looking.

It was incredibly annoying.

Gabe's muscles were gleaming lightly with sweat from his workout, his dark curls held back with a headband. He looked like a European soccer player, not some small-town, all-American doctor.

Could Soren really be blamed for wanting to take a bite out of him?

Alicia followed his gaze out the window, smirking slightly at Soren. "Oh man, he's hot, isn't he? I went to high school with him. He's a doctor too. Whole package."

"Mm." Soren chose to take a sip of his drink rather than answer with real words. He hadn't considered that the workers here might have noticed the specific purpose of his favorite viewing spot, but maybe little Alicia had been paying closer attention than he'd thought.

Bliss washed through him, dimming his annoyance at having his ogling pointed out. Humans had come such a long way with their uses of sugar. It was one of Soren's favorite things about the present day.

Alicia leaned in closer conspiratorially. "You know," she whispered, "the new girl hooked up with him when he first moved back to town." She pointed to her coworker, a pretty blonde girl Soren hadn't seen before, manning the espresso machine. "Cammie said he rocked her world. She was a total mess when he ghosted her."

Well. How *interesting*.

Something dark pulsed in Soren. He stared at little blonde Cammie, feeling a familiar manic grin gracing his lips, and he briefly wondered how terrible it would really be if he committed murder in this coffee shop.

Tempting. Super tempting. But it was probably a bad idea. Danny would inevitably be pissed when he heard about it. And a pissed-off Danny would lead to an absolutely murderous Roman.

Soren sighed into his coffee, uncaring that Alicia was waiting for a response from him.

It wasn't worth the risk, really.

Especially considering Soren hadn't *actually* murdered anyone since his first accidental killings in his early, bumbling days as a vampire.

Little Cammie would live to see another day.

Alicia, belatedly realizing he wasn't the right audience for her gossip, returned to her post at the counter. Soren sipped his drink, trying not to sulk. She'd taken all the joy out of seeing a sweaty, tank-topped Gabe walking to his car.

Whatever. Soren sat up straighter in his seat, tossing his head back. He refused to be brought down by this. He wasn't just another townie lusting after the local doctor. He was a dark, dangerous predator, doing what dangerous predators did best. He couldn't help that his vampire instincts urged him to hunt and stalk his prey.

And that his stupid inner vamp was fixated on one prey in particular.

Sure, Soren still had to feed regularly, and Gabe wasn't exactly on the menu—at least not *yet*—but that side of things was more about survival than fun lately.

And Soren lived for fun.

Or at least he used to, before he set foot in this stupid town.

The problem was that Gabe kept him at arm's length. He made sure Soren wouldn't be there when he came over to Danny's for family dinners. He sat as far away from Soren as possible those few and far between times they had to be in the same room together. And he very pointedly ignored Soren's various flirtatious comments, refusing to even look Soren in the eye. As if Soren would stoop so low as to compel him into bed.

And yes, maybe Soren *occasionally* teased the human mercilessly just to get a rise out of him. But wasn't that what everyone did when they had a crush?

It was almost enough to make Soren think Gabe really *was* immune to his charms. Soren hadn't ever seen the human romantically involved with a man, for that matter. Maybe Soren was barking up the wrong tree entirely.

But...no. He'd caught the way the human eyed him when he thought no one was looking. There was a heat to his gaze that Soren had centuries of experience translating. The human was *not* immune.

And rightly so. Soren was a goddamn catch.

Plus, would fate really be so cruel?

It was a stupid thought. Soren already knew the universe was a vindictive bitch. He had no reason to expect good things to come his way. Roman and Danny's happiness was the exception, not the rule.

Still, Soren was tired of this standstill.

So he decided, sipping his liquid sugar, he'd do something about it.

He *wasn't* some mooning townie. He was Soren fucking Iversen. He could seduce one measly human.

He had three weeks to try, anyway. If Gabe still hated him by the end of it, then Soren would admit his instincts were off. He'd move on. Leave this town like he should have already.

He didn't let himself think about what he'd do if Gabe decided he *didn't* hate Soren.

Soren would cross that bridge when he came to it.

Three

Gabe

"Paging Dr. Kingman to the ER."

Gabe looked up from his patient notes and glanced reflexively to the ceiling on hearing the overhead page. Since there was no one else in the dictation room to hear him do it, he indulged himself for a moment in groaning dramatically.

Fuck. He was supposed to be finishing up by now, giving a report to the day-shift ICU doctor, but so far they hadn't even shown up yet. Most likely because today the oncoming doctor was Dr. Monroe, and that motherfucker *always* stopped in the cafeteria for his morning coffee *after* clocking in for the day. It was infuriating, even on a good day.

And today was not a good day.

The overhead page repeated, and Gabe logged out of the hospital computer and hustled down to the ER. A patient there must have ended up with a breathing tube down their throat. Gabe's fellowship was centered on critical care and pulmonology, meaning he focused specifically on lungs. He mostly took care of patients requiring breathing machines on the hospital's two ICU floors.

It suited Gabe, taking care of ventilated patients. He wasn't like Danny, who was warm and sweet and had the kind of presence that made people—patients, coworkers, randos at the coffee shop—feel immediately at ease.

Gabe didn't put anyone at ease. He could be charming sometimes, sure. A leftover sheen from his days as a high school prom king. But it was a superficial charm at best. Because when it came down to it, he could also come off as a bit of an asshole. Gruff when he should be gentle, firm when he should be soft.

But Gabe's patients were often sedated, and they couldn't talk with a breathing tube anyway, so Gabe was able to care for them in the way he did best—with good medicine, genuine respect, and a healthy amount of emotional distance.

As Gabe walked through the ER, his gaze darted to the nurses' station before he caught himself. Apparently he was too used to keeping an eye out for his brother to stop now. He pulled his focus to looking for the charge nurse on duty, hoping they could tell him where his new patient was. He spotted Dr. Monroe first, consulting with an ER doctor in one of the bays.

The asshole raised his coffee cup to him in greeting.

Fucking Dr. Monroe. At least the ER didn't need Gabe anymore, if the day-shift doctor was already there.

"What's up your ass this morning, Doc?" asked a bright, absurdly cheery female voice. Gabe knew it well. He looked down to see Chloe, nighttime charge nurse and his brother's work bestie.

Gabe shrugged, suppressing the urge to glance at his watch. "Nothing. Just ready to get out of here."

"Funny. You usually seem like you couldn't care less what time you leave." The short brunette raised an eyebrow at him, but Gabe ignored the gibe. "Have you heard from Danny?"

Gabe's little brother had left the day before for his belated honeymoon, and Gabe was officially on puppy duty. He wanted to be annoyed with Roman for not waiting until *after* the honeymoon to get Danny a puppy, but remembering the ecstatic look on his brother's face as he showed off the little fur ball made it hard to hold a grudge.

"He texted me when they landed," Gabe answered. "Then Roman texted to tell me I wasn't allowed to text *them* unless Ferdy had some kind of emergency."

Chloe laughed brightly. "That's actually pretty sweet. Little lovebirds."

Gabe fought the urge to roll his eyes at her blanket approval of Danny's husband. It wasn't her fault she didn't know Danny's husband was a monster.

Then what do you call Danny? a snarky voice in his head asked.

Different. It's different, Gabe told himself for the hundredth time.

He honestly didn't know what was true anymore. He'd thought, when he moved back to Hyde Park, that he'd have...time. Time to get back into the swing of things after the hell of residency. Time to reconnect with Danny. Time to reconcile his anger at and love for his mother.

But by the time he was even close to settled, his mother had forgotten him, Danny had been practically a stranger, and Gabe had been wondering why he'd even moved back to a town he felt never actually knew him.

Now it was a year later and Danny didn't really need Gabe at all—he was married to his honest-to-God literal soulmate, for fuck's sake. Their mother was declining every day, despite the supernatural assistance, with Gabe no closer to unfurling the tangle of emotions she invoked in him.

And Gabe was still trying to wrap his head around the fact that *vampires* existed. That he was somehow now surrounded by them. That the world he'd fought his whole life to make sense of didn't come close to what he'd imagined it to be.

Gabe took a deep breath in through his nose and out through his mouth, doing his best not to spiral into that familiar mess of thoughts, focusing instead on Chloe and chatting for a few minutes more while he waited on Dr. Monroe. Chloe even offered to walk Ferdy if Gabe needed some backup.

Danny had somehow found himself some good friends in this stagnant mountain town. For his part, Gabe always felt like he was seeing the same old people from high school everywhere he went. Same former friends. Same former teachers. Same former hookups.

It was all just...exhausting.

After Chloe left, promising to check in about the dog in a few days, Gabe lost the battle and glanced at his watch. It was six o'clock in the morning already. *Fuck.* Gabe should have been heading out the door already.

He looked over to the patient bay where Dr. Monroe was apparently done with the medicine side of things, focusing his attention now on attempting to flirt with one of the nurses. She, to her credit, looked more bored and annoyed than anything else.

The man was notorious for trying to fuck anything that moved. He'd even tried to figure out which way Gabe swung when he first started at the hospital. No go though. He wasn't Gabe's type.

Not that Gabe *had* a specific type. But Dr. Monroe, smarmy bastard, definitely wasn't it.

As far as who might be... Gabe pointedly ignored when those thoughts immediately led to him picturing a certain beautiful monster. It was clearly time to leave, if his tired brain was going to such stupid places.

"Monroe," he barked. "Can we get started?"

Dr. Monroe glanced up from his reluctant prey, eyes widening in surprise at Gabe's harsh tone. "What's your rush, King? You got a hot breakfast date?" The douchebag sounded a little jealous at the thought.

And then, in a classic case of the world's worst possible timing...

"Morning, Highness." The words, coming from directly behind Gabe, were a silky-sweet purr. He hadn't even noticed anyone approaching.

How did that fucker always move so quietly?

Gabe turned, already knowing what he'd find waiting for him. A bright, maniacal grin. Artfully tousled blond hair. Pale-blue eyes.

The very reason Gabe had been so eager to get out on time that morning. To avoid a situation exactly like this one.

Soren had arrived.

He'd insisted on picking Gabe up at the hospital and driving to the care home together, but Gabe had been hoping to meet his designated chaperone in the parking lot, away from the prying eyes of his coworkers. Clearly Soren had other ideas.

Roman's little vampire friend was, as always, looking ridiculously fashionable for their small Colorado mountain town, in tight black jeans and some flowy designer top. Gabe didn't get it. No one needed to look like they just stepped off the runway in a place where the main highlights were hiking trails and winter sports.

At least Soren wasn't wearing a fucking fur coat, like the first time Gabe had met him. Small mercies.

He didn't think Soren's greeting had been loud enough for anyone else to hear, but Gabe went on the defensive anyway. "Stop calling me that."

He hated that it had only taken a single instance of Soren hearing one of the locals call Gabe by his high school nickname, King, for him to forever mock Gabe for it.

Soren only grinned at him, looking pleased with himself for riling Gabe up with two simple words.

Meanwhile, Dr. Monroe sidled closer to them both, his eyes lighting up in obvious interest. "Who's your friend, King?"

Gabe resisted the sudden and irrational urge to tell the other doctor to fuck right off. "This is Soren. Friend of Danny's." It was immensely satisfying watching the smile on Soren's face slip at being designated the little brother's friend. "Soren, this is Dr. Monroe."

"Charmed." Soren gave Dr. Monroe a thorough once-over, practically batting his blond lashes, and Gabe bit back his irritation at the slow perusal. His coworker was a manwhore, and Soren was a compulsive flirt. It would make perfect sense for the two to get it on, and Gabe definitely didn't care enough about either of them to be bothered by it.

He focused his gaze elsewhere, pointedly ignoring their small talk. He just didn't like it when his two worlds mixed was all. It had nothing to do with Soren's almost ethereal beauty, or the way Gabe's blood boiled when he pictured the slimy ICU doctor pawing at the vampire's delicate frame.

Oh, for fuck's sake.

Gabe needed to get out of there.

"I'll go get changed out of my scrubs," he broke in gruffly, turning away without waiting for a response. It wasn't his business who Soren flirted with, but Gabe didn't have to stand by and watch it happen.

Today just wasn't a good day.

—ele—

Gabe was badging into the employee locker room before he even noticed Soren had followed him. He gave the vampire a stern look over his shoulder. "You're not allowed in here."

Soren's only reply was a blank stare, as if arbitrary human rules like staff-only locker rooms were so foreign a concept they didn't even merit a reaction.

Gabe opened his mouth, closed it again, then settled on, "Just don't look." He made his way over to his locker, allowing the blond vampire to slip in through the door behind him.

He didn't really care if Soren tagged along. Gabe didn't have to get fully nude to change out of his scrubs. Besides, Gabe didn't have anything to be ashamed of. He worked out religiously—the best way he'd found to deal with persistent anxiety—and watched what he ate.

He didn't suffer from a lack of offers to share his bed; that was for sure.

Not that Gabe had been taking anyone up on those offers lately.

Frequent hookups used to be the next best thing to relieve his stress and clear his mind, but ever since his attack, he hadn't felt inclined.

Gabe tugged at his scrub top with clumsy fingers. His complacence with Soren's presence had nothing to do with feeling pleased the vampire had walked away from Dr. Monroe, choosing to follow Gabe instead.

Nothing at all.

Soren was unnervingly quiet while Gabe changed. It was enough of a switch from the brat's usual chattiness that Gabe found himself glancing over at the mirrors after pulling his scrub top off, looking past his own head of loose brown curls to Soren's face in the reflection. The vampire was gazing at Gabe's bare torso with open appreciation in his eyes.

The little monster even licked his lips.

Fuck. Gabe didn't want to think about what that look did to him. Soren was *not* an option for him. The fucker was odd, unhinged, and—most importantly—not even *human.*

It didn't matter if he was beautiful.

It's a false beauty, Gabe reminded himself. *The allure of a predator. Designed to lure in unsuspecting prey.*

"Told you not to look," Gabe grumbled, trying to ignore the way his dick plumped up at the sight of Soren licking those pink lips.

"I never agreed to anything," Soren replied brightly, not averting his gaze for a second.

Of course he didn't. As far as Gabe could tell, Soren lived to be contrary.

Gabe rushed through getting dressed, not wanting to linger in the locker room with any of the strange feelings the petite vampire aroused in him. He clearly needed to get laid, if having someone watch him get changed was having this effect on him.

Soren slipped on a pair of sunglasses as they headed out the hospital doors to Gabe's car. The way Danny had explained it, sunlight wasn't technically detrimental to vampires, but the brightness *did* irritate their eyes, especially if their inner demon was out and about.

There were a lot of misconceptions out there Danny had been slowly educating Gabe on. Vampires didn't need an invite to enter a home. They didn't need to kill to feed. They could eat human food if they wanted; it just didn't nourish them. And their fangs stayed hidden, except for the times their inner demon—that was what Roman and Danny called the vampire side of themselves—took over.

Gabe had only seen Soren with his demon out once. The morning Gabe had been attacked by Lucien. Soren must have been following the other vampire, because he'd appeared out of nowhere and rescued Gabe, calming him down with his vampire compulsion.

Gabe had subsequently been too freaked out by finding out about the existence of vampires to ever thank Soren properly, a fact that he occasionally felt a twinge of guilt about.

But, even if it had been for a good reason, Soren had used his powers to mess with Gabe—had affected his mind, his perceptions, his emotions.

Was Gabe really expected to feel thankful for that?

And for that matter, Gabe wouldn't even have *been* attacked if Roman and Soren hadn't come to town and brought their vampire drama with them. He didn't really owe the blond vampire anything.

Gabe pushed down the unpleasant memories of that brutal attack. Thinking about it wasn't helping the anxious knot building in his stomach.

Before Gabe was anywhere near ready, they were pulling into a familiar parking lot. Here was the reason Soren had even met him after work at all, like they were some kind of pals.

The care home, with Gabe's mother waiting inside. Well, not *waiting*. The dementia kept her from knowing they were coming. But she was there.

Gabe could drive off right now and she would never know.

Gabe *wanted* to drive off.

His fingers felt fat and clumsy as he unbuckled his seat belt, and his stomach twisted further into knots.

Fuck.

He knew what was coming. And sometimes it was like the knowing *made* it happen.

Like now.

Gabe's chest started to feel tight, and his throat felt thick, like he couldn't swallow properly or get enough air. Logically, he knew he was fine. His throat wasn't *actually* closing up. But that didn't change the feeling that he couldn't breathe.

His skin prickled as he broke out into a cold sweat.

Fuck. Fuck. Fuck.

Not here. Not in front of *him*.

A small hand landed on the back of Gabe's neck. Delicate but strong. Firm. Immovable. "Breathe, Highness." Soren's voice, without its usual teasing notes, was sweet and smooth. Like cool water on a hot day.

"I. *Can't*." Gabe managed to grit out the words between gasps.

Soren used the thumb of his gripping hand to gently rub the side of Gabe's neck. "You can. Tell me five things you see," he ordered gently.

"Um." Gabe searched his surroundings with frantic eyes. "Steering wheel. My jeans. Rearview mirror. Glove box." He glanced to the right, unable to help himself. "Your eyes."

Those eyes. Such a light, pale blue. With all their intensity now focused on Gabe.

Soren's lips twitched. "Good. Four things you can feel."

Gabe knew this exercise. They'd learned about in med school, during their psych classes. A tool to help cut through panic attacks. "My seat underneath me. My feet on the floor. The seatbelt. Your hand."

"Three things you hear."

Gabe's breaths were starting to come a little easier as Soren's voice and soft commands kept him grounded to the present moment. "My breathing. Voices outside. You talking to me."

Soren gave his neck a light squeeze. "Good, Highness. Very good. Two things you can smell."

Gabe spoke without thinking. "The ocean. Pine trees."

Soren arched a brow at his words, but Gabe was too exhausted to be defensive.

"That's what you smell like. Like if the sea met a pine forest. And, um...cold. I don't know how a person can smell *cold*, but you do."

Soren didn't mock him, but those pale eyes lit with an internal fire. Gabe couldn't tell if he was offended or pleased. The vampire continued the grounding exercise. "Something you can taste."

But Gabe shook his head. "I'm fine now. Thank you. That helped." He wasn't *fine* exactly, but the panic had receded. In its wake was a shaky sort of weak feeling, the same one always left behind after any attack like that. Like Gabe could sleep for a week. Or burst into tears at any moment.

God, he hoped he didn't burst into tears.

Soren's gaze was steady, searching. After several long moments, the vampire removed his hand from the back of Gabe's neck.

Gabe did his best not to mourn the loss of that steadying grip.

"We're not doing this today," Soren declared.

Gabe felt his panic rising again at the words, but also a sense of...relief. Still, he protested. "What do you mean? We have to."

Soren tossed his head regally. Ironic that the vampire always called Gabe "Highness," when he acted like a little demonic prince himself. "We don't, actually. Wait here. Stay calm." He got out of the car.

Gabe did stay, waiting in the car while Soren walked into the care home, but he hated himself a little for it.

Why couldn't he do *better*?

He *should* have been doing better. He'd been visiting his mom regularly with Danny. Roman used his vampire compulsion to help their mom with her dementia, a skill Danny had learned now too. Sometimes it helped her remember who they were; sometimes it only served to keep her calm and happy. Either way, it had made the visits more bearable to Gabe than they'd been in the past.

Which was why Soren was with him now. To use his compulsion to help continue their visits while Danny was on his honeymoon.

Because the visits were still...tough. Gabe's feelings were always complicated when it came to his mother. The woman who had raised him with love, only to leave him to fend for himself much too young. He always felt raw in her presence, flayed open by the emotions she elicited in him. He should have known the prospect of showing that vulnerability in front of Soren would set him off.

Because instead of doing better, Gabe had been getting worse. His world had stopped making sense a year ago. His anxiety kept building; his emotions kept spiraling. He felt like he was...*pretending* all the time. Pretending to have it together. Pretending to be happy. And he was terrified of anyone seeing through it.

And now here he was, failing his family. *Again.*

Gabe was pulled out of his thoughts by Soren opening up the car door. "She's fine," the vampire reported, scanning Gabe's face like it would give him answers to his mental state. "Happy and calm."

"Um, okay." Gabe felt lost, unsure of his next steps. "What now?"

Soren climbed back into the driver's seat with catlike grace. He turned to Gabe, arching a brow. "We're going out to breakfast."

That wasn't what Gabe had been expecting Soren to say. He'd been thinking it would be something along the lines of, "I drop you off and go do my own thing, loser. Obviously."

Who wanted to hang out with someone who'd just had a complete meltdown in a parking lot?

"Breakfast?" Gabe repeated stupidly.

Soren's answering grin was bright and fierce.

"I'm craving pancakes."

Four

Soren

A bell rang as Soren led Gabe through the door of his favorite diner.

At some point during the drive over, the bigger man had grabbed Soren's hand, seemingly without noticing, and now he was still clinging to it like some sort of lifeline, his usual cocky swagger completely gone. The rare sign of vulnerability was doing very strange things to Soren's heart.

A large blonde woman with Sheryl on her name tag led them both to a corner booth. *Excellent.* It was an incontrovertible fact that booths were infinitely better than regular old tables and chairs.

Rudy's was a breakfast spot Danny had introduced Soren to, on one of the few occasions he and Soren had been on their own together. Soren was fond enough of his friend Roman's adorable mate, but he wouldn't say he and Danny had a lot in common, necessarily. Danny was sweet, compassionate, caring. And Soren was...Soren.

One thing they did share, however, was love for a good greasy spoon.

Soren reluctantly let go of Gabe's hand as they sat in the booth. It was so rare the human allowed any physical contact between them. Soren was tempted to try to pull Gabe over to sit on his side instead. But that would probably be pushing his luck.

Soren ordered coffee for himself and Gabe and ignored the menu in front of him. He had it memorized at this point.

Technically, Soren didn't need human food at all to survive, but he liked the taste of it anyway. The ritual of it too. No one realized how important the act of eating was to human society until they were no longer a part of it. And as long as Soren had his regular diet of human blood, his inner vamp didn't care what else he put in his body.

Sheryl placed their coffees in front of them moments later, and Soren eyed Gabe critically while the other man ordered his breakfast. The human was still looking dazed, his golden-brown eyes glassy. Not surprising after the full-blown panic attack he'd had in the car.

Soren should have read the human better.

He'd realized Gabe was tense back at the hospital, acting more irritable and nervous than usual. But Soren had just thought Gabe was annoyed at him for showing up without warning instead of waiting for him outside.

The human could be a stick in the mud like that.

Soren supposed he *could* have waited outside. But he hadn't been able to resist the idea of seeing Gabe in his natural habitat. There was something about the man that made Soren want to study him, like an insect under a microscope. Was Gabe a blustery douchebag in his official doctor capacity? Or was he secretly tenderhearted, holding patients' hands and convincing them all was right with the world?

Plus, Soren had wanted the full white-coat visual, but Gabe had disappointed him in that matter. The man wore scrubs but no coat.

The human really lacked a proper sense of drama.

But then he'd more than made up for it by disrobing right in front of Soren in the locker room. A fact that Soren was regretting a little now. After the emotional moment in the car, he didn't feel quite right about his lingering arousal. But he'd never been very good at denying himself anything he wanted, and given the opportunity to watch Gabe take his clothes off, he hadn't been able to resist the temptation.

And Christ, that man had a scrumptious body. Tanned and well muscled, with a lean edge to him from all those long runs he went on. Soren had had no shame in ogling that shirtless chest.

"How did you know what to do back there?" Gabe's hesitant question broke through Soren's thoughts. *Probably for the best*, he reflected, shifting in his seat and fighting the urge to adjust his hardening cock. It really had been too long since he'd had a man.

Right, Soren. Focus.

He debated dodging the question. Evading probing questions was one of Soren's many talents. But for some stupid reason, he was compelled to go with the truth.

"I've been there myself," he offered.

Gabe scoffed at that, but it lacked his usual bite. Definitely not fully back to himself, then. "You've had panic attacks? What is there for you to possibly be afraid of? You're, like, invincible."

"Immortal, not invincible," Soren corrected, taking a sip of his coffee. "We can be killed. Beheading. Fire." Why was he giving the vampire hater information on how to kill him? His mouth went on without his permission. "Besides, there is a world of hurt beyond just killing."

Gabe gave him a sharp look at that.

Maybe Soren had given too much away with that answer. Because that was the annoying thing about Danny's boorish brother. The fact that, when it came down to it, he wasn't really boorish at all.

He was an idiot, of course. Classic American male with too many emotions and no idea what to do with any of them. Like the way he'd been pushing his family away for years when it was clear to anyone with half a brain they meant the world to him. Idiot, for sure.

But Gabe still picked up on a lot despite all that. Maybe he could read hints of Soren's past in his face. It was unlikely. Not even Roman, who'd somehow wormed his way into becoming Soren's closest friend these past decades, knew Soren's whole story.

Which was for the best. Opening up to people meant opening up to future pain.

Soren knew that well.

But Gabe's panic attack in the car had left Soren...curious. He found himself wanting to crack his human's head open and peer inside. See if he could untangle the mess he was sure he'd find there.

Well, not *his* human. Just *the* human. Regular, old, boring human.

Right.

They drank their coffee in silence until their breakfast arrived. Pancakes—lightly cooked, doughy on the inside, the only right way to make them—with whipped cream and berries for Soren. Eggs and toast with bacon for Gabe.

Soren eyed his companion's plate distastefully.

"Boring," Soren accused, needing to say it out loud.

"Classic," Gabe corrected, narrowing his eyes, unable to hide his annoyance. It was his go-to look when it came to Soren.

For some reason, it made Soren want to smile. And, since he always did what he wanted, he did. Grinned wide and bright.

Gabe blinked at him.

Soren grinned wider. "Have some," he ordered, cutting off a portion of his pancakes and placing them on Gabe's plate.

Gabe shook his head. "I don't need the sugar."

Soren huffed. "It's not about need; it's about *want*."

"People want lots of things that are bad for them."

And didn't Soren know it. "That's half the fun, Highness."

Gabe gave him a skeptical look. Soren didn't know why he was pushing this—annoying Gabe to death was probably at odds with Soren's grand seduction plan—but he couldn't seem to stop. "Come on, take a bite. Don't you ever just do what you want?"

It took Gabe, staring at the pancake piece on his plate, a moment to answer. When he did, he sounded...blank. Void.

Soren didn't like it at all.

"No, not really," Gabe muttered. "Not for a long time, anyway."

Soren shook his head. This man. "You and Danny have the same kind of sickness. You just exhibit different symptoms. He never did what he wanted either, until Roman came around."

Gabe gave a bitter laugh, ignoring Soren's pancake offering for a bite of his bacon. "Well, he's certainly doing what he wants now. How long do you think before he runs off into the sunset and leaves this god-awful town for good?"

"Why would you think he's going to do that?" Soren raised his chin, his voice indignant. He ignored the fact that he agreed with Gabe on the god-awful town part.

Gabe kept his gaze on his plate. "That's what I would do, if I was suddenly immortal, with another immortal, rich lover to foot the bill. Why stay here?"

Soren spoke before thinking it through. "Because your brother is a sweet boy, mindful of his responsibilities. You're projecting your own selfishness onto him."

Gabe winced, a look of real hurt crossing over his face, and Soren tried to ignore how that expression felt like a knife twisting in his own gut.

A thought came to him. "Is that why you hate Roman so much? You think he's going to take Danny away from you? Your little brother, who you've always counted on being exactly where you left him?"

"I don't *hate* Roman." Gabe didn't deny the rest.

Soren leaned across the table, smacking Gabe—lightly, mindful of his superior strength—on the side of his head. "Idiot."

Gabe hissed and held a hand to the spot Soren had smacked. *What a baby.* "Why am I an idiot?" he asked, glaring at Soren.

"Your brother isn't going anywhere. At least, not anytime soon. You should focus on appreciating what you have, not on some hypothetical future of pain."

Gabe ran a hand through his hair, his glare dropping. "Well, maybe he *should.* It's my turn to shoulder some of his burden. I didn't realize, before, how thin he'd been stretching himself. I should have, but I didn't. I can do more."

When Roman and Soren had first met Danny, he'd been working too much, struggling to pay care home bills he hadn't told Gabe he was even paying, visiting their mom on his own when Gabe was refusing to be there. Soren had been judgmental over Gabe's lack of agency at the time, but he was realizing now there was maybe more to it than just willful denial.

"And how are you going to do that when you couldn't even get out of the car today?"

Gabe's face paled at Soren's question. Christ, Soren really was the worst. Why was he taunting a man who'd just had a full-blown panic attack in front of him?

But Gabe seemed hell-bent on ignoring his own limits, and if Soren needed to remind him of them, he would. It seemed both men in the Kingman family were determined to do it all on their own, no matter what the pressure did to them.

Well, if Gabe needed someone to push him, to force him to acknowledge his own emotions instead of leaving them inside to fester, Soren could definitely do that.

Soren was excellent at getting under people's skin.

Hyde Park really was the worst town.

Soren sipped his too-sweet cocktail, eyeing the bar he'd found himself in skeptically. It was the closest thing he could find to a decent gay bar without driving an hour away, but the "closest thing" wasn't nearly close enough.

The yokel in flannel currently grinding on some poor girl in yoga pants was a prime illustration of that fact.

Still, it wasn't the worst place. Decent drinks, with a dance floor that, despite current evidence to the contrary, could get lively enough on a weekend night. But it was nothing compared to the clubs Soren had frequented in his travels. Soren licked his lips as memories of slick skin and tight bodies gyrating under glowing lights ran through his mind.

Paris, New York, Dubai. There were so many better places to be. *This is what happens when you settle in Nowheresville, Colorado, instead of moving on like you're supposed to.*

Soren could head to Mexico City right now if he really wanted to. Find a beautiful man with a big cock and delicious blood to spend the night with.

But the thought just didn't hold the appeal it once had. Plus, Soren had...obligations. To Danny and Roman. At least for the next three weeks.

Right.

Like that would be enough to keep him here, if he really wanted to leave. Soren was loyal, true, but he wasn't anyone's lapdog.

Not anymore, you mean. Soren brushed the thought aside, taking another sip of his drink.

"Fancy seeing you here." A voice said from behind him. It was deep and smooth, but Soren could spot the smarminess in it a mile away.

Still, Soren was here for a reason. He wasn't looking for Prince Charming. He turned to the side, peering up at the man who had appeared over his shoulder. He was tall, nicely muscled, with blond hair kept shorter than Soren's own.

It took Soren a moment to place him. The flirty doctor from Gabe's work. *Dr. Morgan? Murphy?* The one who had looked at Soren with such obvious interest.

A look very similar to the one he was giving Soren now.

"We met this morning. Dr. Monroe, if you needed a reminder," the larger man said teasingly.

"What a coincidence," Soren murmured, downing the rest of his drink in one swallow.

Monroe motioned the bartender over. "What are you having?" he asked Soren.

Soren let the man buy him a drink, studying the doctor as they chatted about mindless, inane nonsense. He should have been exactly what Soren was looking for tonight. Handsome, passably charming, big enough that Soren would enjoy the power play of taking control.

He waited for the familiar pull of his inner vamp looking for prey. The thrill of the hunt.

There was nothing.

But that was no reason to go hungry. Even if this man was...wrong. Too blond, too smooth, too *nice*.

Soren put up with a little more of the doctor's attempts at flirtation, then leaned in close, flashing him a grin. It was a toned-down version of the one that left so many people unsettled in his presence. The one he loved giving a certain *other* stuffy doctor, just to watch him squirm.

"Want to get out of here?" Soren purred, placing a hand on Monroe's arm. The man nodded eagerly, practically drooling as they paid their bill.

Ten minutes and one minor compulsion later and Soren was gently licking Monroe's bite mark closed in the alley behind the bar. His saliva could do that, with small enough wounds. Part of the ol' vampire magic.

Soren had chosen Monroe's wrist, not wanting the intimacy of a neck bite tonight. More out-of-character behavior. In the past, Soren had loved the false intimacy of a neck bite with a stranger.

But the smell was all wrong.

Soren sighed. He supposed Monroe didn't *objectively* smell bad. He wore some sort of sandalwood aftershave, clearly expensive. But he didn't smell...clean. The way Gabe always smelled. Like citrus and soap. Even after a twelve-hour shift, or one of his long runs on the town's trails.

And why the fuck does it matter what Gabe smells like?

Soren chose not to answer himself. He and his brain weren't on speaking terms anymore.

He finished his task quickly and perfunctorily, just long enough for the small bite to completely heal. Monroe was panting, looking dazed and flushed, his hard cock tenting his slacks. The man hadn't *quite* come in his pants from the bite, but he'd been close.

Vampire feedings could do that to a person. Their bite in itself was usually pleasurable, unless they were aiming purposefully to create pain. It was an evolutionary trick that made it easier to compel people into remembering only pleasure afterward, rather than fear. It also lent itself to the delightful combination of blood and sex, a combination most vampires craved.

A combination Soren *should* be craving.

But there he was, closing the man's wound and leaving them both unsatisfied.

It just wasn't *like* him.

Soren had gotten used to indulging all his baser instincts a long time ago. Those instincts Roman called his demon, what Soren just called his inner vamp. The voice inside them both that called out for blood and violence and a good, hard fuck.

Roman had been fearful in the past, of giving in to that side of his nature. He'd worried indulging his demon would lead him more quickly onto the path of becoming feral, of losing his humanity. But Soren had always felt fighting against his vampire nature did more harm than good in that regard. And so he generally chose to give in to his own debauchery.

It had served him well. He was still sane at this point, even after more than three centuries as a vampire. Even without finding a mate like Roman had to tether him to his humanity.

But since coming to this boring-ass town, Soren's inner vamp didn't *want* to get up to any of its old habits. It didn't want to fuck this doctor, really. It wanted only one thing. One *person*.

Soren huffed, annoyed with himself, then turned to Monroe.

The man blinked at him slowly. "Your eyes."

Soren knew what Monroe saw. What anyone saw when his demon was out. If he smiled, Monroe would see his fangs as well. But he wasn't in the mood for smiling. He looked deep into Monroe's eyes, which were a murky green.

Soren preferred a golden brown these days.

Compulsion was Soren's specialty. He matched his breathing to the man's, syncing their rhythms. "My eyes look like they always do. Nothing unusual here. We made out for a bit here in this alley. You tried to take me home. I told you, another time. I'm a tease like that."

"A tease," Monroe repeated blankly.

Soren smirked. "Go home now. Rub one out, if you like. I don't even mind if you think of me while you do it."

Soren turned and left the alley quickly, frustrated with himself for his own moderation.

Moderation wasn't his *thing*. Debauchery was. Random hookups. Endless parties. More blood than he could stomach.

But he hadn't been himself since coming to Hyde Park and seeing *him*.

Because wasn't that how he'd rather be spending his night? He wanted to be back at the house, with eyes on Gabe, making sure the human was okay after the panic of that morning.

Except Gabe was at his stupid *work*. The only reason Soren had come out at all.

Soren's phone dinged on the way to his car. A text from an unknown number.

Where is my angel?

No, no, no.

Soren's blood ran cold, his fingers trembling around his phone. It took everything in him not to freeze where he stood. He forced himself to get calmly into his car, refusing to let his steps falter.

Hendrick didn't know where Soren was. He'd already be there if he did.

But the text was a message: he was looking.

This was it. It was time for Soren to leave—he'd officially stayed in one place too long. Soren should heed the warning.

But he didn't drive out of town. Didn't text Roman, telling him he needed to leave, to find another family babysitter.

Soren drove back to Danny's house.

He waited for the human to return.

Soren was an idiot.

Five

Gabe

Gabe blinked awake slowly. Something was off. He could hear the gentle chatter of birds in the pines behind the house. There was no blaring alarm rousing him from sleep.

Meaning he'd forgotten to set one.

Fuck.

He reached blindly for his phone and winced when he saw the time. Five p.m. He hadn't meant to sleep that late at all. Usually the first day of a stretch of time off, Gabe tried to wake up as early as his body would allow him. Sleeping this late after a night shift meant he'd probably end up staying up all night again, and his sleep schedule would be fucked for the next few days.

And then there was Ferdy. He hadn't even walked his brother's puppy before falling asleep, too exhausted to do anything but throw some food in the dog's bowl and crawl under the covers.

Fuck. *Fuck*.

Gabe rolled himself out of bed, looking for a pair of sweats in his suitcase, to throw on over his boxers. He stumbled down the stairs, blinking blearily. His eyes didn't want to open fully, but his body knew the way, even if he was only half-awake.

"Ferdy," he called out. "Here, puppy."

No answering bark. No clacking of puppy paws on the hardwood. He turned into the living room and stopped short at the sight in front of him. There was Ferdy, ears cocked and tail thumping slowly. He was snuggled up in a lap.

Soren's lap.

The petite blond vampire was curled up in a corner of the couch, petting the little bundle of fur lazily, his blond head resting on his other hand. "Good evening," Soren purred. "Or is it morning for you, Highness?"

Gabe hadn't seen much of the vampire in the past few days, despite staying in the same house. Gabe had been either working or sleeping, and Soren had, strangely enough, not been taking advantage of the opportunity their close quarters provided to pester him. And Gabe for his part hadn't sought the vampire out, not wanting to bring up the very necessary conversation of trying another visit with his mom.

Familiar guilt coursed through him. *Bad son. Bad brother. Coward.*

He pushed the thoughts aside and blinked blearily at the puppy Soren was holding. He'd never known the energetic dog to not come when called. "Is he sick?"

Soren took a second too long to tear his eyes off Gabe's bare chest—Gabe was so used to living alone he hadn't even thought to put a shirt on—before answering, "I tired him out. Used my vamp speed to run with him in the woods behind the house."

The image of Soren—fashionista, club hopper, literal monster—running around with a puppy in the forest made Gabe laugh out loud.

Soren pursed his lips in annoyance. "What?" he asked defensively.

"Nothing. Just the thought of you on puppy duty."

"What about it?" Soren narrowed his eyes.

But Gabe was too foggy-headed just now to properly tease the vampire. "Just...thank you. You didn't have to. It was, um, nice of you."

Soren shrugged casually, but he looked pleased by the thanks. "You're welcome, Highness."

Gabe sighed. He was never getting rid of the nickname.

Feeling more alert, he was struck still for a moment by the picture Soren presented, all curled up in the couch. The vampire was wearing some sort of knit loungewear that looked unbelievably soft.

Gabe had had no idea the little monster could look so...domestic.

He cleared his throat. "You hungry?"

Poor choice of words. Gabe held his breath as Soren's pupils dilated, a new heat filling his gaze. "You offering?" Soren asked, arching a brow.

"Shit." Gabe blanched. "I didn't mean… I just need to eat some dinner. You interested?"

"Just messing with you, human. I drank a few days ago. Don't need yours." Soren grinned his usual grin, but the heat left his eyes in an instant.

Oh. Of course. Gabe opened his mouth, then closed it again, not sure what to say. He knew from Danny that vampires often liked to mix sex and feedings (which was, frankly, more information than Gabe needed to hear from his own newly vampified brother).

So if Soren had fed recently…

Gabe wasn't sure why the thought of Soren feeding off someone else in town made his gut clench.

Sure you do. He ran a hand through his hair.

"I don't cook," Soren said out of nowhere, the words sounding like a challenge.

"Okay…?" Gabe frowned at him. "Yeah, why would you? You don't have to eat."

"Roman cooks for Danny."

Gabe wasn't sure why Soren was making that comparison. Roman was Danny's *husband.* His fated mate. It was an entirely different situation.

"Don't worry," he found himself reassuring the vampire. "I don't cook either. I'm well versed in ordering in though. You like Thai?"

Soren's answering grin was…softer than usual. Less manic, more genuine. "I could be persuaded."

An hour later, they were eating from takeout containers on the kitchen table, both having agreed that using real plates was just a way to create unnecessary dishes. Gabe had put on a shirt, not missing the way Soren had pouted in disappointment when he'd told the vampire he was going to go cover up.

Gabe had been nervous about living in the same house as Soren. Beyond nervous. He'd been half-convinced that without Danny or Roman to chaperone, Soren would try getting into his head again.

That he'd try to mess with Gabe's mind, manipulate his emotions. But Gabe was realizing he'd misjudged that risk.

Soren could have used his freaky compulsion to ease Gabe's panic attack the other day. He could have easily coerced him into visiting the care home, to get their visit over with. But instead, he'd comforted Gabe with calm words and a steady presence. He'd taken him to breakfast and given him time to get his thoughts together.

And once Gabe let himself relax in Soren's presence, it was weirdly...nice.

Gabe wasn't used to having someone to eat dinner with. Someone like Soren, who had a million interesting stories. Who didn't quiz Gabe on being a doctor or expect him to lead the conversation. So many people thought Gabe—high school football player, former prom king, ICU doctor—was some kind of alpha male or social butterfly, but in truth Gabe liked to listen more than he liked to talk. Liked being able to focus on someone else instead of pretending to have it all together.

Soren didn't seem to mind that at all.

Gabe took a small bite of a ridiculously huge, ridiculously fancy cookie that Soren had insisted they get delivered in addition to dinner. According to him, they needed sweet to balance the spicy.

Gabe would never admit how delicious the cookie was. Nobody needed that kind of sugar on a regular basis.

"Tell me about your mom."

Gabe choked on his bite. "What?"

Soren nibbled his own treat delicately, and Gabe tried not to stare as the vampire's pink tongue darted out to lick a dab of frosting from the corner of his mouth. Tried to ignore the vague feelings of arousal sitting this close to Soren stirred in him. "The issue you're having visiting her."

Well, that did the trick.

Soren took one look at Gabe's expression and clarified, "I'm not asking you to divulge all your emotional secrets. I just need to know. Is it me? Because I don't need to go with you. You can visit her without me there for compulsion. Or I could go ahead of you, try to ease her mood, and then leave you to it."

It would be an easy cop-out, to say the only issue was that Soren made Gabe uncomfortable. But for some reason, Gabe didn't want to leave the little monster thinking this was all his fault. Not when he'd been so patient with Gabe the other day in the car.

"No, it's not you," Gabe murmured, sliding down a little in his chair.

Soren looked unconvinced.

"Not *just* you," Gabe amended. "It brings up...a lot. Visiting her. I hate to think of someone else seeing...all that."

Was that the lamest explanation in all of history? Probably.

Soren sighed and put down his cookie, clasping his hands together on the table in front of him. "Do you know how old I am, Highness?"

"Not exactly. Older than Roman, right?"

"I was turned in Denmark in the seventeenth century."

Holy. Fucking. Shit. Gabe did his best not to let his shock show, but judging by Soren's amused look, he failed miserably. "Um...you don't look a day over twenty-two?"

That part was true enough, but Soren still giggled at Gabe's comment. The sound was bright and melodic. Like a little bell.

It made Gabe's stomach flip.

"I'm just saying," Soren said after his giggling died down. "I've seen a lot. There's nothing you could do that would shock me." He paused, a thoughtful look on his face. "Well, if you drop-kicked your mom in the face, I guess I would be a little surprised. But I *know* people. And you're good people. I'm not going to judge you."

Gabe snorted at that. "You love judging me."

"Exactly," Soren agreed, as if Gabe had proved his point. "If you weren't a good person at heart, I wouldn't love judging you. I would dismiss you. I wouldn't have any time for you at all."

The vampire's words were harsh, but his tone was...gentle. It reminded Gabe of the comfort he'd felt with Soren's strong, delicate hand on the back of his neck, his voice giving Gabe soothing commands.

"I love her," Gabe found himself saying.

"I know you do." Soren scooted his chair closer, leaning forward.

"I just have…complicated feelings." Gabe hated how weak his voice came out.

"Only boring people's feelings are uncomplicated," Soren reassured him.

Gabe watched in amazement as the vampire leaned closer, patting him gently on the arm. His time with Soren was turning out to be…disorienting.

He'd spent so long holding on to his mistrust of Soren, keeping his distance, trying to convince himself his fixation with the vampire was based on fear. But now here he was, on the verge of opening up more than he had with anyone in the past decade.

Gabe had never even had a real conversation with *Danny* about his feelings concerning their mother. It wasn't like he'd told Soren any real details, but still…there was a weight lifting off his chest, just in saying it out loud: he had complicated feelings around his mother, beyond just unconditional love and devotion.

Why was a vampire the first person Gabe had opened up to in years? And how was it *Soren* of all people who'd made him feel so much better with just a few words?

He would be worried about compulsion again if he couldn't see the pale blue of Soren's eyes, so clear and calm and focused wholly on Gabe.

He didn't move away from Soren's hand.

"Pick a hand." Soren was hiding both of his behind his back, bouncing on his toes with mischief painting his face.

Gabe pointed to Soren's left.

"Aha!" Soren brought his left hand forward to reveal *Jurassic Park* in its clutches. His blue eyes gleamed. "Excellent."

"You were hoping for that one?" Gabe asked, amused in spite of himself.

Soren nodded gleefully. "One of the best movies ever made."

Gabe snickered. "You told me at dinner that you're over three hundred years old...and a movie about *dinosaurs* is one of the best ever made?"

Gabe wasn't sure how he had already progressed from complete shock to joking about their incomprehensible age difference, but it was hard to stay too serious around the blond vampire when he was in such a playful mood.

Soren gave him a truly savage look. "One, dinosaurs are cool. Irrefutably. Two, it's a matter of storytelling. Subject matter isn't even the key part. It's about pacing. Suspense. Amazing acting. And, of course"—he pointed at the DVD cover in demonstration—"Laura Dern and her khaki shorts."

Gabe shook his head, grinning in spite of himself.

Soren was full of surprises.

The picture Soren had painted for Gabe of his past life made him seem like some kind of lascivious, fanged party animal. Why Soren would want to stay here and watch one of the DVDs from Gabe's childhood with him was a complete mystery. After dinner the vampire had simply instructed Gabe to make them popcorn and then disappeared into the living room to "narrow down their selection."

Gabe nodded at Soren's right hand. "What was the other option?"

Soren's grin was bright and manic as he revealed the second DVD. *Interview with a Vampire.*

Gabe snorted. "Really?"

"Just thought you could bear reminding how alluring and sexy the rest of the world finds my kind." Soren's grin turned sly.

As if Gabe needed any reminding. He'd been doing his best for over a year to ignore just how alluring and sexy a certain vampire was.

Soren was just...way too enticing.

And he was only becoming more so as he revealed new facets of himself to Gabe. The petite vampire's loungewear was apparently an outfit of his own making. When he'd stood from the couch, it had been revealed to be a crop top with matching high-waisted, flowy knit pants. The shirt was short enough that glimpses of Soren's slim pale midriff peeked out when he was standing. Like now. Gabe swallowed hard, his cock beginning to harden in his sweats.

The microwave dinged. Saved by the bell.

"I'll get the popcorn," Gabe offered. So what if his voice came out a little raspy?

Soren smirked at him, moving to pop the DVD in. Ferdy was still on the couch, snoozing away, his ear twitching in his sleep. Apparently the key to tiring out energetic puppies was having a speedy vampire on the premises. Who knew?

When Gabe returned with the popcorn, he settled on the opposite end of the couch as Ferdy. Soren, instead of sitting back with the puppy, planted himself in the middle, leaving zero space between his and Gabe's bodies.

At Gabe's look, Soren widened his eyes in faux innocence. "What? I need to be able to reach the popcorn."

Gabe said nothing. He'd been right—Soren's outfit *was* soft, the sleeve brushing against Gabe's bare arm.

Gabe swallowed, his mouth suddenly dry, and tried to focus on the movie, willing his cock not to harden again as Soren's pine-and-ocean scent drifted over him. There would be no hiding a hard-on in these sweats, and he didn't want to give Soren the satisfaction of knowing how he affected him.

The vampire was too gorgeous by far, and he knew it, the little brat.

As the movie played, the dinosaurs meting out their own brand of prehistoric justice on their makers, Gabe held himself stiffly, his right leg bouncing. He was trying to avoid their bodies touching any more than necessary, but the awkward stiffness was starting to make his back ache.

Soren glanced at his jittery leg, huffing in annoyance. "What's going on, human?"

"Nothing." Gabe stilled his leg, trying to subtly stretch his upper back without bumping into the vampire.

Soren sighed, grabbing the remote to pause the movie. "Tell me."

"It's just an old back injury from an unruly patient during residency. I get stiff sometimes."

"Hm." Soren eyed him for a moment skeptically, then reached over and lifted the popcorn bowl from Gabe's lap, placing it on the coffee table. He pushed and prodded until Gabe found himself leaning forward, seated at the very edge of the couch. He looked over his shoulder to watch Soren clamber up behind him, placing himself between Gabe and the back of the couch.

The scents of ocean and pine washed over him again.

Gabe gritted his teeth as blood rushed to his cock. "What are you doing?"

"Hush," Soren commanded.

Strong, delicate fingers dug into Gabe's neck, moving in sure strokes. Gabe let out a groan before he could help himself. "Fuck. Your hands feel amazing."

"I know," Soren murmured. "Press play."

Gabe complied, reaching for the remote. It felt too good to put up any sort of fuss.

As Soren worked his back muscles, Gabe found himself melting into a relaxed state that bordered on drugged.

This was becoming a mysterious theme of Soren's presence. Up to a point, having Soren around increased that restless, anxious feeling that lived ever-present in Gabe's gut. But as soon as Soren was touching Gabe, it was like it all...dissolved. That tightness in his chest gave way to a loose, warm, fluid state.

None of that would be a problem, per se...except he was also incredibly turned on.

He couldn't *help* it. Gabe usually made a point of keeping some physical distance between him and Soren, but now Soren's lithe body was pressed up against his back. His scent surrounding Gabe. His hands all over him.

"Fuck," Gabe groaned, as Soren dug into a particularly tight spot on his lower back. "Is this part of your vampire magic?"

"No, this is you having more muscles than sense and me being good with my hands."

Another rush of blood shot to Gabe's cock at the thought of how else Soren might be good with his hands. He went on the defensive. "I'm not *that* bulky. I run a lot."

Soren hummed. "You're bulky enough." The clear appreciation in his voice took any potential sting out of his words.

Soren clearly liked Gabe's muscles. Gabe liked that Soren liked them.

He didn't protest as Soren tugged at the bottom of Gabe's shirt, moving to lift it over his head. "It's in the way," the vampire breathed into his ear, sending a shiver down Gabe's spine.

His shirt removed, Gabe groaned again at the feel of Soren's hands on his now-bare back. "Your hands are so warm."

Soren must have heard the unspoken question in his voice. "Another false myth," he told Gabe. "We only get cold to the touch if we haven't fed for too long. Shows we're in the danger zone."

Gabe struggled to focus on that tidbit of information. It was hard to manage—Soren's hands were sent from heaven. "You can die that way?"

"No," Soren started pressing his knuckles along Gabe's spine. "But we can be severely weakened. End up comatose."

The conversation should have been the reminder Gabe needed for his hardening cock to go down. That Soren was *other*. Not human. A predator.

And one who wouldn't possibly be sticking around in this town for much longer. He'd been here a year already. Why would Soren possibly want to stay, with the life he'd led so far?

But Gabe was too blissed out to care about anything other than the feel of Soren's hands on his skin. Those hands that were now drifting down Gabe's sides, stroking gently rather than kneading. Gabe shivered again, goose bumps erupting on his skin.

Soren hummed behind him, pleased at Gabe's reaction.

"Feels good." Gabe's words were practically slurred.

Jesus, he needed to get a grip.

But before Gabe could collect himself, one of the hands on his side snaked around to the front. Gabe held still, hardly breathing as delicate fingers just barely cupped his now rock-hard cock.

His body felt hot. "It's a natural reaction," he grunted, not sure whether he wanted to push that hand away or press it down harder against himself.

"Oh, very natural." Soren's hand didn't move, and Gabe shivered again as the vampire's nose nuzzled behind his ear.

Fuck.

Gabe had never been this sensitive to another person's touch before. Had never been driven to this state by a few simple touches and a hand on his clothed cock.

He should put a stop to this. Now, before things went any further. There were a million and one reasons this was a bad idea.

But then Soren was shimmying his body forward to press himself even more firmly against Gabe's back, and Gabe felt the outline of Soren's own hard cock pressing against him.

The immense satisfaction that Soren was just as turned on by him as he was by Soren momentarily stunned him, and Gabe didn't protest as Soren's hand dipped beneath his sweats, under the waistband of his boxers, to wrap itself around his cock. The feel of Soren's hot hand on his bare skin had Gabe moaning softly before he could stop himself.

He hadn't been touched this way in so long.

Soren pressed a soft kiss to the back of his neck. "Let me make you feel good, Highness?"

The hint of vulnerability in Soren's voice was the final push in melting Gabe's reservations. He found himself nodding, opening his legs wider before leaning his head back against Soren's shoulder. "Yeah, okay. Please, Soren. More."

Soren growled softly before complying, his delicate hand grasping Gabe's cock with a firmer hold. And then he was stroking Gabe with an expertise that was almost alarming.

That's what comes from hundreds of years of sexual experience. Gabe pushed the unfair thought from his mind. He wasn't exactly a virgin himself. And as Soren's hand twisted around his cock, the vampire's pale thumb circling the drops of precum beading around the head, Gabe found himself thankful for every bit of experience that was helping Soren make Gabe feel *so damn good.*

Gabe let his full weight fall back against him, giving in to the blissful sensation. "I don't care what you say. Your hands *are* fucking magical, brat."

Soren hummed behind him, somehow managing to make the simple noise sound smug.

Pleasure tingled along Gabe's spine with each stroke of Soren's hand. He hadn't expected any of this, his defenses were down, and it wasn't long before a familiar tightening in his balls had him warning the vampire. "Fuck. Fuck, Soren. Gonna come, baby."

He was only half-aware of the endearment leaving his mouth. He could be embarrassed about it later, when he didn't feel so fucking good.

Soren hummed again, increasing the speed of his strokes, twisting around the head at the end of each pass. He started pressing warm, wet kisses along the back of Gabe's neck, and that was all it took for Gabe to find his release, moaning as his cock pulsed in the vampire's hand. His eyes wanted to close with the force of it, but he kept them open at half-mast, watching ropes of his white cum coating Soren's pale fist.

The sight of it was way fucking hotter than it had any right to be.

Gabe was panting, his head still resting against Soren's shoulder. *Fuck.* He'd been going through a major dry spell. He couldn't think of any other reason a simple hand job would feel so amazing.

He found himself turning his head to press a kiss against Soren's neck, unable to resist the silky-smooth skin there, only slowly becoming aware of the rhythmic sounds coming from behind him.

Soren was jerking himself off.

Gabe wanted to see it.

"Let me," he offered, lifting his head and moving to turn around.

But Soren pressed a hand to his back, halting his movements. "Hush, human," he purred. "Stay still."

Another kiss on his nape, and then Gabe's back arched as he felt the pressure of Soren's blunt teeth pressing into the back of his neck.

Little monster.

Gabe should be freaked out. He should remind Soren that he didn't want to be anyone's dinner. But he was too mesmerized by the sounds of Soren finding his own pleasure. The little pants and whimpers, muffled by Gabe's skin, as the vampire approached his release. Soren's free hand roamed frantically along Gabe's stomach, his shoulders, his pecs. As if touching Gabe's skin was in itself a turn-on for him.

Fuck. That thought was hot. Gabe didn't even care that Soren was smearing Gabe's own cum over his body.

He felt the wetness and heard the low, sweet moan as Soren finished behind him. The moment was punctuated by Soren's teeth pressing even harder into Gabe's neck, a move that for some reason had Gabe's spent cock twitching in interest.

Gabe braced himself for sharp fangs, cursing himself for not pulling away.

But Soren's teeth remained blunt, bruising rather than puncturing, and after a long moment, he released his hold on Gabe's neck, pressing a small kiss onto what was most likely going to an impressive mark.

They both sat there, panting heavily, Soren's hot breath against Gabe's neck, as the credits rolled on their movie.

"What now?" The words were so quiet Gabe almost didn't hear them. But he did. And he heard *it* again. That hint of vulnerability, an emotion he'd never before associated with Soren.

Any freak-out Gabe might have had over what they'd just done got pushed to the side. He didn't want to make Soren miserable. For once, Gabe didn't want to be the jerk after a hookup.

"Put in the second movie?" he offered.

He felt the curve of Soren's lips against his skin as the vampire smiled. "You do it," Soren said. "I need to wash my hands."

So Gabe found himself watching *Interview with a Vampire* with an actual vampire.

His life no longer made any sense.

Six

Soren

Soren woke up with an overwhelming feeling of *rightness* coursing through him. The body under him smelled amazing. Citrus and soap.

Of all the scents in the world, why was this simple one so intoxicating?

They'd almost gotten through the whole second movie before Gabe had fallen asleep. Soren had considering carrying the larger man upstairs to his room—the benefits of vampire strength—but then Gabe had sighed in his sleep and pulled Soren on top of his reclined body, and Soren had decided right then and there that a night on the couch was just fine for both of them.

He had followed Gabe into sleep not long after. Soren didn't need as much as the average human, but he hadn't gotten any at all the past few days. He'd been wandering the city at night while Gabe worked and staying close during the day while Gabe slept.

Soren had been on edge ever since getting that text, but instead of sending him running like it logically should have—like it would have in the past—it had left him feeling...protective.

Protective of his human.

His human.

Soren hadn't actually *planned* on seducing Gabe last night. Hendrick's text had left him feeling conflicted over his grand seduction. What was the point, if at any minute, Soren would be forced to run? But he hadn't been able to resist touching Gabe. The human usually had his defenses up so high around Soren. To see him melt like that from just a simple massage...

The man was clearly touch-starved.

When Gabe had been holding himself so stiffly, Soren had worried their relationship had regressed. That Gabe was afraid of him again.

The thought had hurt more than it should have.

Soren still had very vivid memories of the year before when, finding out what Soren was, Gabe had thrown him out of his hospital room, calling him a monster.

The human had become more accustomed to their kind over the past year—he didn't have a choice, really, when his only brother had become one of them—but Soren had still worried that underneath it all, Gabe feared him.

That normally wouldn't bother Soren. He usually took pleasure in frightening big, strong men. The type that would have pushed him around before finding out he was stronger and faster than they would ever be. But, for whatever idiotic reason, he didn't want Gabe to feel that way.

Probably the same idiotic reason Soren couldn't seem to leave this town. The same reason he'd been drawn to this man from the moment he'd laid eyes on him. The same reason Soren kept accidentally referring to him as *his* human.

Not going there.

Soren had been there once before. He'd tried his hand at belonging to someone, and it had caused him nothing but pain. *Continued* to cause him nothing but pain.

But when Gabe had melted so beautifully under Soren's touch, he hadn't been able to resist taking it further. To see just how close Gabe would let him get.

And Soren had gotten very close indeed.

Just thinking about it had him nuzzling deeper into the warm, hard body underneath him. Gabe had his arms wrapped tightly around Soren. As if, even in his sleep, he didn't want him to get away.

Soren should have felt trapped.

He didn't.

For reasons beyond just the obvious: that he was ten times stronger than the human and could escape quite easily if he wanted to.

Something hard was poking into Soren's stomach. He wiggled against it experimentally.

He really should get up. Leave this human alone for good. Continue on his way. He thought about the other two texts he'd received since the first.

Looking for you, my angel.

You know you can't hide from me.

But the usual fear was blunted; it was hard to stay focused on the bad when the good was so close. When the good smelled so goddamn amazing. Soren didn't *want* to get up.

And Soren was an expert in doing exactly what he wanted.

He hadn't gotten a proper taste last night. Was Gabe's cock as delicious as the rest of him?

But one night of touching wasn't blanket permission, so instead of scooting down Gabe's body, Soren scooted himself up. He nuzzled his nose behind Gabe's ear, inhaling more of that delicious scent. Gabe stirred beneath him.

"I want to taste you," Soren whispered into his ear, licking around the rim.

"Hm?" Gabe's sleepy mumble sent desire shooting through Soren. It was the kind of noise only a lover would hear. Intimate. Soft. Sweet.

He let his fingers trail over the hard ridge of Gabe's cock through his sweatpants. "Can I taste you, Highness?"

Gabe's breath hitched and his arms tightened briefly around Soren as he woke up enough to comprehend what Soren wanted. Soren waited breathlessly for Gabe to stiffen, to push Soren off him, but Gabe just nodded, letting out a sleepy affirmative, groaning when Soren nipped his ear with blunt teeth.

Soren should have been embarrassed by how quickly he moved to scramble down Gabe's body. But he couldn't find it in himself to care. He tore Gabe's sweatpants off, mindful not to rip them. He hadn't gotten a good look last night, but he'd felt enough to know he'd like what he'd see.

And he was right.

Gabe's cock was perfect. Hard and thick, with a slight curve that Soren just knew would feel amazing inside him. Gabe didn't leak as much as Soren did, but there was still a drop of precum on the flushed tip, just waiting for Soren to take a taste.

He darted his tongue out, savoring the burst of salty flavor, humming a little when he felt Gabe's fingers curling into his hair. *Delicious.*

Soren took his time, mapping the size and shape of Gabe's cock with kittenish licks. Not sucking, not yet. Just feeling his way around with his tongue.

Gabe groaned again, a helpless sound. "You're killing me, brat."

Soren grinned. "I know."

But he'd been waiting a long time to get his hands on this human, and he didn't want to rush the experience. He licked his way down the shaft to Gabe's balls, moving to roll one after the other experimentally in his mouth.

Gabe's fingers tightened in his hair. "Please. Please, Soren."

Ohh yes. Soren liked that word on Gabe's tongue. It left him feeling generous, and he obliged, finally engulfing all of Gabe's length into his mouth. Gabe made an incredibly gratifying, strangled sound as Soren's lips closed around him. His hips bucked shallowly, and Soren reached a hand up to press on his hard stomach, keeping the man from thrusting into Soren's mouth.

This was Soren's show.

And it didn't take long once Soren got to work. A few minutes of hard, frantic sucking, just this side of rough, and Gabe's abs were tightening under his hand, the bigger man pleading, "Please, baby. Gonna come. Please. Don't stop."

Baby. Gabe had called him that last night. Soren's stomach swooped again at the sound of it. He doubled down, increasing his pace, and was rewarded with a long, low groan and the salty, bitter taste of Gabe's cum flooding his mouth.

So. Damned. Delicious.

Soren licked the remains off his lips slowly as he peered up into Gabe's golden-brown eyes, reveling in the slight trembling of the man's torso he could feel under his hand. "You're a quick draw, Highness."

He watched in delight as Gabe flushed, running a hand over his face in his embarrassment. "I mean, this morning, I, uh, kind of woke up already turned on."

"Thinking of me, were you?" Soren teased.

Gabe's flush only deepened, which was answer enough. "And then last night it had, um, been a while?"

Soren was incredibly satisfied to hear that.

He'd had a hunch though. After all, he'd been keeping an awfully careful eye on Gabe's whereabouts this past year. Especially after Lucien's attack. So he already knew more or less that Gabe wasn't exactly dating lately.

Still, the admittance gave him a thrill of pleasure. Soren grabbed at his own cock, painfully hard and leaking copiously.

Gabe reached for his arm. "Let me? Please?"

There was that *please* again. Soren nodded, hoping the heat in his face wasn't a sign that he was blushing, because that would have been just...fucking embarrassing.

Humans did *not* make Soren blush.

He slid himself up Gabe's legs, giving a small yelp when Gabe's hands clasped him firmly on the ass, pulling him up to straddle the man's face.

Soren barely had time to take a breath before Gabe was swallowing his cock down.

"Jesus Christ," he gasped.

Gabe mumbled who the fuck knew what around his cock in response, and the vibrations shot licks of pleasure up Soren's spine.

He didn't know what he'd been expecting when it came to reciprocity from this human he'd only seen with women before, but it wasn't this full-bore, no-holds-barred enthusiasm.

Gabe's hands were on his hips, his hold firm enough that Soren felt secure but loose enough that Soren could find his own rhythm, fucking gently into Gabe's mouth. When Gabe nodded in approval, hollowing his cheeks and gazing up at Soren with soft eyes, Soren started moving his hips with more force.

"Tap my hip if you need me to let up," Soren ordered, his voice hoarse.

Gabe's fingers only gripped his hips more tightly. Christ.

Soren lost himself to the pleasure of fucking Gabe's mouth, holding his heavy lids open so he could take in the sight of Gabe's full lips stretched around Soren's cock. It was a heady thing, having this big, strong man at his mercy.

When he felt himself getting close, his thighs trembling and his insides quivering, Soren slid himself out of Gabe's grasp, grabbing his spit-slick cock and leaning down to claim Gabe's lips, licking his own taste out of the human's mouth.

He tasted so sweet underneath.

Soren devoured Gabe's mouth, sucking his tongue and nipping his lips, his hand moving furiously on his cock until he was spurting his release onto Gabe's chest, moaning helplessly into their kiss.

Gabe groaned and huffed a laugh, breaking away after Soren was fully spent. "You have a thing for covering me in your cum, don't you?"

Soren hummed noncommittally, capturing the human's lips again.

He was a vicious predator. He was allowed to claim his territory if he wanted to.

It was a long minute before he could bring himself to release Gabe from his kisses, giving the human's lip one final bite before sliding down to Gabe's side, curling up against him on the couch.

"Wasn't sure if you'd be comfortable with that," Soren murmured.

Gabe peered at him, one dark brow raised. "What? Sucking cock?"

"Mm-hmm."

Gabe grinned goofily down at him, still looking fairly cum-drunk. "That wasn't my first cock, brat."

"Are you— You don't—" It was rare Soren found himself at a loss for words, but his brain was pleasantly fuzzy postorgasm, and he'd only seen Gabe with women before... A thought that in his current blissed-out state only made him a *little* murderous.

Not the women part, the Gabe-with-anyone-fucking-else part.

"I'm not closeted," Gabe supplied. "I'm bi. It's not a secret, but I don't go out of my way to let people know. Most of my experience with men comes from when I was off at college, so I'm pretty sure most people in this town assume I'm straight."

Soren had a thought. "Does Danny know?"

"I told him when he first came out to me. He was so nervous." Gabe smiled at the memory. "So I told him I found dudes pretty hot too." He laughed, and the sound made Soren's heart flip in his chest. It was a new thing, getting to see this human so relaxed, so...soft.

It pleased Soren to no end.

They stayed there on the couch for a long while, Soren half expecting Gabe to freak out at any moment. For him to remember that Soren was a monster and a creep and that Gabe didn't want anything to do with him.

What came out of Gabe's mouth instead was a surprise. "We should go to the care home today."

Soren peered up at him, eyes narrowed. "You're sure?"

Gabe's body had stiffened slightly at his own words, some of that blissed-out relaxation leaving it, but he didn't pull away from Soren. "I'm sure. Just give me five minutes, then we'll shower."

An hour later, Soren held his body deliberately still, more so than he was used to. He didn't want any restless fidgeting to be interpreted as impatience.

They'd been sitting in the parking lot for ten minutes.

Soren had driven them there, half-afraid Gabe would have another panic attack, this time while at the wheel. Soren could survive pretty much any car crash, but humans were...disturbingly breakable.

Now Gabe was staring out the passenger window at the care home in front of them, a glazed look in his eyes. It was a little concerning, but his breathing was steady and even, so Soren was letting it go for the moment.

Plus, the human was holding Soren's hand again, seemingly without realizing it, and that gave Soren some annoyingly fuzzy feelings, making him reluctant to move. He closed his eyes instead and basked in the sunlight coming through the window, his dark shades negating any irritation his inner vamp might feel at the brightness.

They sat that way a few more minutes before Soren's phone dinged. He tensed and fished it out of his pocket with his free hand, glancing down with trepidation, half expecting another threatening message from *him*.

Instead, it was Roman.

You and Gabe have not murdered each other, have you? Danny has not heard from Gabe these past few days. It is making him...distracted. Fix it.

Soren looked up with a grimace. Sounded like Roman was getting blue balls on his honeymoon.

Gabe had let go of his hand and was watching him, one knee bouncing rapidly. "I'm sorry. I'll be ready to go in a minute."

Was the human worried Soren had better things to do? He shook his head, reaching back for Gabe's hand. "Not in a rush, Highness. It was just Roman checking in. You should text your brother."

"Oh, right." Gabe's knee stilled as soon as Soren touched him. He cleared his throat. "Sorry. Other things on my mind lately."

An incredibly adorable revelation over these past twenty-four hours was that Gabe apparently blushed almost as easily as his younger brother. He had a more golden skin tone than Danny, so it was harder to tell, but it definitely happened. It was blooming beautifully on his cheeks now, a result of Gabe recalling what exactly had been on his mind.

Soren much preferred this bashful blush to the faraway look that had been in his eyes these past ten minutes. He stroked his thumb over Gabe's knuckles, and Gabe took a deep breath in response.

"You smell like my shampoo," Gabe blurted.

Soren grinned. "That's because we showered together, Highness."

Just the thought of it sent heat shooting down Soren's spine. They had kept the shower fairly chaste, but the act of washing each other had somehow been more intimate than getting each other off with their mouths.

At least to Soren.

Maybe to Gabe too, judging by the way that blush was now traveling down his neck.

But then Gabe changed the direction of the conversation abruptly, his hand tightening on Soren's. "When my dad died, my mom sort of shut down. She stopped—I don't know. She just stopped. They were really in love, I guess. I remember that. They were happy. And my mom couldn't deal."

Gabe looked over, and Soren nodded. He knew some of the basics. Danny and Gabe's father had died very suddenly, in a car crash, when they were still quite young.

Gabe continued, his hand squeezing Soren's to a degree that might have been painful had Soren not been a vampire. "I was fourteen, but Danny was only eight. He was too young to just...go it alone. So I took care of him. Packed his lunches. Got him ready for bed. Held him when he cried." Gabe looked out the window, avoiding Soren's gaze now. "It took her a few years, but she got it together again, and I was able to go back to being a teenager, more or less, but I was...resentful. For a long time. My dad was my person. I was grieving. And suddenly I had to be a parent too?"

"I'm sorry," Soren said. It didn't feel like enough.

Gabe shrugged, his gaze still firmly elsewhere. "I don't know. It wasn't that long, in the grand scheme of things. But it hurt. I threw myself into school and friends after that. I wanted—wanted that normal teenage life, I guess. And after... I was so happy to get away from here, to go to med school. To maybe make my dad proud." Gabe's voice grew thick, and his eyes shone with unshed tears. "When I heard that she was sick, what it was, my first reaction was...anger. I was so *angry* at her. That here she was again, leaving us to fend for ourselves way too young."

Gabe finally looked at Soren then, eyes frantic, clearly desperate for understanding. "I know that was unfair—I *know* that—but by the time I started to come to terms with it, she was already forgetting me. She had made Danny wait to tell me...didn't want to worry me." Gabe gave a bitter laugh. "I didn't realize until too late that *I* was the one leaving Danny to fend for himself, to pick up the pieces. I'd see him, and he'd seem fine. Tired, but what person in healthcare isn't tired? But I'd been abandoning him the same way she'd abandoned me, caring more about my own emotional bullshit than his well-being."

He broke off then, clearly drowning in his own self-loathing.

It wouldn't do.

Soren released Gabe's hand, reaching over to grab the back of Gabe's neck. He squeezed gently, then pulled Gabe down to his level, looking him firmly in the eyes. "Do you know what, in my very long life, I've considered the most troubling of human emotions?"

Gabe stared back at him. "What?"

"Shame."

Gabe's eyes widened slightly in surprise. Had he been expecting Soren to condemn him for his anger?

"Shame infects every other emotion it touches." Soren squeezed the back of Gabe's neck again. "What I've just heard is the story of a boy—because fourteen is still a *boy*—forced to grow up too fast. To become a pseudoparent right after the loss of his own. Your anger at your mother is justified."

Gabe opened his mouth to protest, but Soren cut him off. "It *is*. But because she's sick, because of the responsibility you feel toward your brother, you're ashamed of that anger. You try to bottle it up, to guilt yourself out of it. But that's no way to heal. All it does is allow things to fester. You can be angry and still love your mom. You can hate seeing her like this, hate that she's forgotten you, and still do right by her. You're not a bad person."

That seemed to break something in Gabe, his eyes finally watering fully, tears spilling over onto his cheeks. Soren let go of his neck and leaned over the center console to cup Gabe's face with both hands, wiping at those tears with his thumbs.

"Fuck," Gabe swore. "I never cry."

Soren huffed. "That's not anything to be proud of."

Gabe gave him a watery smile. "Guess not. Why are you being so nice, brat?"

Soren shrugged, not letting go of Gabe's face. "I can be nice. When people deserve it."

"You really think I deserve it?"

The vulnerability in Gabe's voice was a knife to the heart. Who was this human, to affect Soren this way? It wasn't even a unique story. Family expectations and resentments. Loss. Soren should have been immune to it, living as long as he had, seeing all that he had. But hearing the guilt and self-blame Gabe had been dealing with made Soren ache to protect his human, this man so much bigger than Soren but so much more fragile.

Instead of answering Gabe's question, Soren kissed him, a gentle brush of lips. "So typical," he murmured as he pulled away.

"What is?" Gabe asked thickly.

"One blow job and you're admitting all your deepest, darkest secrets. It's just such a classic guy move."

Gabe looked stunned for a moment, and Soren worried that his big mouth had ruined things. It wouldn't be the first time. But then Gabe laughed. It was a muffled sound, his nose still stuffy from crying, but it was genuine.

"Guess I *am* pretty typical, huh?"

Except the annoying thing was, to Soren, Gabe was anything but.

Gabe took another few minutes to compose himself, then they went to see his mother.

Their visit wasn't the best, but it wasn't the worst either. Soren's compulsion wasn't enough to remind Gladys of who Gabe was this time; her dementia had progressed to the point where, even with supernatural aid, those memories weren't always accessible. Instead, she'd called Gabe by her brother's name.

Gabe had still managed to smile and greet her with a kiss on the cheek. Soren was immensely proud.

His compulsion may not have brought back her memories, but it had kept her calm and happy, enough to go for a walk and play a game of checkers after. Watching Gabe with his mother was fascinating but for no real reason Soren could discern. Gabe was just so...gentle with the woman. For all the anger and resentment he'd professed, he offered her nothing but soft smiles and calm reassurances. Almost like he was channeling Danny but with a certain charm that was all his own. He made her laugh and projected a confidence that had many of the other little old ladies staring after him.

Soren resisted the urge to hiss at them to stake his claim.

Golden boy. That was what Danny called his brother. And he was. It was easy to see why he'd been so popular in high school. Good looks and charm were enough on their own, but there was a genuine kindness and goodness underneath, even if Gabe wasn't aware of it himself, and that was a rarity in this world.

Just another reason Soren should leave.

Soren wasn't kind and good, not really. He was selfish and flighty. A monster, Gabe had called him. And it wasn't far from the truth. Soren generally didn't feel too bad about it. There were plenty of monsters in this world, and many were much, much worse than him.

But Gabe had apparently only ever wanted normalcy—to be a normal kid, a normal adult—and Soren had never even *liked* the word. Normalcy wasn't something Soren could provide a partner.

But on the drive home, Soren still found himself letting Gabe hold his hand again. Because he *was* selfish. And he wanted this man with every fiber of his being. He'd had a taste now, and he could see it quickly becoming a true addiction.

Soren didn't want to let this human go.

His phone dinged as they entered Danny's house.

Coming for you, angel.

Seven

Gabe

"Chill, little guy." Gabe removed Ferdy's leash, struggling to get ahold of his wiggling body. Apparently Gabe's runs did nothing to tire the puppy out. Only Soren's.

He watched as Ferdy ran back into the house, Gabe taking a minute to catch his breath before following. His run had done wonders to settle the jittery nerves left over from the care home.

They'd visited his mom for the second time together that morning. It was getting easier, walking in there. Knowing Soren would be there to keep him together if he started to fall apart was a comfort Gabe hadn't known he'd needed.

The vampire kept his distance during the visits, probably not wanting to confuse Gabe's mother with an unfamiliar face, but he stayed close with Gabe afterward, allowing him to let out whatever thoughts or memories or emotions had come up during the visit.

Gabe had no idea why Soren was suddenly so easy to talk to. Maybe it was just the fact that Gabe had never really tried before.

He'd been afraid for so long. Not of Soren, really. Afraid of losing himself, maybe. Of manipulation. Of the unknown. Or maybe just Soren seeing right through him.

But now the fact that Soren had seen Gabe in his weakest moments and still wanted him—a fact Soren had made clear just that morning by swallowing Gabe's cock down in the shower—made Gabe feel...some kind of way.

Gabe normally put so much effort into pretending. For someone to see through it and not run away?

He could get addicted to that feeling.

And for all his teasing, all his surface brattiness, the vampire was weirdly...kind. Understanding. And not afraid to call Gabe an idiot when he let himself get too tangled in his own thoughts. But was it really okay to rely so heavily on someone who could leave at any time? Who had no real roots here, no reason to stay?

Gabe found the object of his musings flopped on the living room couch, watching reality TV. Gabe plopped himself down next to him, hoping the vampire didn't mind that he hadn't showered after his run.

Soren never seemed to mind his smell though. Couldn't seem to get enough of it, in fact. Gabe had never met anyone as okay with his postworkout sweatiness as Soren.

"What is this crap?" Gabe griped, relaxing back into the couch.

Soren waved a hand without looking at him. "Hush, human. You know not of which you speak."

Gabe rolled his eyes, unable to help scooching closer to the vampire until he could rest his head easily on Soren's shoulder. It was as though, after a year of trying to keep his distance, now that Gabe had allowed himself to touch Soren, he *always* wanted to be touching him.

He'd opened the floodgates, apparently.

Something about it soothed him. Touching Soren had a way of settling the swirl of messy emotions that usually roiled in Gabe's gut. He nuzzled his head on the vampire's shoulder, groaning in pleasure went Soren started absently scratching a hand through Gabe's curls. It was pure bliss.

They sat like that for a while, Gabe melting slowly but surely into the vampire's touch. Soren's petting was even better than a run.

"You're kind of a homebody," Gabe said after a few more minutes of quiet cuddling.

Soren paused his scratching. "What about it?"

Gabe shrugged, pushing his head back into Soren's hand, encouraging it to start moving again. "Isn't it, like, kind of boring? After everything you've done? Staying here?"

Soren hummed thoughtfully. "I don't seem to mind it. Maybe I'm getting old." He giggled wildly to himself, like that was the funniest thing in the world. "And what about you, Highness?" he asked after his laughter quieted.

Gabe shifted, turning his head so Soren could pet the other side. "What about me?"

"Shouldn't you be going out with old high school buddies? Playing beer pong or whatever?"

Gabe grunted. "You do know I'm a doctor, not a frat boy, right?"

Soren's answer was to tug Gabe's curls in a way that forced him to look up and meet the vampire's eyes. "Tell me the truth," Soren teased. "You were in a frat in college, weren't you?"

Gabe felt himself flushing. "It's a good way to make connections."

Soren giggled again. Gabe was realizing he liked that sound an awful lot.

"So why don't you hit the town more?" Soren asked again, releasing his tight hold.

Gabe shrugged, resting his head down. "It's not really that fun, I guess. It all feels...superficial. They all know this old version of me. Makes me feel like a faker. Like I'm pretending all the time."

"So you just *pretend* to be an asshole?"

Gabe laughed. "No, I *am* an asshole. I pretend to be a carefree one."

"And you don't think people will like the real version of you?" Soren asked.

Damn, always one to cut to the heart of things.

"Not really," Gabe answered hesitantly.

Soren's pale eyes narrowed. "And why don't you think people will like the real Gabriel Kingman?"

Gabe cleared his throat, toying with the bottom of Soren's shirt. "Um...because he's a coward? He pretends to know what he's doing, but he's really just, like, terrified all the time?"

"What are you terrified of?"

"I don't know. Just...everything. It always feels like something awful is about to happen at any moment. I've always struggled with it, but it's gotten worse this past year."

That put a strange expression on Soren's face. "Why this past year?"

Gabe gave him an "are you kidding?" face. "Because something awful *did* happen. I was attacked. Danny was kidnapped. He almost *died.* He kind of did, in a way."

Gabe could still remember the shock, the gut-wrenching *loss.* Having to hear from Roman and Soren that Danny had been hurt beyond healing, turned into something *other.* That he and Gabe were somehow no longer the same species. That his little brother was forever changed.

Soren pushed Gabe lightly until he was sitting up, the vampire leaning back until they were face-to-face. "Danny's *fine,*" he said firmly.

Gabe tried not to panic at the loss of Soren's touch. "Danny's not human anymore though."

Soren glared at him. "*I'm* not human."

Gabe was putting his foot in his mouth in all sorts of ways. "That's not— I'm not— It's just a little freaky, okay?"

Soren arched a pale brow. "Why is it, as you say, *freaky?*"

Gabe ran a hand through his own curls roughly, frustrated with himself. "You know what makes me feel less scared? Knowing things. Knowing how things *work.* Knowing how bodies work is how I'm able to fix them. It's how I make a living. Vampires were never part of that equation. I have no idea how *your* body works."

Soren smirked at him. "You want to know how my body works, Highness?"

Gabe ignored the innuendo. "What if something happens to Danny? I won't be able to fix it."

Soren's eyes softened in realization. "Danny is much, *much* stronger now than when he was human, Highness. He's not in any danger. There's nothing for you to fix."

Gabe had nothing to say to that.

Soren was right, even if Gabe didn't like to admit it. Danny was going to live years—*centuries*—longer than Gabe could even dream of. His brother didn't need his protection.

Not that Gabe had ever been good at protecting Danny anyway.

He sighed, grumbling to himself, but he leaned his head back onto Soren's shoulder, pleased when Soren didn't push him away.

He grabbed at Soren's hand and placed it back on his head, and Soren resumed his petting.

Gabe let out another deep breath, melting back into Soren's touch. He felt...lighter somehow. Was this how everyone felt, opening up about their feelings all the time? It was kind of awesome.

Or maybe it was just Soren that made it that way.

They watched Soren's stupid show for a while, Gabe only half-aware of what was on the television.

"What do you want out of life, Highness?" Soren asked out of nowhere.

"I don't know. What everyone wants, I guess. To be happy. Just not sure I know how." The truth of that slipped easily out of Gabe's lips, in his relaxed state.

Soren hummed. "Maybe you should stop being such a stick in the mud all the time. Fun can make people happy."

"Did it make you happy, all these years?"

"I thought so. For a long time." Soren sounded thoughtful. And a little sad.

Gabe sat up. "I can be fun." He lunged, digging his fingers into Soren's ribs.

Soren just stared at him, unimpressed, while Gabe ran his fingers along every would-be ticklish spot he could find. "What are you doing, human?"

"Huh." Gabe sat back, eyeing the vampire. "That used to work on Danny."

Soren huffed. "I'm not your brother."

"Good thing, huh?" Gabe grinned. He went back to his cuddling position, this time with his head in Soren's lap. He inhaled the vampire's comforting scent, allowing it to relax his muscles even more. There was a low-level arousal humming through his body, at Soren's smell and his nearness, but he chose to ignore it.

Maybe he and Soren would get each other off before he left for work, but Gabe liked this part of it too. When the flirty, teasing vampire let Gabe be soft and needy.

Gabe was apparently turning into a cuddle slut in his thirties. It was weird; he'd never been one before.

Breathing in deeply, Gabe had a thought. "I haven't seen you smoke."

Soren's petting paused again. "Is that so?"

"You were smoking the first night I met you," Gabe pointed out.

Soren hummed that noncommittal hum he loved. "Flattered you remember."

There was an extended pause.

"Soren," Gabe pressed.

"Yes?" Soren asked innocently.

"Why did you stop?"

Soren huffed. "Well, you don't like the smell, do you?"

Gabe didn't know what to do with that information. Soren had stopped because Gabe didn't like it?

"Do you like Hyde Park?" he found himself asking. It suddenly seemed very important to know.

Soren was silent for so long Gabe thought he wouldn't answer. "Not particularly."

"Oh."

Soren cleared his throat, his hand lifting off Gabe's head. "I probably— I can't— I'll most likely move on soon enough."

Gabe nodded to himself. That made sense.

That made perfect sense.

But the warm relaxation that had been building in Gabe cooled in an instant. The knot in his stomach was back in full force.

Still, he couldn't bring himself to leave the couch. He wanted to keep touching Soren. Wanted to keep feeling this good.

Even if it wouldn't last.

Gabe sighed, tilting his head to one side, then the other, trying to work out the kink in his neck. He was close to done putting in orders for the patient he'd just visited. He was hoping they'd be able to get the breathing tube out by morning. When he'd told her, she'd had tears of relief in her eyes—it was painful, being on a breathing machine when you were awake enough to be aware of it. She had grabbed Gabe's hand in gratitude, and it had taken everything in him not to shed some tears himself.

He was a little...extra emotional lately. As if his new habit of opening up to Soren had released something inside him.

When Gabe's dad had died, the medical staff were the only people who had been any source of calm in the storm, the only ones who had seemed to have any sort of control over the situation.

His mom had been too out of it. Danny had been too young. And Gabe had been...lost. Too old to have a meltdown the way he wanted, too young to have any idea what was really going on. When a doctor had taken them aside and explained his dad's injuries, Gabe had been so grateful that here was an *adult*, someone competent and capable and in charge.

Gabe hadn't gone into medicine for the same pure reasons Danny had gone into nursing. Gabe didn't have the compulsion his brother had to save everyone, to *care* for everyone. Gabe had just... He'd wanted to be that person. The competent, capable adult. The one with the answers, for once.

He'd wanted the world to make sense. To cover his messy emotions with his own version of proficient authority. But somewhere along the way, he'd come to like being a source of comfort for people. Most patients didn't care that Gabe wasn't naturally warm and fuzzy—his skill set in and of itself made them feel safe.

He was just finishing up his notes when a familiar figure filled the doorway of the dictation room.

"How's it going in here?"

Gabe looked up, trying to hide his annoyance. "Monroe. What are you doing working tonight?"

All the ICU fellows had to work night shift at some point, but Monroe's and Gabe's schedules didn't usually overlap. A fact for which Gabe was very grateful.

Monroe dropped into the chair next to him. "Filling in for Dr. Birch. Lucky you, huh?"

"Mm." Gabe turned his eyes back to his computer. He wanted to get all his notes and charting done. He didn't want to run late today. He wanted to get back home and...sleep.

Hell, who was he kidding?

He wanted to get back home to the little monster. Somehow Soren had become the highlight of his day. Not just because he could make Gabe come with a force that had his eyes rolling to the back of his head either.

Gabe had friends, sure. At least, sort of. He had...acquaintances. Superficial bonds with people he'd known since high school. But none that he opened up to about deep, emotional stuff. The last person probably would have been his ex-girlfriend, a woman he'd dated briefly during residency, but any moments of vulnerability from him had seemed to turn her off more than anything. As if she expected Gabe to be the strong one and hated if he fell out of that role.

And Danny... Danny had enough he'd been dealing with—partly *because* of Gabe and his denial over their mom—he didn't need Gabe dumping his own shit on him too.

But Soren listened. He comforted. He teased a little, yes. But he didn't make Gabe feel lesser just for having feelings.

"I saw your friend the other night." Monroe's too-smooth voice broke through Gabe's thoughts.

"Which friend?" Gabe asked without interest.

"The pretty blond one." That got Gabe's attention. "Soren. He's a wild one, eh?" Monroe waggled his eyebrows.

"Yeah, he's a riot." Gabe's stomach churned at the implication in Monroe's words. When had this been? He didn't want to give Monroe the satisfaction of asking any follow-up questions.

It didn't make sense. He and Soren had been staying in together on all Gabe's nights off.

Except... Gabe had worked the night before.

Had Soren gone off and, what...fucked Monroe?

Gabe tried to curb his rage at the thought, spots flashing in his vision. Soren was a vampire. He had to feed. Gabe knew that. And if vamps mixed sex and blood, it only made sense.

Then why did the thought make Gabe so miserable?

He tried to make himself take a full breath. He was jumping to conclusions; he knew that.

"You've hit that?" Monroe didn't seem to realize how close he was coming to getting decked in the face. "Didn't mean to step on your toes, man. He was desperate for it though. Little minx."

Well, never mind the whole "jumping to conclusions" thing. Gabe logged out of his computer, leaving the room without another word, ignoring Monroe's calls behind him. His orders were in. His notes could wait.

He needed to get home. He needed answers.

Gabe tried his best to get his emotions under control on the drive to Danny's, but his hands were clenching on the steering wheel hard enough to hurt.

He knew he was being unreasonable. He and Soren weren't anything to each other. Temporary roommates who'd taken to getting each other off. And Soren wasn't even human, for fuck's sake. He probably had no concept of fidelity, monogamy.

Roman worships the ground Danny walks on. Gabe pushed the unhelpful thought aside. Roman and Danny were mates. Tethered souls. Gabe was just...convenient for Soren.

So what if Soren was nice to him? So what if holding Soren on the couch made the tight ball of anxiety ever-present in Gabe's stomach suddenly melt away?

Gabe slammed the front door on his way into the house.

So much for getting his emotions under control.

He found Soren settled on the couch with Ferdy. He was...crocheting? Gabe refused to find that adorable. Who knew where Soren had been before this? Maybe he'd tired himself out banging random dudes at the club.

Jesus. Gabe was disgusted by his own thoughts. He'd never been a jealous person before. He didn't understand this monster that was suddenly under his skin.

"What's wrong?" Soren eyed him and his clenched jaw, his own welcoming grin dropping.

"Nothing," Gabe gritted out.

Soren rolled his yes. "I highly doubt that, Highness. You look like you're about to punch someone."

"I'm fine."

Soren tsked. "Liar."

"Why is it any of your business anyway?" Gabe knew he was putting his foot in his mouth, but as always happened when he was overwhelmed, he couldn't seem to stop.

"I guess it's not." Soren's voice had gone cold.

Fuck. Gabe was fucking everything up. "When did you last feed?"

Soren raised a brow at him. "A week ago."

"Did you feed from Monroe?"

"Ah, I see." Soren's gaze shuttered. "You're pissed the monster fed from your friend? I didn't hurt him, Scout's honor."

Gabe felt like someone had just knifed him in the chest. "But did you *fuck* him?"

Soren's eyes widened at the accusation. Weirdly enough, the vampire...grinned.

"Interesting...," Soren murmured. He took his time setting down his crochet hook, tilting his head to the side and studying Gabe intently. "Very interesting."

"Did you?" Gabe asked again. He couldn't help it. He needed to *know.*

Soren rose slowly from his seated position. Considering how much smaller he was than Gabe, the move shouldn't have been intimidating, but it was.

"You're jealous." Soren approached Gabe with a shark's grin on his lips. "How silly of you."

Gabe ran a shaky hand through his hair. "I just think, if you're going to fuck around, you should at least have the decency to stay away from my coworkers."

Never mind the fact that he and Soren hadn't even been hooking up yet a week ago. Gabe's mouth was running entirely separate from his brain.

"You're going to shut up now," Soren ordered calmly. He was still grinning, the little lunatic. His body was right up against Gabe now. The vampire reached a hand up, batting Gabe's away, and slid his own fingers into Gabe's hair, tightening his grip to pull Gabe's head down toward him.

Gabe drew in a sharp breath at the sting.

"Do you know how many men I've fucked since coming to this town?" Soren asked, his voice mild.

Gabe was going to be sick. He really didn't want to know that number.

Soren chuckled at his silence. "Zero," he whispered into Gabe's ear. "None. Not a one. Do you know *why?*"

Gabe shook his head, or at least as much as Soren's tight grip would allow.

Soren's pale eyes peered into his own. "You're not ready to know, Highness. Suffice it to say, the beast inside me—the one driven to feed and to fuck—it's a little *fixated* lately. On one single idiot in particular."

Gabe's skin burned. His whole body was on fire. Had Soren really been celibate? Was he really saying what Gabe thought he was saying? This achingly beautiful vampire, this little psycho flirt who could have any man he wanted, only wanted Gabe?

Soren bit his earlobe with blunt teeth, and Gabe groaned, his cock swelling rapidly at the onslaught. "Apologize," Soren demanded, biting down again.

"I'm sorry," Gabe panted.

Soren licked around the shell of his ear, soothing the sting. "How will you make it up to me?"

"However you want." Gabe was putty in his hands.

"I want you to fuck me, Highness."

Jesus. Gabe was a goner. He was drowning, and Soren was both the water and the life raft.

"Yes," he managed, leaning forward into the vampire's hold, pressing his lips to Soren's.

Whatever Soren wanted, Gabe would give it to him.

Eight

Gabe

Their trip up the stairs was a fumbling mess of lips and limbs.

Gabe didn't want to stop kissing Soren for a single moment, only releasing the vampire's mouth when Soren growled at him impatiently, demanding he start removing his clothes.

Bossy little monster.

The relief Gabe felt at knowing Soren hadn't hooked up with that sleazeball after all had his hands trembling. Why it mattered so much—why Gabe had turned into such a jealous beast—well, he'd examine all that later. Right now he barely had the brainpower to find his own room. All the blood in his body had traveled down to his hard cock, straining against his pants.

By the time they entered Gabe's temporary bedroom, they were both naked, their mouths fused once again. Soren bit Gabe's lower lip with blunt teeth, then broke away to push Gabe onto the bed with firm hands. The little vampire seemed to love manhandling Gabe.

Fuck, why was that so hot?

Gabe had always been the bigger, stronger partner when it came to his hookups. By all appearances, this pairing should be no different, but Soren's vampire strength turned the tables. It was strangely sexy.

Soren looked so delicate, all lithe angles and petite build. But he was strong enough to do whatever he wanted to Gabe, to *make* Gabe do whatever he wanted. And that contrast for some reason had Gabe mindless with lust.

"Lube," Soren demanded, his hands on his slight hips, his flushed cock jutting out in front of him.

Gabe's breath caught at the sight. Soren's dick was just as lovely as the rest of him—long and thin and such a pretty fucking pink. Gabe wanted it back in his mouth, wanted to suck Soren down and work some more of those little whimpers out of him.

But Soren had other plans. The vampire growled with impatience, and Gabe made himself find his words. "My bag. Outside pocket."

He watched as Soren padded over to Gabe's duffel bag on light feet, graceful as a house cat.

God, he was beautiful.

All pale skin and toned, slender limbs. A pert ass that bounced lightly as he walked.

And he wanted *Gabe*. Enough to feed on humans without going any further, without looking for sex.

For a whole goddamn year.

Soren approached the bed again after claiming his prize, climbing up onto his knees to straddle Gabe's hips. Gabe's cock was hard as stone, bobbing gently above his stomach as he stared up at this little demon who had him by the metaphorical throat.

He watched as Soren poured lube onto his fingers, reaching behind himself with one slicked-up hand. God, he was going to open himself up for Gabe's cock.

So fucking hot.

Gabe wanted to feel him. "Can I do it?" he asked desperately, aching to touch, to get his hands on that perfect ass.

Soren smirked down at him, shaking his head slowly. "You've been a naughty boy, Highness," he taunted. "Accusing me of all sorts of nasty things."

Gabe flushed, but it was hard to focus on the reprimand. He was mesmerized by the movements of Soren's arm, the rhythmic motion of it. The little minx was opening himself up *while* chastising Gabe.

It was fucking hotter than sin.

"I'm sorry," Gabe said for the second time, needing Soren to know he meant it.

Soren hummed, not giving him anything else. His slender pink cock was flushed and leaking, and Gabe again wanted nothing more than to put his mouth on it.

Maybe Soren would move up and let Gabe suck him down again?

But he had a feeling Soren wouldn't allow that just now. So Gabe placed his hands ever so gently on the vampire's thighs instead, gratified when Soren let them stay there. He stroked the smooth skin of Soren's inner thighs. The vampire's skin was like silk.

"Why is it you think you have any right to dictate who I sleep with?" Soren demanded, his breath coming in short bursts now as his hand worked behind him.

"I don't," Gabe admitted, gazing up helplessly.

Soren arched an eyebrow, the imperious effect only slightly ruined by the desperate movements of his hips, thrusting in time with his hand's movements.

"I just—the thought of you with someone else...," Gabe started, but he didn't know how to end the statement.

"You don't like it," Soren finished for him.

"I hate it," Gabe bit out. "I wanted to strangle Monroe."

Soren grinned at him, his hand and hips stilling. When had that manic grin stopped looking unsettling and instead become sexy as hell?

"Good," Soren declared, baring his teeth even wider. "Because if I see you with anyone else, I'll rip their throat out."

Jesus.

That should have been a statement that made Gabe's cock soften, not harden even more. He rubbed his hands over Soren's pale thighs, resisting the urge to palm the vampire's ass. "I don't want anyone else," he reassured.

Soren's grin changed then. Softened in that way it sometimes did just for Gabe. He brought his hand forward, and Gabe's back arched as Soren's delicate fingers rubbed the excess lube onto Gabe's cock, readying it for Soren. And then he was lowering himself, his movements graceful and fluid as ever, even as the thick head of Gabe's cock breached his hole.

A little demon princeling.

Gabe shut his eyes, trying to keep himself from coming immediately at the sight as Soren's tight heat enveloped him. He bit his lip almost hard enough to draw blood as Soren slid down further. The vampire's channel was squeezing the life out of Gabe's cock. It was too much and not enough all at the same time.

When Soren's ass was touching Gabe's thighs, Gabe's cock bottoming out inside him, Gabe moved his hands from Soren's thighs to his hips, rubbing his thumbs along the equally silky skin there.

He couldn't stop touching him.

But he kept his grip light. Soren may have asked Gabe to fuck him, but Gabe was in no doubt of who was running the show.

And Gabe was happy to let him. So fucking happy.

He was rewarded when Soren started to move in an easy rhythm, his hips swiveling every other thrust in a way that made Gabe see stars.

Gabe slammed his head back into the pillow, groaning. "Fuck. Baby."

Soren giggled. Fucking *giggled*, the movement jostling him around Gabe's cock in a way that had Gabe groaning again. "Baby?" Soren questioned, finally calling Gabe out on the pet name that kept escaping every time Soren got his hands on him.

"Fuck. Yes. I don't know." Gabe was practically delirious with pleasure. "Baby. Brat. Baby brat."

Really, this was unfair. Soren was far too coherent.

Gabe flattened his feet on the bed, raising his hips to meet Soren thrust for thrust, gratified when Soren whimpered, leaning forward to dig his fingers into Gabe's shoulders.

He opened his eyes again, unable to resist the sight of Soren riding him, those pale eyes so close to his. "You're so fucking beautiful, brat."

He should be embarrassed by the reverence in his voice, but it was true. He was the most beautiful thing Gabe had ever seen.

Soren responded by increasing the speed of his hips, gripping Gabe's shoulders harder. Gabe moved his hands to finally grab that perky ass, pulling Soren flush against him as they ground together. Pleasure traveled from his cock along his spine, his balls tightening against his body. "Fuck. Gonna come, baby. Gonna come."

"Not yet," Soren ordered breathlessly.

Gabe groaned in distress, but his body complied with the order somehow. He didn't have to wait long, luckily. A few more thrusts and Soren was coming with another whimper, his hot release coating Gabe's stomach.

"Thank fuck," Gabe breathed. It took less than a minute for him to follow suit, his vision whiting out as he finished inside Soren, his thighs shaking as his cum filled the little vampire.

Fuck. Jesus fuck.

Gabe had never gone bare with anyone before. Had never wanted the risk. Or the intimacy. But there was something so primal about it, knowing a part of him was left inside Soren. Gabe didn't want to pull out. He wanted to stay connected in this unbelievably intimate way.

But Soren gave a sigh of satisfaction, lifting himself in one smooth motion off Gabe's cock, rolling off his body and onto his side. Gabe immediately curled himself around the vampire, tucking Soren's slight body into his chest.

"I'm not some virgin maiden," Soren grumbled. "I don't need a cuddle after every time."

Gabe knew better now than to be offended. "*I* need it," he said lightly.

And it was true. He seemed to only be able to breathe fully when he was touching some part of Soren.

Soren huffed but obligingly burrowed his head into Gabe's chest, his warm breath tickling Gabe's skin. They spent a few minutes like that, Gabe stroking Soren's back gently, before Soren spoke up. "Why did you think I fucked Monroe?"

Gabe didn't want that asshole's name anywhere in their bed, but it *was* Gabe's fault for bringing it up in the first place. "Something he said," he answered, his fingers tracing along the knobs of Soren's spine. "About you being desperate for it."

Soren giggled. "That's just what the compulsion made him remember. I fed on him, nothing else."

"I know. I believe you."

But something unpleasant still itched under Gabe's skin at the thought. "Soren?"

"Mm?" Soren hummed, pressing a kiss to Gabe's chest.

"You said you fed a week ago."

"Yes?" Another kiss.

"Then you need to feed again soon?"

Soren raised his head to peer at him. "In the next few days. Why?"

"Would you— I could—" Even though Gabe had started this conversation, he struggled to get to his point. "Would you want to feed...from me?"

It was something Gabe had never thought he'd offer. Something he'd thought he feared. But apparently even stubborn assholes could change.

Soren's body went still as stone, and his pale eyes darkened. "You'd let me?"

"Um...yes?" Gabe would. He couldn't remember anymore why he'd once found the idea so disgusting. Blood was something Soren needed. Something essential that Gabe could give him. Something Gabe was realizing he didn't want Soren getting from anyone else.

Soren gazed at him for a long moment before nodding slowly. "Okay. Yeah. But...not tonight."

Gabe's brow furrowed. "Why not?"

Soren tucked his head back into Gabe's body, directing his words there. "You're sex-drunk. I'm not sure you know what you're saying. If you still want to tomorrow, I will."

Gabe felt something warm unfurl in his chest. Here Gabe was offering himself up on a platter, and Soren was giving him time to back out. Gabe knew he wouldn't, but the thoughtfulness behind the move had him pulling Soren even closer.

"You and your cuddling," Soren griped.

But he didn't pull away.

Nine

Soren

Soren fucking loved the modern world. The freeness with which humans were now able to live and love and fuck whomever and however they liked.

It wasn't perfect, obviously. Prejudices still existed, and people still suffered for their own desires in a multitude of unfair ways, but it was miles away from the uptight eras of the past. Soren had hated the fifties in particular. A goddamn terrible decade, in his less-than-humble opinion.

He eyed the gyrating bodies through the flashing lights of the club. He was watching one couple more than the others, a particularly attractive pair of men who were grinding up against each other. He reveled in the blatant lust radiating off of them.

Soren didn't *want* them, not really. He didn't want to take them home and play with them in tandem in the way he might have in the past.

But he liked watching them.

He tore his eyes away and searched the crowd for the one he *did* want.

There.

Gabe was squeezing his way through the pulsing bodies on the dance floor, a beer in one hand and a cocktail in the other. Soren drank in the delectable sight of him.

He had let Soren dress him. The human had grumbled against it, of course, but in the end, he'd complied beautifully anyway.

And Soren had shown such restraint, really.

He'd kept it simple, decking Gabe out in a pair of tight black jeans and an even tighter black T-shirt, putting Gabe's golden skin and lickable muscles on delicious display. The black set off the human's dark curls, which he'd let Soren put a little gel in, slicking them back from his face.

Soren's cock twitched as he admired his sartorial work. The human looked like walking sex.

As did Soren, obviously. He'd decided to play into the drama of the night—the night where Gabe was going to let Soren bite him—and was wearing tight leather pants with a sheer baby-blue long-sleeved top. A dash of black eyeliner set off his pale-blue eyes, making them practically glow.

Gabe had swallowed hard at the sight of him, and Soren had been tempted to forgo going out at all. To feed at home after feasting on Gabe's body in...other ways.

Feeding on Gabe. What a fucking concept.

Soren had been stunned at the offer, honestly. The night before had been a bit of a whirlwind in more than one way. First there had been Gabe's unexpected jealousy. Soren had thought they were backsliding—that Gabe was upset at the thought of Soren, resident monster, drinking the blood of someone he knew. He'd been tickled pink to realize it was simple jealousy over Gabe thinking Soren had fucked Monroe.

As if Soren would ever have such poor taste.

But the fact that Gabe wanted Soren enough to wish him to forgo not only sleeping with other people but also drinking anyone else's blood was a heady thing. It was frankly ridiculous that Soren had even had the restraint to give Gabe a day to think it over. His inner vamp had been raging, not used to being denied something Soren wanted so very much.

But, watching his handsome human move through the crowd, Soren was starting to think good things came to those who waited.

Gabe finally reached their little table, setting the two drinks down before sliding into the booth next to Soren, both of them facing out to the crowd. He nodded to the couple Soren had been watching, who were now making out somewhat ferociously, practically humping each other on the dance floor. "Do you know them?"

Soren shook his head, grinning at his human. "No. I just like to *watch*." He put deliberate emphasis on the last word, making it sound as salacious as possible. He kept a careful eye on Gabe's expression, looking for any signs of disgust or jealousy.

It was one thing for Gabe to be jealous of Soren fucking someone else—after all, Soren didn't want Gabe fucking anyone else either, as the idea made him positively murderous—but it was another for him to want Soren to act like some kind of monk.

Some kind of *angel.*

But Gabe just nodded, smiling almost shyly around a sip of his beer. "They're a beautiful couple. Did you want to go dance?"

Soren arched a brow. "And if I did? You wouldn't mind us dancing like that? In public?"

Gabe cocked his head, then asked, his deep voice mild, "Tell me, brat. Is tonight supposed to be some kind of...test?"

See? This human, for all his emotional blockheadedness, was way too perceptive for his own good.

Because Soren had to admit, if only to himself, that bringing Gabe here was in some ways a fucked-up kind of test. Soren had deliberately chosen a wild spot, one where public groping and bathroom fucking were the norm. They'd had to drive over an hour to get there, so it wasn't like they'd run into anyone Gabe knew, but still...the atmosphere was a little intense for someone used to a mostly straight lifestyle.

But Gabe had taken it all in stride, holding Soren's hand on the way in, accepting the male bartender's flirtations with ease. And now he apparently wanted to dance with Soren, to grind against each other in a very public setting.

Soren fiddled with his glass. This human was making him...*feel* things. "Well...I've been quite...*homey* with you, up until now. But I like the nightlife too, you know. I like flirting. Dancing. Drinking. *Biting.*"

He flashed his teeth at Gabe in a not-quite smile.

Gabe smirked, taking another sip of his beer. "Okay. I knew that about you already. You all right doing those things with me? Because I like all that too. Just haven't had much time in my adult life to explore them. First residency. And now, you know, Hyde Park doesn't have the best nightlife in the world."

Gabe scooted a little closer, so the sides of their bodies were touching, and reached over to brush a lock of Soren's hair behind his ear. Soren did his best not to shiver at the gentle touch.

"And I don't mind who you flirt with, brat, as long as I get to be the one who takes you home at the end of the night."

Christ. The human couldn't just *say* things like that. They were about to enter dangerously mushy territory.

To hide how touched he was, Soren fisted the front of Gabe's shirt and pulled him close. "Why wait until the end of the night?"

Soren could feel Gabe's answering smile as their lips met. He plundered the human's mouth with his tongue, claiming it all as his territory. And Gabe let him. He moaned, opened wide, and let Soren dominate him however he liked.

He kept *doing that*. Letting Soren run the show. Letting him play with that beautiful, muscled body in whichever way he pleased.

At this rate, Soren was going to have to keep him.

Soren broke the kiss before he did something stupid like offer himself up on the table. He pushed Gabe out of the booth with both hands and pulled him to the crowded floor. "Dance time, Highness."

They moved together in a sultry rhythm. Gabe had surprisingly good moves, for a former football player. They danced with his front to Soren's back, Gabe's hands sliding over Soren's hips, across his stomach. The touch was so distracting, Soren's cock firming under his leather pants, that it took him a minute to notice Gabe was maneuvering him slowly over to the hot couple they'd been watching.

The other duo took notice of them right away, taking the hint of their close proximity and bracketing Soren and Gabe with their bodies. For a few songs, they were all a jumble of writhing limbs. Soren lost himself to the music, all thoughts and doubts leaving his brain, simply dancing to his heart's content. Every now and then, Gabe would catch his eye, grinning broadly.

Who knew the human could be so fun?

Soren decided they needed a break when the dark-haired twink of the pair, who'd been gyrating against Gabe for most of the current song, started running his hands more deliberately over Gabe's ass.

Soren growled to himself, tugging Gabe out of the other man's arms, standing on tiptoe to whisper in his human's ear, "I'm about to break some fingers."

Gabe shook his head but smiled down at Soren, mouthing an apology to the other couple as Soren pulled him away through the crowd.

Soren was mostly kidding—the other pair had been good dance partners, and he didn't begrudge a little groping—but he didn't want anyone getting the idea that Gabe was up for grabs.

He was, most decidedly, *not*.

Soren could feel his inner vamp itching to stake its claim. He didn't particularly want to be fucked in this club, but there was something else they *could* do.

Soren guided Gabe into a dark corner on the other edge of the dance floor, pushing his human up against the wall.

Soren had worked up an appetite.

Gabe gave a dopey smile as Soren backed him into the dark corner. There was a looseness to the bigger man now. It could have been the dancing, or possibly Soren's human was a little tipsy at this point.

Either way, Soren didn't mind taking advantage. He had already confirmed on the car ride over that Gabe was still a willing victim.

Soren grinned his shark's grin as Gabe's hands landed on his hips, the man's thumbs sliding just under Soren's shirt to rub at the tender skin there. "You still want what you offered me last night?" Soren asked in spite of himself.

Look at him, being so good, asking for permission a third time.

Gabe stiffened, his hands gripping Soren's hips a little tighter. But he didn't jerk away, instead using his grip on Soren to pull him even closer.

"Yes." Gabe's voice was barely audible over the music, but it was steady. "I want you to drink from me."

Soren rubbed a soothing hand over Gabe's hard chest. He didn't scent any fear from his human, only desire built up from all that dancing.

Or maybe the idea of getting bitten turned Gabe on?

Soren grinned wider at the thought. It sure as hell turned Soren on. He'd been wanting to sink his fangs into this man since the first day he saw him. The little taste he'd gotten on the day Soren had healed him from Lucien's attack hadn't been nearly enough.

Gabe placed his own hand over Soren's on his chest. "Will it hurt? Danny said it doesn't usually hurt. Was—was he just saying that?"

So not fear, exactly, but his human was definitely nervous. Soren shook his head. "Maybe for an instant, but I promise you I'll make you feel good. Very, *very* good."

Soren licked his lips, his gaze moving to Gabe's neck. He knew he should feel more empathy for Gabe's nerves, but the predator in him was focused on only one thing right now.

Soren wanted this—wanted *him*—and he was beyond ready to take what he wanted.

"Close your eyes, Highness," he purred.

Warmth bloomed in Soren's chest when Gabe complied easily, dark lashes fluttering. Soren let his vamp come to the surface. If the corner weren't so dark and hidden, the changes might be evident to those around them but not necessarily. Vampires were subtle monsters. Adapted for blending in with their prey. Soren knew his eyes were darkening, black taking over his pale irises and the whites beyond. He felt his fangs drop.

But that was it. Easy as pie.

He reached an arm up, placing a hand on the back of Gabe's neck to bend him down to Soren's level, rising onto his toes to meet the human halfway. He liked Gabe's size normally, was delighted and turned on by taking control of the larger man, but it was a little inconvenient for feeding.

Maybe Soren should have worn his heeled boots.

When Gabe was right where he wanted him, Soren dropped a soft kiss on his neck, directly over his pulsing jugular. Gabe's breath hitched. Soren tongued the same spot, lavishing it with attention.

"Soren..." Gabe's voice came out strained.

"Yes, Highness?" Soren smiled against his salty skin.

"You're teasing me."

Soren licked his mark again. "Just warming you up."

Gabe's fingers spasmed on Soren's hips. "Please, Soren."

Well, when he asked so nicely...

Soren couldn't possibly deny such a polite request. He sank his fangs in with one smooth motion, moaning around the burst of flavor on his tongue. Gabe tasted as delicious as he smelled—clean and bright, with earthy undertones that had Soren's head swimming.

Or possibly that was Gabe's blood alcohol level. Soren had gotten buzzed off drunk victims before—it was actually a faster way for vampires to feel the effects of alcohol, rather than consuming booze themselves.

He drank deep, gratified when he felt Gabe's cock hardening against his stomach, the human moaning in surprise at his own reaction. Soren couldn't blame him. His own cock was hard as well. *Blood and sex.* This was what life—a vampire's life—was all about.

If he wanted, Soren could enhance the pleasurable sensations his venom was sparking along Gabe's neurons with compulsion, but Gabe didn't seem to need it. Soren had never been so pleased with the side effects of a vampire's bite as he was now, feeling Gabe's undeniable reaction against him.

Because he didn't just want to claim Gabe. He wanted Gabe to feel *good.* To crave being fed on the same way Soren already knew he was going to crave feeding on his human.

Ending a bite had never been a problem for Soren—not since his very first days as a vampire—but it took every ounce of willpower to release his hold on Gabe's neck.

The human just tasted so *goddamn good.*

Soren placated himself by lapping up stray drops as he licked the wound closed with his healing saliva, humming to himself.

Gabe was panting against him, his fingers still in bruising grips on Soren's hips. "Fuck. I mean—fuck. Danny told me it felt good. I just— I thought he was trying to keep me from worrying."

Soren dropped a last kiss over the now-healed bite. "No. It's usually very...pleasant...for humans."

"And—" Gabe paused, and Soren swore he could see a flush forming on the man's cheeks under the club's flashing lights. "You could do that just with me, right? I have enough blood to...satisfy you?"

A pang of desire shot through Soren at the thought. Feeding on Gabe. Feeding *only* on Gabe.

But he couldn't resist teasing. "If that's what you like... In the old days, vampires often kept a favorite human pet to feed on exclusively."

As expected, Gabe's brow furrowed immediately. "I'm not your *pet*."

Soren smirked up at him. "Then what are you?"

But Soren didn't get to hear the answer to his question, because out of the corner of his eye, he saw a familiar face in the crowd.

One that couldn't possibly be there.

Every muscle in Soren's body tensed. *He can't have found me already.*

"Stay here," he barked, pressing Gabe back against the wall. Gabe opened his mouth to protest, but Soren was gone before the words could leave the man's mouth.

He pushed through the crowd in the direction he'd seen him.

Not there.

Soren tore through every inch of the club, aware that he was moving faster than a human should be able to, unable to find it in himself to care. Hopefully the flashing strobes would hide it, make the crowd think it was a trick of the light.

Not *fucking* there.

Had Soren been seeing things? Was his fear making him paranoid? Maybe the strain of over a century of running was finally catching up to him.

Unsuccessful, he eventually made his way back over to Gabe, who was standing in the same corner he'd been left in, arms crossed over his chest, an impressive scowl on his handsome face.

"What the fuck, Soren?" Gabe glared at him. "You feed off me, call me your 'pet,' then just disappear? What, you saw something tastier-looking across the way?"

There was real hurt in Gabe's tone, hurt Soren should address, but he could feel old defenses coming to the forefront. He rolled his eyes. "Your jealousy was cute at first, human, but it's quickly growing old."

Soren watched as the color drained from Gabe's face. *Fuck, fuck, fuck.* Soren was fucking everything up, too frustrated and overwhelmed to be patient the way he should with Gabe's insecurities.

Normally, this was where Soren would just...walk away. He hated misunderstandings, considered them an easy excuse to let someone go. Explaining himself took emotional energy Soren didn't usually care enough to give.

But he found himself walking toward Gabe instead of away, placing his hand on Gabe's chest, over the man's heart. Gabe held himself stiffly, but he didn't reject Soren's touch.

That was something, right?

"I'm sorry." The words tasted like ash in Soren's mouth. A perfect night, ruined by Soren's shitty baggage. "I can explain, but I want to go home first. Is that okay?"

He waited for the yelling, for the accusations, but Gabe only nodded, his lips pressed together tightly.

The drive home was tense.

Soren took the long way back, or at least his version of it—taking unnecessary turns, backtracking down the same streets. He wasn't a fucking secret agent; he had no idea how to actually lose a tail if he had one.

Soren's strategy had always been based on avoiding detection as long as possible, not so much the escape part once he was found. But he did his best.

Gabe didn't comment. He'd closed his eyes, slumping down in the passenger seat, apparently unwilling to deal with Soren until he had some sort of explanation.

Soren knew he had fucked up badly. Gabe had let himself be vulnerable in a real way with Soren—let himself be literal prey to a monster—and Soren had immediately, if unintentionally, messed with the man's head. What was supposed to be a moment of carefree teasing had turned into something else entirely.

At least it left Soren free to drive like a lunatic.

Now if only he could ease some of the tightness in his chest. Because Soren knew, even if he fixed things with Gabe, it wouldn't make any difference. None of it would help. It was only a matter of time now.

Even if Soren hadn't been able to find him in the crowd afterward, he knew what he'd seen.

Hendrick had found him.

Ten

Gabe

Something was off. Clearly.

Gabe eyed the blond vampire across from him warily. Ferdy had greeted them with exuberance at the door, yipping excitedly, sniffing first Soren's pant legs and then Gabe's own. Gabe was sure that, after the club, they had many interesting smells between the two of them. Soren was using it all as an excuse to avoid Gabe's eyes, focusing all his attention on the wiggling puppy instead.

The night had started off so *well*.

Gabe hadn't gone out like that in...he didn't even know how long. His big nights out since moving back to Hyde Park had usually just consisted of a few drinks at the local bar with old acquaintances or a prospective hookup.

But dancing with Soren had been so fucking *fun*. Not to mention an unexpected turn-on. Seeing the way the vampire translated his otherworldly grace on the dance floor, his hips moving in a hypnotic rhythm, had left Gabe practically panting. And then that hint of possessiveness when their dance partner had gotten overly handsy...

And not to mention the bite. *The bite.*

Talk about an unexpected turn-on. Fuck.

Danny hadn't been exaggerating when he said vampire bites felt good. Gabe thought back on their past conversations about it with new embarrassment. Now that he knew what a bite felt like—like there was a direct line from his neck to his cock, like two seconds more and he would have been begging Soren to let him fuck him in that corner—he was more than a little mortified to have even discussed it with Danny. He didn't need to picture *that* between Roman and his little brother.

But then it had all gone to hell.

The bite may have felt amazing—Gabe's cock twitched at his even thinking about it—but it had left him feeling...vulnerable. On edge. He'd let another person drink his *blood*, for fuck's sake. Had even gone so far as to offer himself up on a platter weekly, in exchange for being Soren's...what, exactly? One and only?

He'd felt like a blushing virgin asking for exclusivity from his more experienced boyfriend, a position Gabe had never found himself in before.

But the moment had been so...intimate. Gabe didn't want to imagine Soren doing that with anyone else, now that he knew what it felt like.

And Soren had *mocked* him for it. Likened him to a pet.

Well, okay, Soren *always* mocked him; that was nothing new. But then the vampire had just...vanished. Leaving Gabe there in the corner, stewing over the whole encounter.

And now here they were, Soren still studiously avoiding Gabe's eyes. For a vampire that was usually pretty in-your-face with his personality, he was being awfully cagey.

It was all just...off.

Sex between them hadn't made things nearly this awkward, so why had this bite? It had to be something else, something *more*. Gabe was aware that driving home had taken way longer than it should have, like Soren had been going some roundabout way. Avoiding someone? Was he worried that Lucien was back? Then why wouldn't he just tell Gabe that?

"You need water." Soren's eyes were still on the dog, but Gabe had to assume the comment was directed at him. "The drinking and dancing. The blood I took. You're probably pretty dehydrated at this point."

Gabe shrugged but didn't argue. He headed toward the kitchen, Soren and the puppy both at his heels. He downed a glass of water, only for Soren to take the empty cup and refill it for him, then fish a sports drink out of the fridge and shove it into Gabe's hand.

"Should I make you something?" Soren asked, biting at his nails. Gabe had never seen him do that before. It was a surprisingly human gesture.

"You don't cook."

Soren huffed. "I'm not completely useless. I could...peel you a banana?"

Fuck. It would have been adorable, if Gabe weren't already at the end of his rope. He took a seat at the kitchen counter, patting the stool next to him. "Stop offering me shit. Just...sit. Explain."

Soren shook his head, tucking his hands into the pockets of his pants, possibly to keep from chewing on them.

Those fucking leather pants. They should be illegal.

"I think I'll pace, actually," Soren said. "Take a page out of Roman's book."

Whatever. Soren needed to talk, and Gabe didn't care if the vampire floated around midair to do it. He sipped his drink and waited, watching Soren move from one end of the small kitchen to the other.

Gabe's beverage was half-empty before Soren's voice finally rang out. "I wasn't like Roman. I wasn't dying when I was turned. I was...chosen. For a purpose."

"Like, to do a job?" Danny had always said Soren was exceptionally good at tracking people.

Soren cleared his throat, not breaking his stride. "No, not a job. I was turned *for* someone. To be with someone."

Gabe felt his stomach drop. "A *mate*? You have a mate out there already?"

He tried to take another sip of his drink but stopped when he realized his hand was trembling. The thought that Soren had a mate out there...hurt. Quite a lot, if Gabe was being honest with himself.

But Soren was already shaking his head. "No. Definitely not. Although, he tried to convince me of it at one point, after I found out they existed. Evil bastard." Soren gave a bitter laugh. "Really, he just chose me for my looks. He thought I seemed...sweet. Delicate. Called me his angel."

Gabe resisted the urge to snort. Soren was nobody's angel.

That was part of what made him so great.

"He came from a small community of vampires. A den," Soren continued. "They were of the mind that if you turned a human, they were yours. To do with as you wished. To *serve* you however you wished."

Gabe caught the unspoken message in Soren's story. So Soren had been turned to be someone's...sex servant? "That's— That's fucking awful." It was beyond awful, but Gabe couldn't find any other words at the moment.

Soren paused his pacing, approaching the kitchen counter, although he kept his gaze on the counter itself, still avoiding Gabe's eyes. "It wasn't always, honestly. Hendrick was handsome. Powerful. Seemingly enchanted by me. And I was...young and stupid. I thought we were partners at first. He let me think that."

Gabe didn't think it made someone young and stupid to expect respect from a partner, but he kept silent, not wanting to interrupt the story.

"But as you know"—Soren gave a wry twist of his lips—"I'm no angel. And over the years, anytime I would act contrary to the way he wanted...anytime I acted like *myself*, it made him...angry. And he let me know it. In many varied, creative, violent ways."

Gabe's stomach hurt. His chest hurt. His fucking *heart* hurt.

Poor Soren.

Soren kept talking to the counter. "I stayed with him, in that den, for over a century before I finally fled, venturing out on my own. He left me alone for a while. But eventually he found me again. He always finds me. And he likes to remind me, periodically, that I'm only alive at his whim."

Fuck. This was all so fucking *horrible*. Gabe gripped the kitchen counter with white fingers. "Because he turned you?"

"Because he didn't kill me when I left." Soren finally met Gabe's eyes, and the pain Gabe saw in the vampire's gaze made his chest ache that much more fiercely. "Roman has told you vampires don't always get along? Our...inner beasts don't always play nice. Turning someone to be your companion naturally doesn't always work out. In that den, when it didn't, the new vampire would be executed, not released."

Gabe's stomach gave another twist. "What the fuck?"

Soren laughed, but there was no humor in it. "He considers himself merciful, actually, for not killing me then. Personally, I think he just likes knowing he has a plaything out there. Someone he can use and abuse whenever he gets the...itch."

It was...wrong. All so *wrong*. Soren was strong. Powerful. Spirited. The thought that there was another vampire out there thinking he *owned* the mischievous blond imp made Gabe feel absolutely ill. "Where is this guy now?" he asked, afraid he already knew the answer. Soren's odd behavior at the club was beginning to add up.

"Here, possibly." Soren's tone was light, but there was no mistaking the tension in his body. The thought clearly terrified him. "I thought I saw him at the club. I usually keep track of his movements—that's part of how I got so good at tracking people to begin with. But I got a little complacent here, I guess."

Gabe felt like a thousand different emotions were competing for space in his mind at once. Fear. Sadness. Worry. Regret. "Shouldn't we be packing? Do you need to leave? You should leave, right?"

He didn't even know what he was saying, but the thought that someone might be coming to hurt Soren—someone strong enough that Gabe had no chance at stopping him—was making him panic.

Gabe's instincts had been right. Bad things *were* going to happen.

"I'm not leaving." Soren's pale-blue gaze held his, and Gabe had a feeling the vampire's words had surprised even himself. "He could hurt you, Gabe. He probably saw us together. And he's not beyond petty jealousy. I'm not leaving you to be hurt by him."

Gabe had known moments of feeling helpless in his life. When his dad had died. When he'd heard his mother had Alzheimer's. And now here he was again, scared and helpless and hating the feeling just as much as he ever had. "So what do we do?"

Soren shrugged. "I don't know. I could have been wrong." He reached out across the counter and placed a tentative hand on Gabe's arm. "I'm sorry, Highness."

Gabe shook his head. "No, it makes sense now. Why you got...distracted back there."

Soren squeezed his arm. "No, dummy, not that. I'm sorry I brought this to your doorstep. I should have left a long time ago."

The thought was like a knife to the chest. "Don't say that. I'm glad you stayed. I wish— I wish I was stronger. I wish I could help you. Protect you." Gabe took a deep breath, hoping he could keep off a panic attack. The pressure in his chest just didn't want to let up. "So...you stay. For now."

Soren nodded. "I stay. Danny and Roman will be back soon... It sometimes helps to ward him off, having other vampires around."

They had a week left of Gabe's brother's honeymoon. It seemed in that moment like an awfully long time, with so much potential for something to go horribly wrong.

But...the selfish side of Gabe didn't *want* Soren to disappear. Not even with an evil ex on the horizon.

Gabe took another deep breath. "Come here." He motioned with his arms to Soren, who arched a brow at him.

"Why?" Soren asked.

"I want to hold you." Gabe made "gimme" hands at the reluctant vampire.

Soren was smirking now, the little brat. "Why?"

Gabe sighed but kept his arms up. "Because you just told me a sad story, and I want to comfort you."

Soren crossed his arms. "I don't need comfort."

"Then I want you to comfort *me*." It wasn't even a lie. "Will you?"

Soren huffed at him but stepped around the counter to come stand in between Gabe's legs. Gabe wrapped his arms around the petite vampire, holding him as tightly as he could, knowing Soren could more than handle his human strength.

There. That was better.

The tightness in Gabe's chest released slowly as he held Soren in his arms, breathing in that ocean-and-pine scent.

Soren ducked his head into Gabe's chest, mumbling something that was muffled by Gabe's shirt.

Gabe pulled back slightly. "What was that?"

Soren stared firmly at his chest, avoiding his eyes, but repeated himself. "I don't want you to pity me."

"I don't," Gabe reassured. When Soren scoffed in response, he explained further, "I hate that this happened to you. Hate that you had your humanity taken away by someone who didn't appreciate you, who didn't take responsibility for what he'd done. I hate so much that someone out there wants to hurt you. But I don't pity you." He slid a hand around to cup Soren's face, gently guiding his vampire to look him in the eye. "I know how strong you are. How loyal you are to those who deserve it. You haven't let your past define you."

Soren bit his lip. "Even though I still run from it, like a little coward?"

Gabe stroked Soren's cheek with his thumb. "Self-preservation isn't cowardly. You've been protecting yourself."

Soren pulled his head from Gabe's hand, moving instead to rub it against Gabe's chest. Gabe had a feeling his vampire liked cuddling more than he let on. Soren was such a physical creature; how could he not?

"I wish I were stronger. I wish I could protect you."

Soren tilted his head away from Gabe's chest just enough that his words came out clear. "I don't need that from you."

"I don't get what you need from me at all, I guess. Other than blood."

"Orgasms." Soren smirked at him again.

Well, shit. That was all Gabe was to Soren? He shouldn't really be surprised. The wealth of this vampire's life experience was over-whelming. What could Gabe, small-town rube turned small-town doctor, really offer him?

But before he could go to a dark place with his thoughts, Soren continued, the smirk dropping from his face, "Not *just* orgasms, human. I've never told anyone that story. I spent over a century in a community where any vulnerability was immediately taken advantage of, with a beast who took any opening to punish me for—for my own feelings. You don't take advantage. You don't begrudge me my strength. You don't make me feel...lesser."

Gabe laughed. "That's like, the bare minimum of a healthy rela-tionship, brat."

Soren looked up to frown at him. "Don't belittle it. It *means* something to me. To feel safe. And don't put yourself down. You don't have to be the big, bad protector to be a worthy partner." Soren grinned his manic grin, and Gabe's heart lightened just a little to see it again. "I've got that part covered."

Gabe smiled back at him at that, but there was still that nagging doubt. Could he really be an equal partner to Soren as a human?

But what was the alternative? Jump on the vampire train like his brother? *Turn?*

Soren hadn't given him any indication that they were anything long-term. And an eternity as an otherworldly creature was the definition of long-term.

Gabe tried to put the thought aside and focus on the vampire in his arms. This was about Soren, not his own insecurities. "What do you need from me right now?"

Soren met his eyes. "Orgasms."

"I'm being serious, brat."

"So am I." Soren reached a hand down to palm Gabe's cock, which hardened rapidly under even that simple touch. "I want to feel you inside me, Highness. I want to forget the bad memories. I want to feel good. I want to have *fun.*"

Gabe's breath hitched as he watched Soren's eyes darken in arousal. He knew there was more to discuss, but it was a tough offer to pass up. Soren wanted to feel good, and Gabe wanted to make that happen.

He leaned his head down to claim Soren's lips. Just a gentle, brief caress, a tease of tongues. He was rewarded with the softest, sweetest sigh from his vampire.

"All right, brat." Gabe's voice came out husky. "I'll take you to bed."

Eleven

Soren

Soren's initial thought had been to have Gabe fuck him in the kitchen. For his human to bend him over the counter, or maybe let Soren ride him on one of the kitchen chairs. But then Gabe had kissed him so sweetly, so gently, and before Soren knew it, he'd let himself be led up to the human's bedroom.

Like this was some kind of...*romantic interlude.*

It was a far cry from the vampy, bloody sex he'd been imagining earlier in the night, pressed up against each other at the club. But the gentleness of Gabe's kiss after the shock of thinking he'd seen Hendrick's face had Soren all sorts of messed up.

Maybe that was why, up in the bedroom, he was still letting Gabe kiss him so fucking *sweetly.*

Gabe had both hands cupping Soren's cheeks, holding his face like he was something precious. He was claiming Soren's mouth with warm, gentle, openmouthed kisses, and Soren was letting him.

To be fair, Gabe was a fucking dreamy kisser, so Soren couldn't really be blamed, could he?

Gabe was using his hold on Soren to angle his head the way he wanted, sucking gently on his lips in between smooth, silky strokes of his tongue.

Soren was letting out a whimper before he knew it.

Christ. He needed to breathe. Needed to take control of the situation before he drowned in all this sweetness. He took a step back, pulling his head out of Gabe's grasp. "Strip," Soren ordered, panting a little.

Gabe swallowed hard before following his command, pulling his shirt over his head in an instant, revealing all those delicious muscles. Soren rid himself of his own top quickly, pulling off his leather pants next.

Gabe groaned in appreciation, watching him undress. "Those fucking pants," he muttered.

Soren paused in toeing them off his ankles. "Don't like them?" he teased.

The heat in Gabe's eyes could have melted steel. "Like them too fucking much," he corrected.

As he should. Soren looked amazing in them.

"Grab the lube," Soren demanded.

He lay down on the bed as Gabe complied, spreading his legs wide and watching in satisfaction as Gabe's eyes darkened at the sight.

"Open me up," Soren ordered.

"Fuck, yes," Gabe sighed, moving forward to climb up on the bed. And then Gabe was kissing him again.

Soren took control quickly this time, sucking on the human's tongue savagely, giving in a little to the ferocity that lived ever-present inside him. Would Gabe protest? Ask Soren to be sweet again?

But his human only groaned in satisfaction, doing that addictive thing he did where he melted so easily under Soren's ministrations. Gabe's thick, hard cock was pressed against Soren's, his body weight bearing down in a way that should have left Soren panicked but instead left him feeling just so goddamn good.

Soren whimpered as a slick digit probed at his entrance urgently. Gabe pushed the tip inside, and Soren sighed in satisfaction at the stretch—Gabe's fingers were so much bigger than his own.

Gabe kissed his jaw, his ear, his neck. "Open up for me, baby."

Christ. Soren was getting addicted to that *baby*.

One finger turned to two, to three, and then Soren was grabbing at Gabe's muscular ass, pulling him closer. "Fuck me, Highness. Now."

Gabe smirked down at him as he lined the fat head of his cock up to Soren's entrance. "How am I 'Highness' when you're the one ordering me around?"

But Soren didn't have to answer the silly question, because then Gabe was entering him in one smooth push, filling Soren up with that goddamn perfect cock.

"Yes," Soren sighed, pushing up into that sensation. "More."

He yelped in surprise when Gabe sat back onto his knees, using his hands on Soren's ass to pull Soren's lower body with him, until Soren's upper back was pressed into the bed and his hips were high in the air. The action was smooth enough that Gabe's cock never left his body, still inside him to the hilt. Soren clenched his hole around it, and Gabe moaned in response.

"You want to be the boss?" Gabe asked, his voice husky. "Fuck yourself onto me, baby."

Hell yes. Soren could to that.

He planted his feet firmly on the bed, pushing up onto Gabe's cock, watching with satisfaction as those golden eyes went to half-mast. Gabe was meeting him thrust for thrust but letting Soren set the pace. Again.

This human kept doing all the right things.

Soren's breath caught as Gabe's hands slid all over him, caressing his hips, his stomach, his chest—everywhere but Soren's desperate and aching cock.

"So perfect," Gabe murmured, running his thumbs over Soren's nipples.

They were just words. But they sounded so fucking sincere. Was that why Soren's chest ached to hear them? He thought he'd long ago given up on the idea of being perfect to anyone else. His only experience with another's expectations for him had led to nothing but pain. But Gabe wasn't thinking of some idealized version of Soren when he said those words—his human had seen every side of him tonight.

The monster. The rude brat. The coward.

And still the human seemed to want it all.

Soren panted. He suddenly wanted...something. Something different. Something *real*. He didn't want to keep his human at arm's length anymore. Soren's hips paused as an overwhelming sensation flooded over him.

Gabe's heated gaze softened in concern. "Soren?" he questioned, stilling his own movements.

Soren wrapped one leg around Gabe's hips, then the other, pulling the muscled human firmly on top of him. "Fuck me properly," he ordered. Somehow it came out sounding like a plea.

Gabe smiled down at him, brushing a lock of Soren's hair out of his eyes. The move was unbearably tender.

Soren should have hated it.

Then Gabe's weight crashed fully down on him, and he did as Soren asked. He fucked him properly, setting a brutal pace that left Soren gasping as the human angled his thrusts in a way that hit Soren's prostate repeatedly.

So goddamn good.

It had been so long since Soren had willingly let someone else take control. But he didn't feel dominated. Gabe was gazing at him with what could easily be considered adoration in his eyes, even as he was pounding Soren with a force that might have left bruises had Soren been human. Every now and then, the phrase "so beautiful" escaped the human's lips, in between groans.

"Yes," Soren sighed. "More, Highness. *More.*"

His orgasm hit him hard and suddenly, a cry escaping his lips as electricity shot up his spine and he coated their stomachs in his cum. Gabe wasn't far behind, his hips stuttering, and Soren gasped at the sensation of Gabe's cum filling him up. Gabe kept grinding into Soren, thighs trembling, as if he couldn't bear to leave his body just yet.

Soren understood the feeling.

They lay together, Gabe blanketing Soren's body with his own, for what felt like endless moments afterward, Gabe's head on Soren's chest, Soren stroking his dark curls gently. The tension and fear of the last few hours had finally left Soren's body, and he felt soft, pliable.

Vulnerable, a voice in his head taunted.

He pushed it aside. Gabe's weight felt comforting, like a big security blanket. Soren was done listening to that fearful, cowardly side of himself. Because there was another, deeper-rooted voice whispering the same word over and over again in his head.

Mate. Mate. Mate.

He'd known it for longer than he'd wanted to admit. Soren had heard the stories. He knew what it meant when a vampire was inexplicably drawn to a human. What it meant when the scent of a stranger suddenly smelled like home.

Soren had a mate.

But if Soren turned Gabe, if Gabe became his equal in strength and power, would his human still stay this sweet? Or would he start seeing Soren as something...smaller. Weaker. Something to own. His pretty possession.

Gabe's words from the kitchen came back to him. *I wish I were stronger. I wish I could protect you.* Had Gabe really meant that? Even if Gabe being stronger meant he would no longer be human?

Soren opened his mouth to ask but stopped himself, glancing down at the head of dark hair on his chest. Gabe's breathing was already the deep, even pattern of the sleeping. Soren should let his human rest. For now, it wasn't Soren that needed protecting anyway.

He would keep his mate from harm.

He'd let the situation with Hendrick go on far longer than he should have. Soren had become complacent. Too grateful for his freedom to try and mitigate the cost. It had seemed worth it—the pain and humiliation of giving in to Hendrick's need to dominate, his need to *hurt*—in exchange for Soren having a life of his own.

He'd made a pattern of avoiding Hendrick as long as possible, until he was inevitably caught, suffering the consequences until Hendrick got bored, and then carrying on as he wished. Overall, Soren had thought he'd had the life he wanted. More or less.

Sure, a snide voice in his head remarked. *Lonely. Wandering. Never getting too close to anybody.*

Had he really been fooling himself all this time? Letting Hendrick push him around, convinced somewhere inside himself that he was still *lesser* just because some dysfunctional group of vampire rejects had told him so?

It was too late to regret it. Soren refused to cry over spilled milk. It didn't matter if he should have dealt with it sooner.

He'd deal with it *now.*

Soren sighed, pressing a kiss to the forehead of the large, sweet human draped over him.

Soren had someone worth protecting now.

It was hours later when Soren finally brought himself to slide out from under Gabe's warm weight. He tucked the covers up around his human, bending over to give him another forehead kiss, since there was no one else around to see how fucking sentimental he'd apparently become in the last few hours.

He paused by the bed after finding a clean pair of Gabe's underwear to put on. It was beyond tempting to crawl back under the covers and press himself against Gabe's steady heat—the man was like a goddamn furnace—but Soren didn't have time for that right now.

Soren needed information.

He closed the bedroom door quietly behind himself and padded downstairs to the living room. Ferdy was on the couch, his tail thumping lightly at the sight of Soren in the doorway.

"Spoiled pup," Soren murmured, walking over to give the mutt a head scratch anyway. He was pretty cute, even if he was an awfully needy creature. Feeding, watering, walking, affection.

Caring for mortal creatures was a full-time job.

He sat down on the couch, dialing a number he was surprised to find he still remembered by heart. A soft voice answered after one ring. "Soren." There was warmth in the simple greeting.

In that entire hellhole of a vampire den, there was only one person Soren even slightly regretted leaving. "Jay."

"Is everything all right?" Of course Jay would know something was up. Soren never called just to chat.

"Everything's fine, Jaybird. Just wondering when you last laid eyes on Hendrick."

"Oh." There was a world of understanding in that one word. "I haven't seen him around for a long time now. Years."

Interesting.

In the past, Hendrick had always gone back to his old crew in the interims between messing with Soren. It was the main reason Soren had never had the guts to attempt to deal with his ex more permanently. Hendrick had...friends...of a sort, who could demand retribution, if they really wanted. It was far easier running from one unhinged vampire than trying to battle a whole damn trio.

"He hasn't come by to see his vamp bros at all? Silas? Anton?"

There was a lengthy pause on the other end. Then, "That would be tough to do. They—they're dead."

"What?" Soren didn't attempt to hide his shock. That was some fucking news. True, he didn't exactly check in regularly, but still...

Jay sighed down the line. "Silas went feral about ten years back. Had to be put down. Anton ran off a little while after. Last I heard he was going feral himself. I figure he's a goner by now too." Jay's voice remained soft, but he didn't sound sorry at all.

Neither was Soren.

He still remembered the early days, when Hendrick had first shown his true colors, begging Silas, the de facto leader of the den, for help. Silas's response had been to tell him it was all the natural order of things. That Soren belonged to Hendrick, and Hendrick could treat him as he saw fit. He had hauled Soren back to Hendrick's house, telling the other vampire exactly what Soren had done.

It had taken weeks for Soren to heal from Hendrick's...retribution.

"And Veronique?" Soren asked.

"She was killed," Jay answered, his voice breaking a little. "Putting Silas down."

"Oh, Jay. I'm sorry." It wasn't exactly a lie. Soren did feel a little bad about that one. Veronique had turned Jay, been his partner for centuries, and had been one of the more decent ones in the community. She'd let Soren stay with them more than once when Hendrick was on a tear.

But "one of the more decent ones" wasn't saying much, in this instance. She'd never put a real stop to any of it, and Soren hadn't truly forgiven her for being part of that shitty den anyway.

Or for taking advantage of Jay's natural sweetness.

She'd at least treated Jay with relative kindness. Or, that was to say, not outright terribleness. But that was partly because it was impossible to be bad to Jay. He was the angel that Hendrick had wanted Soren to be.

A pure, kind soul. Not like Soren.

Gabe likes that you're a brat, Soren reminded himself.

He sighed. He'd apparently reached a dead end, more or less. In the past, he might have hung up by now, but a twinge of guilty conscience had him staying on the line. "Are you still with the others?"

The den fluctuated in size and, by necessity, moved around every few decades, but the loss of Silas, Anton, and Veronique could have broken the whole thing up as far as Soren knew.

"For now." Jay sounded tired. "I don't really know where else to go. And everybody pretty much leaves me alone, even with Vee gone."

"You could go anywhere, Jay." Soren's voice revealed his own frustration, but he couldn't exactly blame the other vampire. He knew how that den was, the kind of brainwashing they did. They did everything they could to prevent their members from trying to leave. Soren had been told by Hendrick often enough that vampires trying to make it on their own went mad. Of course, he had conveniently left out the part that they'd all turn feral eventually anyway, if they didn't find their mates.

Like going mad would have been any worse than the rest of it.

"You could come here, if you wanted. I'm in Colorado. Hyde Park. My friend Roman's mated to a nurse here." The words were out of Soren's mouth before he even realized it. Christ, what was he saying? He didn't even have his own place.

This town was making him soft.

"Thanks for the offer." Jay sounded sincere enough, but Soren knew he wouldn't come. Jay had never been the bravest soul.

"Be careful out there, Soren. With Hendrick."

They said their goodbyes, and Soren sat, scratching Ferdy's ears absently. How strange, to think of three of his past tormentors dead and gone. And Jay still there, still a part of that fucking den.

#

"Johann? Jay?" No answer, but Soren ducked his head into the barn anyway. He immediately spotted a pair of dirty bare feet dangling off the side of the hayloft. Keeping his steps light, Soren leaped softly onto the ladder resting there, reaching up to grab onto one of those ankles.

"Caught you," he teased.

Giggling sounded from above him. It was such a sweet sound. The only laughter around these parts was usually mocking and unkind. Soren released his prey and climbed the rest of the way up the ladder, pausing at the top to eye the dirt-smudged vampire in front of him.

Slate-gray eyes peered back at him from under a dark head of hair.

"Soren." Jay greeted him warmly enough, but there was a hint of concern in his eyes. "Have you come to stay for a while?" His eyes traveled over Soren, the younger vampire looking for signs of injury.

"Not to stay," Soren answered, settling next to him. "Is Vee here?"

Jay giggled again. "Nope. You think I'd be this filthy if she were?"

It was a fair point. Veronique was incredibly picky about appearances. Jay was only able to indulge his love of nature when the other vampire was out and away. "She went to Silas's for a party. Said I could stay here though. Isn't that nice?"

Soren hummed noncommittally. That was Jay. Grateful for even the smallest scrap of kindness. Never mind the way that, underneath the surface consideration, Vee treated him like any other servant. Or the way she didn't seem to care at all that Jay preferred men over women sexually.

Soren knew he wasn't the only one who'd noticed how Jay eyed some of the male vampires in their community. The young vampire was too guileless to hide it.

"Hendrick's over there too," Soren told him. "They're planning a hunting party in the city afterward."

"Oh." Jay pouted a little, pursing his Cupid's-bow lips. "Do we have to go to that?"

Soren laughed, nudging the other vampire with his shoulder playfully. "No, they're bringing the humans back with them. They want us to set up for some playtime though."

"Oh, that's fine." Jay leaned back into the hay pile. "That means I can loll about a bit longer."

"Jay..." Soren had a hard time making the words come. "I won't be here when they get back."

Jay twirled a piece of hay between his fingers. "What do you mean?"

Soren cleared his throat. "I can't stay here anymore. I just...can't. I'm leaving."

Jay sat up with a start, scattering hay every which way. "You can't leave, Soren. I know—I know it's bad. I know that. But you've heard what happens to vampires out there. You'll go mad. Or be caught by humans."

It's what they'd always been told. Leave the den, face the horrific consequences.

That was, if the vampires in the den didn't catch and kill them first.

Soren shook his head. "I don't believe it anymore. Any of it. I just—I know it has to be better than this."

"You don't have to go. I can ask Vee to help more," Jay offered, eyes pleading. "With Hendrick."

Soren smiled sadly. "She's his friend, Jaybird. She wouldn't. And...eventually he's going to get tired of this. Of fighting me. And they'll put me down. I'm not waiting around for that to happen."

"They wouldn't!" Jay cried. "I wouldn't let them."

"And how would you stop them?" It wasn't said with any meanness, and Soren didn't intend to belittle the younger vampire. But Jay instantly deflated, as Soren knew he would.

The young vampire had been turned only a decade before. He was the weakest member of the den by far. He might truly want to help Soren, but he wouldn't be able to. Not really.

"I'll keep in touch," Soren said gently. "I'll write if I can. I just wanted to say goodbye."

Soren didn't ask Jay to go with him. He already knew the other vampire wouldn't dare. Bravery wasn't Jay's strong suit. It wasn't Soren's either, for that matter.

But the time had come.

Soren would risk it all—loneliness, madness, death—if it meant a chance at a free life.

Twelve

Gabe

Gabe set his weights back on the rack with a grunt, removing his headphones and pausing the medical podcast he was listening to. Soren had taken one look at his phone and his choice of workout entertainment and had declared him "the most boring human in the world," but there hadn't been any real bite to the comment. Especially considering how he'd stayed in the garage and ogled Gabe shamelessly for the first half hour of his workout.

The heated look in the vampire's eyes had almost been enough to make Gabe stop lifting weights and opt for an entirely different method of raising his heart rate... But he really needed the endorphin rush of some proper exercise. The swirl of anxiety in his stomach had been building ever since Soren's confessions about his past. Soren's ex...

The thought of someone out there wanting to hurt Soren.

Fuck.

What Gabe really needed was a run—something long and grueling to leave him wrung out and exhausted—but Soren didn't want him leaving the house. It was clear Gabe wasn't the only one feeling anxious.

They'd been holed up at Danny's for the past few days—Gabe had been given a rare full weekend off, and Soren had convinced him to call out sick today. But playing hooky from work wasn't helping his nerves at all, and he definitely couldn't keep it up without running into trouble. He wasn't sure what they were going to do the next night, when he was scheduled to work again.

Ugh. He *really* needed a fucking run.

He was just considering another set when the doorbell rang. Gabe quickly wiped the excess sweat off his forehead with his towel, exiting the garage back to the main house and heading toward the front door.

He was intercepted by a blond blur.

Soren was at the front door before Gabe's eyes could even adjust. The vampire glanced back over his shoulder at Gabe with a frown. "Go into the kitchen."

Gabe laughed in disbelief at Soren's paranoia. "It's just our take-out," he argued.

"The kitchen, Highness." Soren narrowed his pale eyes in warning.

Gabe sighed but complied anyway. It was weird. Gabe had always been tall and strong, even more so after he'd started using exercise to deal with his anxiety. So he'd never had a partner act *protective* over him before. The weirdest part was how nice it felt. Gabe was so used to people expecting him to take charge, to take care of things. He thought he'd found satisfaction in being considered strong and capable. But here was this little brat of a vampire treating Gabe like he was something precious. Something breakable.

Gabe hadn't felt cared for like this since his dad had died.

He was finishing chugging a glass of water when Soren entered the kitchen, hands laden with Styrofoam takeout containers. Truly a ridiculous amount of food, considering one of them didn't even need to eat. But Gabe had learned Soren loved excess in all things, even unnecessary human food.

He realized he was staring when Soren eyed him warily.

"What are you making moon eyes at me for, Highness?"

Gabe grinned innocently from his spot at the kitchen table. "No reason."

"Hm." Soren set the food on the table, passing by Gabe to grab silverware from the drawer.

Though it was subtle, Gabe didn't miss the way Soren leaned in and inhaled deeply as he went by. Gabe protested immediately. "Don't. I've been working up a sweat. I must smell vile."

"You never do, Highness," Soren replied absently. "You always smell good. Clean."

Something warm unfurled in the pit of Gabe's stomach at the casual words. Soren had been...softer...since their disastrous night out. Still a snarky brat, of course, but he'd been grumbling a lot less about Gabe cuddling him, and here he was even saying spontaneous, borderline-sweet things without immediately retracting them.

Living with Soren, sharing this time with him, was like finding out the tiger he'd been so wary of was actually a house cat. Like, a super fancy, *exotic* house cat for sure. Maybe a Savannah. But not exactly the dangerous predator Gabe had feared.

It was all making Gabe feel some kind of way. Bratty, "keep you at arm's length" Soren was tempting enough; protective, "actually letting you close" Soren was fucking irresistible.

"Can I have a kiss, then?" Gabe asked as Soren returned with the silverware.

"Needy human," Soren teased, leaning in anyway.

Gabe took immediate advantage of his proximity, pulling the vampire onto his lap and wrapping his arms around him.

Soren protested. "Ugh! You're still all sweaty, and I'm wearing silk."

He was. With them staying entirely at home the past few days, Soren had committed fully to his loungewear aesthetic. He had on a dark-blue silk pajama set that was severely testing Gabe's ability to keep his hands to himself.

His vampire really was too beautiful for words.

Despite his own protests, Soren settled on Gabe's lap, pulling the takeout on the table toward them. "Eat, human," he ordered. "We need to feed those muscles."

Gabe laughed, rubbing his nose against the back of Soren's silky-soft neck.

Huh. Vampires could get goose bumps. Who knew?

"Make me a plate?" Gabe requested.

"Seriously...needy-ass human," Soren muttered. But he was already piling little bits from the different containers together for him, allowing Gabe to focus his full attention on snuggling the vampire in his arms.

Gabe had never been so drawn to touch and be touched before.

Sex had always been a nice enough release, but PDA—like their dancing and groping at the club the other night—had never exactly been Gabe's thing, and he wouldn't have called himself a cuddler before. But touching Soren was a world apart from touching anyone else. It just was.

Soren's voice broke through his reflection. "Are you going to ask me to feed you by hand too, Highness?"

Tempting. Very tempting.

But Gabe ultimately released one of his arms from its role in holding Soren hostage and pulled the container closer. Soren for his part didn't seem too interested in the food this time, content to sit on Gabe's lap as he ate his dinner.

"Do you, um, need to eat too?" Gabe asked between bites. "I mean, like, feed?"

Soren leaned back against him, keeping his head to the side so Gabe could get his fork to his mouth without interference. "I can last a few more days. I'll let you know."

A little thrill went through Gabe at the thought of Soren feeding on him again. It had been so intense, so pleasurable. He relished the thought of trying it again in a more private location, one where they could explore those...sensations...more fully.

He was halfway through his food when the doorbell rang again.

Soren immediately stiffened in his arms. "Expecting anyone?"

"No."

Soren was off his lap and heading out of the kitchen in an instant. "Stay here," he commanded. "If I yell for you to run, go out the back door immediately."

"What?" Gabe protested, pushing his food aside. "I'm not gonna just *leave* you."

Soren shot him a glare over his shoulder. "I can take care of myself, Highness. But not if I'm distracted worrying about you."

That set off a complicated mix of emotions in Gabe. He'd always been strong, at least physically, and now here he was, cursing his weak-ass human body for not being stronger. He listened carefully to the sounds of Soren opening the front door. There was a soft murmur of voices; Soren definitely didn't sound angry or panicked. And there was no yell for Gabe to escape.

After a few more moments without any drama, Gabe stood and poked his head out of the kitchen, catching the end of Soren's "I didn't think you'd *actually* come. How'd you even find us?"

He was talking to a young dark-haired man, on the shorter side—about the same height as Soren, actually. But whereas Soren often gave off the impression of more height, with his general attitude and penchant for heeled boots, this guy appeared more...dainty. Like a porcelain doll.

The small man was looking wounded at Soren's comment. "I—I'm sorry. I can go."

"Don't be silly," Soren snapped, running a hand through his hair. Oh boy.

Gabe knew his vampire well enough at this point to know he probably wasn't actually angry, despite his tone. More likely he was overwhelmed. Gabe watched as Soren stared at the young man for another moment before sighing dramatically. "Christ. Come inside."

Gabe couldn't contain his own curiosity anymore. He stepped out of the kitchen. "Who's this?"

Soren shot him an exasperated look. "I didn't tell you to come out yet."

The young man leaned around Soren and gave Gabe a little wave. "Hello."

"Hi." Gabe couldn't help giving him a wave back. The guy was adorable.

Soren sighed dramatically for the second time. "You're both killing me. Gabe, this is Johann. Johann, Gabe."

Johann smiled brightly. "Call me Jay. You're not one of us, are you?"

Okay, so this was a *vampire* friend of Soren's. A few weeks ago, that might have sent Gabe into a tailspin, but now he just grinned back. "'Fraid not. Certified human over here."

Jay's eyes widened in delight. "Ohhh. So cool! Soren, you've got a human!"

Soren crossed his arms. "I don't *have* a human. He just *is* a human."

Jay bit his lip, looking thoughtful. "Maybe I should get a human?"

Soren brought a hand to his face. "Jesus fucking Christ."

ele

Hours later and Gabe was on the couch in a Ferdy-Soren sandwich, with Jay curled up in a neighboring armchair. Apparently he'd started at the hospital and tracked Soren's scent from there ("You said your friend's mate was a nurse. I took a chance."). Gabe had expected the two of them to want to catch up, maybe go over some vampire gossip, but Soren had seemed completely uninterested in a heart-to-heart. They'd sat awkwardly in the kitchen together for all of five minutes before he'd asked Jay out of nowhere, "Have you seen _Jaws?_"

And now here they all were, already on the sequel.

Gabe was trying to keep his focus on the shark on the screen, and the foolish beachgoers' imminent demises, but he was a bit distracted. The little vampire in the armchair was making a lot of...noise. Gasps and squeals and the occasional, "Oh no."

Jay caught Gabe watching him a moment later, and gave him a wide-eyed look. "The ocean is really scary, huh?"

Gabe couldn't help it. He laughed. "You're a _vampire_. You've got your spiffy supernatural speed. Couldn't you just...outswim a shark?"

The little dark-haired vampire bit his lip, turning back to the screen. "Oh...no. I don't know how to swim."

Gabe raised a brow. "You don't know how to swim... How old are you again?"

He yelped when Soren's elbow jabbed him in the side. "Hush," Soren scolded. "It's not his fault. Jaybird's been...sheltered."

Gabe decided not to comment on Soren's adorable nickname for his friend. "Sorry. I didn't mean to laugh at you."

Putting his foot in his mouth wasn't new for him, but he still felt pretty bad. Soren had filled him in earlier while Jay was getting settled upstairs. The particular den of vampires they had both come from was fairly old-fashioned. They tended to settle on the outskirts of human communities, keeping mostly to themselves unless they were going on a hunt. Modern pursuits weren't really their thing.

Apparently neither were beach days.

"It's okay," Jay reassured him sweetly. "It's pretty silly, I guess. Over two hundred years old and I can't even swim. Soren, maybe you could teach me sometime?"

"Uh...sure thing." Soren shifted awkwardly against Gabe.

This was an interesting side of Soren to see. He was clearly fond of his little friend. Protective of him, even. But he seemed to have trouble knowing how to show it. Gabe felt a rush of warmth for his prickly, bratty vampire. He planted a kiss on the side of his blond head, laughing when Soren scowled at him.

"I can help," Gabe volunteered, turning to Jay. "I'm a great swimmer."

Gabe wasn't sure exactly why his offer had Soren scowling harder. He was just trying to be helpful. He could see why Soren was so protective of his friend. The younger vampire—fuck, was Gabe really considering over two hundred years old as *younger*?—came off as pretty naive. And, at least on the surface, he seemed sweet as pie. Gabe couldn't really imagine anyone being mean to the guy.

Even if he *had* shown up a little bit out of the blue.

Soren had told Gabe he'd called his old friend for information, offering up a place to stay—"So sweet of you." "Shut up."—without really expecting him to take Soren up on the offer. Apparently the poor guy had lost his partner recently.

Or at least, Gabe supposed ten years counted as "recently" from a vampire's point of view.

The trio finished the movie, complete with Jay's added soundtrack. As the credits rolled, Jay stood from the armchair with a big stretch. "I'm heading to bed. If...that's okay?"

"You don't have to ask permission," Soren told him gently.

Jay flushed. "Oh. Right. Sorry, bad habits." He yawned. Vampires could apparently yawn. Gabe took note.

"I've been up for days," Jay explained at Gabe's look. "I didn't want to miss anything. Flying on a plane and everything!"

Soren huffed. "You've been on a plane before, Jaybird."

"Yeah, but never by *myself*."

Gabe held in his laugh, waving good night as Jay headed upstairs. They'd given him Gabe's old room, since Gabe had been sleeping in Soren's bed these past few nights anyway.

"I'm going to make sure he's got everything he needs." Soren rose from the couch and hurried up the stairs after the other vampire. He'd been completely horrified earlier to see Jay had shown up with one measly backpack.

"Didn't you get Vee's funds when she passed?" he'd asked.

"Oh, sure. I've got money," Jay had reassured him. "I just don't need much."

Soren had eyed the other vampire's outfit skeptically—a ratty, oversize sweatshirt over a pair of fleece pants—but hadn't said anything. It was another sign he was genuinely fond of the other vampire. Gabe was pretty sure any other living creature wearing that outfit would have received a withering takedown of their nonexistent fashion sense, then been forced to change on the spot.

Gabe chuckled to himself thinking about it, heading into the kitchen to look for a beer.

Voices carried from upstairs. "He's so nice, your human."

Gabe smiled to himself at Jay's comment, but the grin left his face quickly at Soren's reply. "He's not *my* human."

Before the bite of that could sink in, Jay protested. "But he is! I've never seen you like that. You were all...snuggled up with him. Do you think he's your ma—"

Soren cut him off. "Hush. Enough of that. Don't throw nonsense words around."

But Gabe knew the word Jay had been about to say.

Mate.

Gabe had thought about it. Quite a lot, actually, in these recent weeks. He could be a little oblivious sometimes, sure, but he wasn't *dumb*. He'd heard enough from Danny about the pull between mates. The way Danny had felt safe and secure with Roman from the start. It could be hard to tell what Soren was thinking, what with all the walls he put up, but Gabe had felt the care and consideration from him. And Soren had stayed here, in Hyde Park, all this time, in spite of the motherfucker who was chasing him from place to place.

And then there were Gabe's own feelings. The soothing contentment he felt when touching Soren. The way he'd been drawn in and fascinated even before he'd seen all the good underneath Soren's bratty exterior.

Mate.

The idea didn't seem all that ridiculous.

Gabe looked up as Soren entered the kitchen. "So are we starting our own vampire den, then?"

Soren gave him a strange look. "*We?*"

Gabe didn't know what to say to that. He wanted to ask about mates, about where this thing between them was going, but he was afraid to disrupt this new, fragile bond between them. Afraid his heart might split in half if Soren laughed him off, or just flat-out told him no.

Soren eyed him from the doorway. "You like him," he said, crossing his arms over his chest. It sounded like an accusation.

"Sure," Gabe answered easily. "He's sweet."

"Sweet," Soren repeated frostily.

Gabe suddenly felt like he was walking on very thin ice, and he wasn't quite sure how he'd gotten there. "Is he...not?"

"No." Soren pursed his lips. "He is." He walked over to Gabe, stealing a sip of his beer.

Gabe watched him warily.

"I'm not," Soren finally said.

"You're not what?" Gabe asked.

"Sweet." He said it like a curse.

"You are to me." It was a rare occurrence, to see Soren blush. Gabe was fascinated by the faint pink stealing over his vampire's cheeks, the tips of his ears.

His vampire. His *mate*, if he wanted to go there.

Did Gabe want to go there?

Soren stepped closer and tucked his face into Gabe's chest. Most likely to hide his blush, but Gabe welcomed the contact anyway, rubbing his hands soothingly over Soren's back.

"He used to call me 'angel.'" The statement came out muffled. "He'd get upset when I wasn't."

Hendrick. That evil motherfucker.

Gabe hugged Soren tighter. "I'm not looking for an angel though."

Soren leaned his head back, peering up at Gabe. "What *are* you looking for, then?"

Gabe smiled. "I'm not looking for anything. I'm just—I just like having you around. You're better than any hypothetical angel, brat."

Soren scowled at him. "Cheesy," he accused. "Way too cheesy for words. You should be ashamed."

But he didn't step out of Gabe's arms.

·

Thirteen

Soren

Soren took a small sip of his vodka soda. It wasn't his drink of choice, but he didn't trust this place to make him anything more complicated than that. The bar definitely wasn't one of his usual haunts, with its surly staff and tasteless collection of neon signs advertising mediocre beer brands. But he was trying to keep as far away from Danny's house as he could without leaving city limits.

He'd been drinking and flirting his way through this part of town all night. It should have been fun—it might have been in the past—but mostly it was just...tedious. There was no heart to the flirting. No real intention. Not even for the sake of hunting.

Soren's inner vamp was still only interested in one particular prey.

It wasn't like Soren had suddenly stopped liking to go out—dancing and flirting with Gabe at his side had been all kinds of delightful. He'd relished getting to study his human's reactions to Soren, to other men. And then the incredible satisfaction at being the one to take him home at the end of the night. But Gabe was at his stupid *work*.

With Jay there for added protection, of course.

Theoretically it should have been Soren with him, but Soren was hoping to avoid drawing attention to his human—if Hendrick hadn't gotten a close look at Gabe that night, then it would be best for them not to be seen together. And while Jay wouldn't be much of a defense against Hendrick, he was still stronger than any human and would hopefully be able to stall Hendrick enough for Soren to get there.

At least, that was what Soren hoped. He worried he was putting an awful lot of stock in Jay's loyalty to him, considering this was Jay's first time away from that fucking den. He caught himself biting at his fingernails and tucked his free hand under his thigh, annoyed at his own nervous tell.

Was Soren making a mistake? But Jay had always hated Hendrick. He could never understand why Hendrick took such delight in hurting Soren, why he didn't take more care with him, like Vee had for Jay. Soren was counting on that hatred to help his old friend hold strong.

He took another sip of his drink. It would be okay. *Gabe* would be okay.

And Jay had been more than happy to help, sweetheart that he was. Moreover, he was nonthreatening and adorable enough that Gabe had been pretty sure Jay could get away with hanging around the hospital cafeteria all night without drawing too much suspicion.

Soren was trying very hard not to feel bitter about it all. At how easily Gabe and Jay interacted. He was painfully aware this was all his own trauma-induced bullshit. Gabe had done more than his fair share in reassuring him, both verbally and in other ways, that he liked Soren just as he was. And he wasn't being subtle about it—having Jay around apparently did absolutely nothing to stop Gabe from wanting to touch and hold Soren all the time.

And Soren was having a hard time even pretending to be annoyed by it. He *liked* being touched by his human. Liked being held by his human.

Soren had never thought he could be so content stuck in the same boring house for days. But Gabe had a way of making staying still easy, for the first time in Soren's lengthy existence.

Soren toyed with his straw, trying to push thoughts of his human away. There was an even better reason to send Jay in his stead. Hendrick may have been jealous in the past, but his obsession was still very much with Soren. If Gabe had to leave the house, Soren wanted to be as far away from him as possible.

Even better if Soren could draw Hendrick out himself.

He'd tried calling the same number he'd been receiving all those goddamn texts from, but either Hendrick had blocked him or he'd already dropped whatever burner he'd been using to taunt Soren. Another aspect of his pointless mind games, no doubt. *Don't call me; I'll call you.*

And so here Soren was, enduring all this barhopping and empty flirting, just to lure Hendrick's attention and to hopefully get that attention off Gabe, if it had ever been on him in the first place. But at this point, Soren was starting to think he'd only imagined Hendrick's face the other night. He was too used to fearing it in every corner; apparently, he'd started conjuring it.

Soren took another sip of his vodka soda, trying to find it in himself to search the bar for someone to make exaggerated eyes at. It was hard to focus on the present, when all his current actions were fixated on the past.

The start of Soren's new existence hadn't been so bad.

More confusing than anything. He didn't even really remember dying. There had been a voice in the darkness, a sharp bite of pleasure, and then unbearable agony. But that had only been for a moment—Soren had lost consciousness fairly quickly.

After all, other than hunger pangs, he'd never really known pain before, at that point in his life.

The real pain would come later.

"You're awake, angel?"

Soren opened his eyes to a dimly lit room. He was in a bed much softer than any he'd ever been in before, the silky texture of the sheets against his skin a foreign sensation.

There was a handsome man sitting beside him, his hair a few shades darker than Soren's own, big and broad and dressed in fine clothes.

Soren blinked. Angel? Had the man been referring to him? "Where am I?"

The big man smiled at him, all teeth. It couldn't have exactly been called a warm smile, but Soren had seen worse. "You're home," he answered, as if it were obvious.

"This isn't my home."

It definitely wasn't. Where Soren lived wasn't nearly as nice as this. His family were peasants, and he was the fourth of six children—they rarely had enough food to put on the table, let alone silver to set it with.

Another toothy smile. "It is now. I've been watching you, little Soren. We've even met before, though I made sure you wouldn't remember. I know the things you crave."

Soren doubted that. Besides the fact that they had definitely never met...this man couldn't possibly know what he craved. No one knew who Soren dreamed of at night, the men he dreamed of touching.

So Soren kept silent, not wanting to give anything away. More than that, he was...distracted. There was a buzzing under his skin. An itching for something, and he didn't know what. It was building and growing to an overwhelming degree every moment he was awake.

"Ah." The man gave him a knowing look. "You must be hungry. Don't worry, I've brought someone for you."

He gestured to the corner, where a woman with a blank look on her face was sitting with unnatural stillness. "Don't worry," the man said gently. "She won't fight you. You can let it out."

Soren didn't know what the stranger meant. Let what out? He didn't move.

"Here," the man offered. "I'll help you."

He moved impossibly quickly to the woman's side, pushing back her sleeve and baring her wrist. He bent over it, broad shoulders hunched, and his dark-blond hair swept over his face, hiding it from view.

Soren very quickly began to smell blood.

Only...blood had never smelled so enticing *before. The familiar metallic notes, yes, but also a richness...a spice...*

Why did it smell so good? Soren's breath hitched as he felt a change come over him. That overwhelming sensation grew and grew until he felt something other *come to the forefront.*

Himself but not himself.

And then he was up and across the room, and his mouth was covering that gentle river of blood, and he was drinking deeply. Big, greedy swallows.

"Good," the man murmured from his place at Soren's side. "Very good. We're going to do well together, angel."

Soren licked his bloody lips. "Who are you?"

That toothy smile became even more sinister with fangs glinting in the candlelight. "I'm your new master, angel. You can call me Hendrick."

Soren had killed that poor woman in the end—had drunk her dry. He'd been too new and too hungry to know any better, and Hendrick had been in no rush to teach him proper control. Humans were expendable to the older vampire. He'd been completely unbothered by Soren's excess, by any destruction left in their wake.

It had taken very little time in his new life for Soren to realize he was meant to be seen, not heard. And a very *long* time for him to realize how stifling that was, with his new and improved condition.

It hadn't made sense at first. His had never been a life full of choice and possibility. He'd been poor and half-starved and long used to playing up to other people's expectations—what was one more person telling him what to do?

But that was something Hendrick and his den didn't acknowledge about turning someone. That change...unleashing someone's inner vampire—their *demon*, as Roman called it—did more than just make someone crave blood. It amplified certain parts of their personality as well, all those inner cravings given new life. For some, like those in that shitty den, it amplified their viciousness, their cruelty.

But for Soren...

Soren craved pleasure, excess in all things. And a pursuit of pleasure necessitated freedom. He wanted to feel and think and say what he pleased. It had taken him many years to realize it fully.

And one night for Hendrick to beat it out of him.

At least, temporarily. The cycle would continue for decades. Until Soren couldn't stand it anymore, and he'd run. And run. And kept running.

"Christ," Soren sighed. He was being fucking maudlin, obsessing over the past. He looked over the latest text from Jay, lips quirking at his friend's unbridled enthusiasm.

No Hendrick. But so many humans! A little old lady called me adorable. I love the hospital!

This was pointless. Soren downed the rest of his drink in one graceless gulp. He'd go back to the house, cuddle that silly puppy, and wait like a sap for his human to return.

"Another one?" the bartender asked.

Before Soren could answer, he felt it: a surge of cold, a new, ominous tension in the air. A familiar, hated scent.

"I've got this round."

Soren shivered.

The man sliding onto the barstool next to him was tall and broad-shouldered, his dark-blond hair combed neatly back from a ruddy face. Soren had once thought him handsome, before he'd seen all the ugliness underneath. Maybe it was turning into a vampire that had corrupted Hendrick, or the toxic culture of the den, but Soren had a feeling he'd always been rotten on the inside.

"You were much easier to find this time, angel," Hendrick murmured, pushing the new drink toward Soren. "Putting down roots, are you?"

"Just a place to rest for a little while." Soren hated how small his voice came out, the familiar jangle of nerves in his stomach. He loathed that Hendrick still had this effect on him, after all this time.

"Mm. With that friend of yours."

Soren's response caught in his throat, his blood running cold. Did Hendrick mean Gabe? Had he been watching them at the house?

"You know," Hendrick continued, drumming his fingers on the bar, "it's a good thing that vampire found his mate. Otherwise, I might be feeling a little *jealous* right about now."

Relief washed through Soren.

Roman. He meant *Roman*.

Soren's friend had been a fixation of Hendrick's before, although not one Soren had ever let him get close to.

Hendrick hadn't taken notice of Gabe.

But Soren's relief was short-lived. Hendrick had mentioned Roman's mate. Christ. Soren hated the thought of his ex knowing about Danny. Roman's mate was sweet, lovely, purehearted—Soren didn't want Hendrick anywhere near him.

He sat unbearably still, trying to resist the urge to bite at his nails. It was happening, exactly as he'd feared. Soren's presence was tainting his friends with Hendrick's attention.

This is why you don't stay. This is why you should have left..

"What do you want, Hendrick?" Soren finally moved, pushing the unwanted drink to the side.

The big vampire chuckled, the sound grating on Soren's already fraught nerves. "I want what I always want, angel. To check in with you. To remind you who you belong to."

Who Soren *belonged* to.

And just like that, Soren's nerves left him. He was just so fucking *tired* of this. These stupid games. This bullshit power trip. "Why can't you just leave me the fuck alone?" he gritted out, turning his barstool to fully face his ex.

Hendrick's shoulders stiffened. "I don't like your attitude, angel."

Hendrick never did.

But this wasn't the place for this particular confrontation; the bar was still pretty crowded, and Soren knew Danny—and Gabe too, most likely—would be upset if humans were hurt in the crossfire.

So Soren rose from his seat smoothly, leaving his still-full drink on the counter. He didn't want to take a thing from Hendrick, even a measly cocktail. "Let's go for a walk," he suggested.

Hendrick's dark eyes glinted. "Lovely idea."

The fucker thought he'd won this round, that Soren was caving to his demands.

Let him think that.

They left the bar, and Soren directed them toward a nearby park. Hendrick loomed over Soren as they walked, but he didn't make a move to actually touch him. That wasn't surprising. Hendrick only ever touched him to fuck or to fight. He had no use for Soren otherwise. No use for any connection beyond the sexual or the violent.

The park was empty this late at night, the abandoned play structure looking positively spooky in the moonlight. Hendrick paused at the edge, his hands in his pants pockets. "This is nice and all, angel. But I was thinking somewhere more...private."

Of course he was. And in the past, Soren might have allowed it. One night of pain and humiliation in return for another few years of freedom.

But he didn't want this slimy cretin's hands on him ever again. "I'm not going anywhere with you, Hendrick."

Hendrick's thin lips pressed together tightly. "Are we feeling rebellious, angel? It's pointless. You know how it ends."

Soren shook his head, casually widening his stance. "Not this time. I don't owe you anything, and you don't have your shitty little squad to back you up anymore. I'm done."

"I think you'll find you owe me *everything*," Hendrick growled.

The larger vampire—aggressive jerk that he was—pounced immediately, tackling Soren to the ground. But Soren was ready for him. His violent response wasn't any sort of surprise. Hendrick had never liked talking things out, preferring to use his physical strength to win his arguments. Why use words when his fists could do the talking?

Soren had his hands out and ready, scratching at the other vampire's face, aiming for the eyes. Hendrick dodged the move, his fangs popping out, murky brown eyes turning black.

Soren screamed as the asshole bit into his shoulder—not drinking, just tearing at the flesh. He managed to jab a knee into Hendrick's balls, but Hendrick only grunted and tightened his arms around him.

Soren could feel his ribs breaking. Goddamn it. Broken ribs were the *worst*.

He shoved his palm up with all his strength, aiming once again for Hendrick's face. He heard an incredibly satisfying crunch, laughing hysterically when blood from Hendrick's now-broken nose sprayed his face.

Hendrick's attack stopped in an instant. He hovered above Soren's body, stunned. "God fucking *damn it*, Soren."

Soren laughed through the pain. Drawing blood from Hendrick was a high he'd never known he needed. "No more 'angel'?"

Hendrick cursed and leaped off, holding one hand to his nose, scowling at Soren as he cracked the bone back into place. It wouldn't take very long to heal, but Soren was still pleased at the sight.

They glared at each other, Soren holding himself ready for another attack. Finally, Hendrick sighed, wiping his bloody hand off on his shirt. "I'm very disappointed in you, angel. *Very* disappointed."

And then he was gone.

Fourteen

Gabe

Gabe gripped the steering wheel with tense fingers, his mind only half-focused on the flood of words coming from the little vampire next to him. Jay was gushing about all the various foods he'd gotten to try in the hospital cafeteria, which—given the twelve hours he'd had to experiment with—was apparently quite a lot. He was currently reviewing the different merits of every single type of candy from the vending machines.

Gabe could only assume one of the lesser-known vampire superpowers was not getting a belly ache from too much junk food.

For his part, Gabe was fighting to keep his eyes open, trying his best to get himself and Jay home in one piece. Work had been beyond exhausting, and he was just *done*. Two of his patients had tried to die on him that night, and he'd had to run codes on both of them. One had made it through the CPR, the other...

Well, the other hadn't.

Gabe knew—he *knew*—it was the way it went sometimes. He knew there had been an amazing team of healthcare professionals working to keep them alive, and that sometimes that wasn't enough. But he still hated it with every fiber of his being.

It felt like losing. He *hated* losing.

And he was glad of Jay's company; he really was. He was especially glad having a chaperone had let Soren feel comfortable with him going to work. But, sweet as the dark-haired vampire was, he wasn't who Gabe wanted next to him after the night he'd had.

Gabe wanted Soren.

He wanted his vampire's soothing touch. Wanted his easy understanding of Gabe's messy emotions. He even wanted him calling Gabe an idiot for expecting to win every single battle of life versus death in the ICU.

But Soren wasn't with him. Soren had better things to do than babysit, apparently.

Gabe wasn't sure exactly what Soren had gotten up to while he was at work. He'd told Gabe he wouldn't feed on anyone else, but...surely he'd gotten restless, stuck in that house with Gabe for days on end? Maybe Soren needed some variety. Maybe he was second-guessing so much time spent with one boring human.

Or maybe he just needed a little space to breathe and spent the day crocheting a new outfit and running with the mutt. Maybe you're just being an incredibly insecure, clingy mess, Gabe's brain taunted.

He sighed, fingers clenching the steering wheel. He *was* being incredibly insecure. Maybe he could talk his vampire onto his lap again for dinner. Or...breakfast? Gabe was never quite sure what to call his presleep meal after a night shift.

Whatever he called it, Gabe wanted to cuddle Soren while he ate it.

Ferdy greeted them at the door, whining in distress. Gabe rubbed the dog's ears. "What's up, pup?"

"Hello, dog," Jay greeted from beside Gabe, waving at the puppy. He apparently hadn't spent much time around animals in the past, and he was still trying to figure out what he called "pet etiquette."

"You're home." Soren's voice sounded from the living room.

Gabe rushed in, not caring if he seemed overeager, but he stopped in his tracks at the sight of his vampire sprawled out on the couch.

Soren's clothes were mussed, his blond hair was in disarray, and...his entire face was covered in blood.

He looked like a fucking horror B movie extra.

Soren greeted them with an ironic wave, his pale eyes oddly blank. "Oh, don't worry," he drawled, gesturing at the mess. "It's not mine. At least, mostly not."

"What the fuck happened to you?" Gabe was aware that his voice was too loud. He didn't know why he was even asking the question...

He knew the answer already. There was only one person out there Gabe knew of who would want to hurt Soren. Only one who would even be capable of it.

Well, two, if you counted Lucien, but that psycho fuck hadn't shown his face in over a year, so Gabe didn't really think he would randomly decide to show up and wreak havoc now.

Gabe walked carefully over to the couch, kneeling in front of Soren's reclined body. "Baby."

Soren's eyes softened, some of that blankness leaving them. "Highness."

"Where are you hurt?" Gabe did his best to gauge the damage with his eyes, but the blood all over Soren's face was pretty distracting.

Soren shrugged in response. The movement brought attention to his right shoulder. His shirt there was torn, the flesh mangled—it looked like he'd been mauled by a fucking animal.

Gabe cleared his throat. "Did he...drink from you?"

"No," Soren answered softly. He was staring at Gabe, like he couldn't get enough of the sight of him. "He was just aiming to damage."

Gabe felt a small amount of solace in that—Danny had told him bites between vampires were a form of intimacy, one that Gabe was sure Soren wouldn't want forced on him—but it was hard to manage too much relief when his vampire was still clearly injured.

Fuck.

Gabe was used to thinking of Soren as practically invincible. Hearing about his past wasn't the same as seeing the evidence. This was the same little monster who'd chased off Lucien, despite being practically half the other vampire's size.

Soren reached out a hand, tracing Gabe's cheek lightly. "You're an ICU doctor, Highness. Haven't you seen worse?"

Gabe shook his head. "Not with someone I care about. Not since—since my dad."

When Danny had been attacked the year before, Roman and Soren hadn't let Gabe see him until he was cleaned up and presentable. Apparently they'd been worried Gabe would have a "complete and utter freak-out meltdown," as Soren had put it.

Gabe had to admit their caution wasn't totally without merit.

Soren sighed softly, his finger still mapping Gabe's face. "It's just the shoulder, really. Plus a couple broken ribs. I was waiting for those to heal themselves before I washed all this off." He gestured at the blood covering his face.

"I'll grab a cloth," Jay offered from the doorway. Gabe turned with a start. He had forgotten Jay was even there.

The other vampire seemed relatively unfazed by Soren's bloody visage. This was the same Jay who'd apparently had his mind blown by—and had gushed for over fifteen minutes about—the different flavors of Starburst candy. Gabe didn't want to think what his blasé attitude over Soren's appearance meant for what the two of them had seen together in that fucking vampire den.

Gabe turned back to Soren. His vampire was grinning broadly. That same smile Gabe had once found so unnerving became even more so with a blood-streaked face. "Why are you smiling?" Gabe asked gruffly, wondering if he should be concerned about a brain injury. "You look like fucking roadkill."

"I fought back," Soren answered gleefully. "I fought back this time."

"Is this a 'you should see the other guy' kind of thing?"

"No." Soren's smile dropped, and he pursed his lips. "I broke his nose and bruised his balls, but those are probably all healed up by now. But still." He grinned again. "I've never stood up for myself with him before. Not like that."

It hurt Gabe's heart to hear. "Why did you this time?"

Soren opened his mouth to answer but closed it again when Jay came back in with a wet washcloth in hand. Gabe took it from the vampire, wiping off Soren's face with it, careful to use gentle strokes. Bedside manner was more Danny's thing, but Gabe could be gentle, if he needed to be.

He could be gentle for Soren.

Gabe still only half believed his vampire didn't have cuts of his own under the mess of blood. But Soren's clean face was coming through unbruised and unbroken.

Beautiful.

Soren watched him through the whole process, a tenderness to his gaze that had Gabe's chest aching.

When he'd cleaned Soren's face as best as he was able, Gabe set the filthy washcloth aside. He wasn't sure where Jay had gone, but that wasn't really his concern right now. "How are your ribs?" he asked.

Soren shifted experimentally on the couch. "They're fine now."

"We should get you washed properly. I don't want any of that asshole's blood on you."

Soren huffed at him. "Well, I don't either. Obviously. Take a bath with me?"

"You're—"

"I'm fine," Soren reassured him, rising into a sitting position. "For once, I'm the one who wants cuddles." He shot Gabe a smirk. "Take advantage while you can."

Well, when he put it that way.

Gabe let himself be led upstairs.

Gabe ran his fingers under the water, testing out the temperature. He tried to ignore the way his hand was visibly shaking under the hot spray. The swirling knot in his stomach was back with a vengeance.

He was feeling too many things—anxious, angry, frustrated—to settle on any one emotion, other than just "bad."

The thing was, Gabe knew his tried-and-true response to this kind of mess of feelings: avoidance. It was what he'd done with Danny and his mother—interact only with surface-level emotions, deny anything negative, push anything and anyone away that threatened to go deeper. But Gabe didn't want to do that with Soren.

He didn't want to be that person.

For so long, he'd put all his focus on being capable at work, on being a person his patients could rely on, but...no one else. And that just wasn't fucking *enough* anymore. Gabe wanted to be someone the people he cared about could count on.

But...what if this turned into another full-blown panic attack? What if it happened in front of Soren, and then the person Gabe should be comforting became the person comforting *him* instead? Gabe couldn't protect Soren physically; he couldn't be strong for him emotionally. What was the point?

Useless. He was useless.

"Highness?"

Gabe turned to find Soren standing in the doorway, a towel slung low around his hips. The vampire had rinsed off in the master bathroom shower, trying to get the rest of the blood off before their bath. He was so beautiful, even with the painful sight of his mangled shoulder on full display.

That shoulder. Gabe eyed the wound critically. It looked like it had already healed substantially in the short time Soren had been showering. There was shiny pink skin around the edges that should have taken days or even a week to grow naturally.

Gabe might not know how Soren's vampire healing worked, but Soren was right—a vampire body was substantially less fragile than a human one.

He watched as Soren stepped gracefully into the bathroom, gliding over to where Gabe was seated on the edge of the tub. As soon as the vampire was in reach, Gabe wrapped his arms around his slender hips, burying his face in the soft pale skin of Soren's stomach.

He sighed in contentment as Soren began brushing his fingers through his curls. The knot in Gabe's stomach was slowly dissolving. But still...

"You're shaking, Highness. What's wrong?"

Gabe lifted his head, gazing up into pale-blue eyes. "What do you mean, what's wrong? He *hurt* you."

"Ah." Soren continued his soft stroking. "That upsets you. I didn't realize you...cared...quite this much." He hesitated over his words. A rare thing for Gabe's bratty vampire.

Gabe ducked his head again, trusting Soren to decipher his muffled response. "I've maybe grown used to you or something."

Soren chuckled, but after a moment, the movement of his hand stopped. "You know,"—his voice came out harder than before—"I'm no damsel. I was hurt. I'll recover. For once, I gave as good as I got."

"Someone can care about you—be upset when you're hurt—without automatically thinking you're helpless," Gabe protested, looking up again.

Soren hummed noncommittally. Gabe wasn't sure he was convinced. "Anyway," Soren mused. "I'm hoping he got the message. I'm not his toy anymore."

"I feel *useless*," Gabe blurted out.

It was horrifying to say it aloud.

Soren tugged at one of his curls, tsking softly. "You're not," he reassured Gabe. "You think I let just anyone in? You think I'd stay in this stupid fucking town for anyone else?"

Gabe swallowed hard. "Why *did* you? Stay, I mean. Why didn't you run this time? I don't mean now, I mean...this whole year. Why did you stay?"

Soren smirked down at him. "You really want me to say it out loud?"

Gabe nodded, his chin brushing against the vampire's soft stomach.

"Let's just say...maybe you're not as boring as I first thought," Soren teased.

Gabe grinned. "You never really thought I was boring though, did you?"

Soren gave him a light tap on the head. "Stop being insightful. And definitely don't go spreading that around. I've got a reputation to uphold."

Gabe tightened his arms around Soren's hips, relief making him feel almost light-headed. Maybe this was something real after all. Something for the long haul. In which case, Gabe had some serious thinking about mortality versus immortality to do...

Soren took his hand off Gabe's head, stepping out of his hold. "Get naked, Highness. The water's going to get cold, and I want to soak."

Gabe stripped hastily, stepping into the warm tub, watching with delight as Soren undid his towel and followed him in. Gabe immediately wrapped his arms back around the vampire as soon as he was seated, Soren's back to his front. He sighed contentedly. It wasn't exactly how he had envisioned the morning going, but he was happy enough to have gotten Soren in his lap in the end.

Soren matched his sigh, leaning more fully against Gabe's chest. Gabe's eyes started closing without his permission. It was just so...nice. He was pretty sure he could fall asleep just like this.

"Loofah me."

"Excuse me?" Gabe opened his eyes with a start.

"Loofah me," Soren commanded a second time, raising his hand. He held a baby-blue loofah with some sort of bath gel covering it. Gabe didn't even know where it had come from.

"Did you just pull that out of your ass?"

Soren snorted. "Don't be crude. Now rub me down. I'm injured. I need some pampering."

Gabe couldn't argue with that logic.

He grabbed the loofah, scrubbing it gently along Soren's chest and arms, careful to avoid the vampire's injured shoulder. He felt like he was on nurse duty for the second time that night. But then again, rubbing down a wet, naked Soren wasn't exactly a hardship.

Soren's shoulder had healed even more—Gabe was fairly sure if he stared hard enough, he would see it healing in front of his eyes. By tomorrow morning, he bet there would be no sign of the bite at all.

"Lean forward."

Soren complied, and Gabe rubbed the loofah along his pale back, making note of all the spots along Soren's spine that made him shiver when touched. When he'd covered everything, Gabe set the loofah on the side of the tub, cupping water in his hands and rinsing off the suds, pulling Soren back against him when he was finished.

"Satisfied?" Gabe asked, pressing a kiss to the side of Soren's wet head.

"No." Soren shifted against him, then placed the loofah back in Gabe's hand, pulling the same hand under the water.

Gabe had already been half-erect just from being in the same vicinity as a naked Soren, but blood rushed to his cock as he felt hard proof of how much Soren had enjoyed that little rubdown.

"Are you sure?" Gabe murmured, squeezing Soren's cock lightly. "You just—"

"I'm sure. I told you I wanted pampering. Pamper me."

Gabe laughed, but the sound came out slightly strangled. "All right, brat." He removed his hand and started stroking Soren again with the loofah. First his lower belly, then his hips, then the insides of his thighs.

Everywhere except for where he knew Soren really wanted it.

Soren squirmed against him more with each pass. After the third sweep, he snapped. He turned his head to glare at Gabe. "I'll do it myself if you won't."

Gabe laughed again, giving in easily. He'd just wanted to see how long it took for Soren to lose patience. He dropped the loofah, wrapping a sudsy hand around Soren's hard cock. "Like this, baby?" he asked, gripping him tightly.

Soren gave a soft sigh. "Oh, yes. Just like that, Highness."

Gabe jerked him with firm strokes, twisting his hand around the head the same way Soren liked to do for him. He was rewarded with panting breaths and delicious little whimpers from his vampire. The water in the tub started churning as Soren chased Gabe's grip. Gabe restrained him with one hand on his hip. "Shh, baby. Be good. Keep still for me."

Soren whined in protest. Gabe could see it becoming an addictive sound. It was so rare that Soren let Gabe take control. So rare that he let himself be the focus of attention.

Gabe kissed along the back of his vampire's neck, making his way over to Soren's delicate ears, nibbling along the edges. The bath soap smelled like lavender, but Soren's own cold pine smell still broke through.

His only warning before Soren came was the vampire gripping the edge of the tub tightly, keening as he found his release immediately after. For such a chatty brat, Soren didn't say much in bed. Gabe didn't mind—he liked the noises Soren made for him better than any coherent words.

Soren sighed in satisfaction as Gabe released his cock, reaching a hand back in search of Gabe's erection. Gabe batted the hand away, nuzzling his nose against Soren's ear. "I'm close already. Just stay where you are?" He rubbed himself against Soren's silky skin, his cock gliding between Soren's pert cheeks in the water.

He kept his movements small, doing his best not to get bathwater everywhere, but it still took barely any time at all for him to finish, groaning into Soren's hair as he emptied himself against the vampire's lower back.

Soren laughed to himself. "That was quick, Highness."

Gabe nuzzled his neck. "I can't help it that you're so fucking sexy, brat."

Soren preened at that. "Too true," he agreed.

They used the showerhead to rinse themselves off again before drying off and climbing into Soren's bed. Gabe gathered his vampire close, pleased when Soren moved easily into his arms. He brought up something that had been weighing on his mind. "Danny and Roman will be back soon."

Soren hummed.

"Are you— Are we— Is this thing between us some sort of secret?" Soren stiffened against him, and Gabe mentally cursed his bumbling words.

"Do you want it to be secret, Highness?" Soren asked lightly.

"No," Gabe answered quickly, gratified when some of the stiffness left Soren's body. "Not at all. I mean...they'll have to find out eventually, right?"

Gabe didn't quite have it in him to ask the rest of it. *Because we're together, right? Because this is long-term. Because you want to keep me? You think we're meant to be?*

He hoped Soren got it anyway.

"Right," Soren agreed.

Something unclenched in Gabe's gut at Soren's easy confirmation. He sighed, tightening his arms around his vampire. "Why didn't you ever tell Roman? About Hendrick. Couldn't he have helped you?"

It took Soren a minute to answer. Gabe waited patiently, stroking Soren's back in the silence. "There were some things that took a long time to unlearn. Asking for help was one of them. Showing weakness at all... And Roman had his own drama. And I liked—I liked that he saw me as someone who could help him. I didn't want him to see me as—as—"

"A damsel?" Gabe offered up.

"Exactly," Soren said, pressing a kiss to Gabe's chest.

"I don't know how anyone could see you that way. You're so strong. So fierce. You scared the shit out of me when we first met."

"Because you thought I was a monster?"

"Because you're so goddamn appealing," Gabe admitted. "Even when you were freaking me the fuck out."

Soren bit his pec with blunt teeth. "Good."

Fifteen

Soren

"Do you think someone could *actually* die by coffee?"

Soren rolled his eyes, pulling Jay forward into the café. He was keeping one eye on the gym across the street and one ear on his phone. There had been no more signs of Hendrick—no threatening texts, no scent of him in the streets—and Soren had agreed to let Gabe work out at his usual spot before his shift at the hospital.

Soren knew he hadn't done any real damage to Hendrick, so he had to assume it was the act of rebelling in itself that had him backing off. He tried not to get lost in self-loathing at the thought. Was this all it would have taken for him not to be stalked and harassed for centuries? Just a single instance of fighting back properly?

A familiar voice sounded in his head. *Pathetic. Weak. Cowardly.*

It lacked the usual sting though. Because Soren had other words running through his mind now. A different voice, full of affection. *Strong. Fierce. Perfect.*

It was a strange thing, having someone see him—*all* of him—and insist they liked every bit of it.

Soren didn't know what to do with himself. He'd successfully seduced Gabe, he supposed. More than seduced. They were...together? And now Soren had fought off Hendrick. So where did that leave him? What was next? He'd never let himself fully consider it.

Gabe was his mate. Soren knew it. *Had* known it.

But...what did that mean?

Soren didn't have the same fear of going feral as Roman once had. Soren and his inner vamp vibed together very well, all things considered. He'd never had to fight it for control. He knew it was inevitable, that eventually he'd go down the same road as all the others, but it could be centuries more before that became an issue.

Everything came to an end at some point, right?

And Gabe wanted *normal*. He wanted a normal *human* life. Could Soren give that to him? He could, couldn't he? He didn't have to ask Gabe to turn for him.

Soren could love him as he was, for however long he was allowed.

If Gabe stayed in this town, Soren would have to leave sooner rather than later, with the whole never aging thing. But Danny and Roman would eventually have to leave for the same reason, right? Maybe Gabe would want to go with them, and Soren could stay close.

Gabe would be a hot silver fox; that was for sure.

And once Gabe hit the end of his mortal life... Soren felt a sharp stabbing pain in his chest at the thought. For the first time since the early days of his vampire existence, he felt his inner vamp rebel—a twisting, itchy sensation under his skin.

His inner vamp really, *really* did not like the thought of Gabe dying.

Well, what do you want us to do? Scare him away? He finally thinks of us as something other than a monster. You want to ask to take his humanity away and reverse all that progress?

Ugh. This was terrible. Soren had been reduced to a poor man's Roman, actually talking to his "demon" like it was a separate entity.

"Soren, we're up!"

Soren was pulled out of his maudlin thoughts by Jay's enthusiastic warning. Alicia was at the counter again, and Soren nodded his greeting before opening his mouth to order—he was graciously inducting Jay to the world of overly sweet coffee drinks—but Jay spoke first. "You guys are hiring?"

Soren looked to where the other vampire was pointing. There was indeed a "Hiring Now!" sign propped up on the counter.

Alicia smiled warmly at Jay. "We are. You interested?"

"No," Soren answered for the other vampire. "He's not."

Jay turned to him, his gray eyes full of dismay. "Why not?"

"Jaybird," Soren explained, the very picture of patience. "You've never had a job in your life."

"Ohh." Jay's eyes widened in realization. He turned to Alicia. "I've never worked before."

The redheaded barista cocked an eyebrow at him. "Good for you, man."

"My friend here has lived a very...sheltered life," Soren offered.

"Hm." Alicia looked Jay over—Jay who was currently staring at the café menu like it was the most fascinating thing he'd ever seen. "It's really not all that hard to learn. And being that adorable does half the work for you when it comes to customer service."

She turned to the back, where there was a door leading to what Soren could only assume was the staff lounge or office or whatever. "Colin!" she shouted, making Jay jump. "Colin!"

After a few seconds, the door opened, and a tall, lanky guy with purple hair and an eyebrow piercing stepped out. "Damn, Alicia. Don't yell like that in front of customers."

Alicia seemed unfazed by the rebuke. "We have an applicant." She pointed to Jay, who smiled broadly.

When Soren smiled like that, it unnerved people.

When Jay did it, people thought he'd fallen straight from heaven.

Colin looked the little vampire up and down. "Got any barista experience?"

"Nope," Jay answered sweetly.

"Food service experience?"

"Nope."

"Customer service experience in any way, shape, or form?"

"Nope."

"Big fan of coffee?"

"I've never had it," Jay said sincerely, smile still firmly in place.

Colin stared at Jay, who stared right back at him. Finally, the tall man ducked beneath the counter before coming back up with a form. "Fill out this application. Come back Tuesday for a real interview."

He turned back, returning through the back door.

Alicia was doing her best to hold back laughter. "Oh my God, you actually charmed him. I didn't think it was possible."

Jay nodded, smiling brightly at her. "I'm very charming."

Christ. Soren pushed Jay toward his table by the window. "Go. Sit. I'll order. Can't have you going to your interview without ever having tasted coffee."

Alicia frowned at him. "You do know what you drink can't be considered real coffee, right?"

See? Bitchy. Soren was becoming fond of this human barista. "Where's Cammie?" he asked snidely.

Alicia shrugged a shoulder. "Oh, she was fired. That's why we're hiring."

Soren tipped extra. This really was a great place for coffee.

He and Jay enjoyed their "not real" coffees together, Jay making appropriate *ooh*s and *aah*s over his drink. Soren found that, when he wasn't using Jay as a comparison for everything he himself was lacking, he was able to actually enjoy the other vampire's company. Soren could see the appeal in all that adorable openness. And there was strength there—that was for sure—more than Soren had given him credit for. How else could Jay have survived that hellhole and still come out chock-full of sweetness?

Alicia stopped by their table a few times, dropping off free treats and filling Jay in on his potential future coworkers.

It was all...nice.

Was this what it would be like? To stay in one place long-term? To have more than one person Soren could call a friend?

It was an almost an hour before Soren spotted his human exiting the gym. It was a familiar enough sight at this point: a tank-topped Gabe, his muscles lightly shining with sweat. This time, though, Gabe didn't head to his car—he made a beeline for the coffeeshop, where Soren had told him they'd be waiting. Soren turned to the door to watch his human enter.

He liked to ogle; so what?

Gabe walked in, a slight swagger to his walk. He was the picture of golden-boy confidence. Soren delighted in watching his human in public for this very reason. The rest of the world got to see this confident front, but only Soren got to see the real deal. The insecurities, the anxieties, the emotional depths. It turned out knowing someone else's flaws was a gift, in its own way.

Soren opened his mouth to greet him but was frozen in place when his human bent over, planting a firm, slightly dirty kiss on Soren's lips. "Hi, brat."

Soren was...stunned. Sure, they'd danced together in that club, and Gabe didn't shy away from affection in front of Jay. But this was Gabe's town. People here *knew* him. They were down the street from his work, for Christ's sake.

Gabe frowned down at him, noting Soren's stillness. "Am I not allowed to do that?" he asked.

Really, he shouldn't be. If Hendrick was still lurking in town and saw that display, they could be inviting a world of trouble. But Soren was having a hard time caring about that. Especially when he saw Alicia staring at them out of the corner of her eye, a shocked smirk on her face.

A feeling of immense satisfaction washed over Soren. *That's right,* he thought smugly. *This one's mine. My human. My mate.*

He relaxed into his seat, giving Gabe a haughty look. "You're allowed, I suppose."

Gabe rolled his eyes, sitting in the chair next to him and greeting Jay with a smile. He threw a casual arm around Soren's shoulder. Soren wasn't preening at all at this public display of affection.

He absolutely wasn't.

He cleared his throat, trying to will away the blush he could feel on his cheeks by force of will. "I heard Cammie got fired."

"Who?" Gabe asked absently, toying with the hair on the back of Soren's neck.

Soren tried not to shiver. He was determined to be petty. "Cammie," he said again. "That blonde barista."

Gabe frowned in thought. "Was she— Am I supposed to know her?" He stole a sip of Soren's drink, wincing at the taste.

Boring human.

Soren felt like he might burst from an overabundance of affection for the idiot.

"No," he said, grinning widely. "You're not."

The next morning, Soren was dealing with a very different version of Gabe. He wasn't exactly sure what had happened during his human's shift at the hospital—Jay had accompanied him again while Soren searched the town for Hendrick—but the swagger in his human's step was gone, and he wasn't saying much.

A sullen, "I'm fine," was the only response Soren had received when he'd asked about it.

Now Soren kicked his heels against the bottom of the kitchen counter he was perched on, watching Jay fiddle around on the stove, his human sulking at the opposite counter. Soren would ask Gabe again when they were alone. If Gabe thought he could keep all his feelings inside, he was vastly underestimating Soren's ability to pester them out of him.

Jay sang to himself at the stove, completely oblivious to Gabe's mini temper tantrum. The other vampire had taken the news that Soren and Gabe had been ordering in for most of their meals as an invitation to try out cooking for the first time. Soren hadn't had the heart to tell him that Gabe mostly stuck with boring toast after a night shift, especially after Jay had begged him to help look up online recipes for omelets, of all things.

"Okay," Jay said cheerily. "I think they're ready."

Soren glanced down at the barely recognizable blobs on the pan. At the moment, he was feeling immeasurably pleased he didn't have to consume human food for survival.

They ate at the kitchen counters. Or at least, they tried to. Jay's omelets were somehow both burned on the outside and runny on the inside. A masterful culinary feat, in Soren's opinion.

He watched in fascination as Jay took a bite of his own food. After a hard swallow, Jay shot Soren a concerned look. "Humans *like* these?" the vampire asked.

"Well, not *these*," Soren answered, fighting to keep a straight face.

"Don't tease him." Gabe finally broke his silence to defend Soren's friend. "These were great, Jay."

"But you only ate your toast?" Jay questioned.

"Um..." Gabe clearly didn't have an answer for that.

"He'll never learn if you lie to him," Soren admonished. "The omelets were terrible." He took one look at the crestfallen look on Jay's face and sighed. "But the effort was sweet. Thank you."

Jay flushed, nodding. "I'll learn. I can be useful, I promise."

"You don't need to be *useful*," Soren told him.

"But I can be," Jay insisted.

Christ. Whatever. Jay had spent the vast majority of his long years of existence in servitude to another. It wasn't a habit Soren was going to break overnight.

He sighed, tugging Gabe up from his spot at the counter. "Thanks for the meal, Jaybird. Time to get cranky pants to bed."

Gabe frowned ferociously at him. "I'm not a cranky pants."

Soren patted Gabe's back soothingly, herding his human up the stairs. "Sure you're not."

They changed into their pajamas, Gabe giving Soren the silent treatment the whole time. Well, Soren changed into his silk set. Gabe just undressed down to his boxer briefs, his preferred sleeping outfit.

Soren had no complaints.

Settling into bed, for once, Gabe didn't immediately pull Soren into his arms. The human was clearly tangled up in his own head. Soren smirked to himself. It had been so long since he'd dealt with brusque, standoffish Gabe. It made Soren feel almost nostalgic.

"How are you doing over there, Highness?" he asked.

Gabe grunted in response.

Soren patted at the space between them on the bed. "It's just so lonely all the way over here, all by myself," he teased.

Gabe gave him an impressively bitchy side-eye. "You don't even *like* cuddling," he grumbled.

Soren shrugged. "Maybe not usually. I don't mind it with you though."

Gabe gave him an inscrutable look. "And why is that, do you think?" he asked.

"How about you tell me all about what bug crawled up your ass, *then* I'll share about my precious feelings?" Soren offered.

That response had Gabe sulking, but after a minute, he lifted an arm, a clear invitation for Soren to come closer. Soren sidled in, tucking himself easily against Gabe's chest. The tension in the human's larger frame eased substantially.

But Soren didn't think his touch was the only reason Gabe had beckoned him closer; at this angle, his human could share without them having to look each other in the eye. Fine by Soren, if it got Gabe to talk.

He pressed a kiss to Gabe's pec, taking a moment to appreciate the human's shiver. "What happened at work?" Soren asked, wanting to get straight to the point.

"My patient died," Gabe said simply.

"I see." Soren didn't, exactly. Gabe worked in intensive care. He must have seen his fair share of dying patients, even if he was a relatively new doctor. "Were you especially close to them?" Soren asked.

"No."

Soren hummed. "Okay."

Gabe took a deep breath, the exaggerated motion lifting Soren's head with his chest. "A patient died last night too."

"Did— Did you make some mistakes or something?" Soren pressed. Guilt could be a powerful downer; maybe that was why his human was so put out.

Gabe sighed heavily. "Not really. I did everything I could."

"I believe that." Soren did.

"It's just... I hate it sometimes. Losing those battles. Feeling like I—like I let someone down. Let everybody down. That's all I do, it seems."

Soren's brow furrowed. "You don't let everybody down."

"I let Danny down."

This again? Soren sat up, tilting his head to meet Gabe's golden-eyed gaze. He grabbed the human's chin, not willing to let him duck away. "Listen. Yes, you had a bad stretch. You weren't the best brother in the whole wide world for a time. Big whoop. You were also there for Danny during the worst time in his life, taking care of him when your mom couldn't. Nobody's perfect. Why is it that you expect yourself to be?"

"I just— I want..." Gabe didn't seem to know how to finish that statement.

"You're being an idiot," Soren scolded. "Modern medicine can't save everyone. You're a doctor, not a magician. And you *know that.* I know you know that."

Gabe made a strangled sound, his chest shaking, and for a horrifying moment, Soren thought he had made him cry. But then Gabe started laughing. "I knew you'd call me an idiot."

Soren huffed. "I guess I'm not the most sympathetic ear."

Gabe pulled Soren back into his arms. "No, I like it. I think I need to hear it sometimes. When my brain runs away from me."

"I can call you an idiot as much as you like," Soren offered happily.

Gabe kissed the top of his head. "Thank you."

He wrapped his arms tighter around Soren, pressing him into his muscled chest.

Cuddle slut.

They rested in comfortable silence for a time. "You know," Gabe said out of the blue, "I never wanted magic to be real."

"Hm?"

"Even as a kid. I remember Danny reading all those wizard books and going absolutely crazy for those movies about the little hairy-feet guys."

"Hobbits," Soren supplied.

Gabe nodded. "Yeah, those. But I never did. I just wanted— I wanted the world to make *sense.* That felt like enough."

"You know, losing your dad at that age...having such a pillar in your life taken away when you were young...it's no wonder you craved stability," Soren mused.

Gabe shrugged. "Even before that. And it's not like it affected Danny that way. He lost our dad even younger, and he still accepted the news of vampires existing like it was just any other thing. He didn't take a full *year* to come to terms with it."

Was that what Gabe had been doing? Coming to terms with the change in his reality? Did that mean he'd be open to other changes, given enough time? Permanent, "turn you into a vampire" changes?

"He had *you,*" Soren said, trying not to get ahead of himself.

"What?"

"He lost your dad, yes. But he still had you. Taking care of him. Holding it together. He had stability because he had you."

Gabe tensed. "Jesus, brat. You can't say stuff like that."

"Why not?"

"I think I'm in danger of...liking you? Like, a lot. You were supposed to be a monster. A manipulative, demonic creature."

Soren laughed. "Is that what you told yourself I was?"

"For a while there, yes."

Soren looked up, catching Gabe's eye. "I'm not a good person though. You know that, right? I'm selfish. Vain. Petty."

Gabe smirked down at him. "You're the one who just told me nobody's perfect. And you're good to me. And to Roman. Danny. Jay, even. You're not as bad as you think."

"Idiot," Soren grumbled.

"Your idiot," Gabe answered, holding him close.

Sixteen

Gabe

Gabe jerked awake to the sound of his alarm blaring. There was a weight on his chest keeping him from sitting up, so he reached out blindly with one hand, grabbing his phone and turning off the hateful sound.

He tilted his chin, looking down at the blond head tucked underneath it. He inhaled Soren's comforting scent, sneezing when the vampire's hairs tickled his nose.

"Christ," Soren said, his voice muffled by Gabe's chest. "First your obnoxious alarm, then you sneezing on my head. Terrible way to wake up."

Gabe rubbed his still-itchy nose more firmly against Soren's hair. "Too bad."

Gabe thought it was a great way to wake up. Soren may not have needed the same amount of sleep as he did, but the blond vampire had gotten into the habit of staying in bed with him anyway, either reading or crocheting to pass the time, usually catching sleep for the last few hours before Gabe had to be awake himself.

Gabe sighed happily and ran a hand along the strip of bare skin between Soren's pajama shirt and pants, the skin just as soft, smooth, and cool as the silk itself.

Wait.

He removed his hand, placing it over Soren's forehead instead. "Hey," Soren protested. "What are you doing?"

Gabe frowned down at the vampire. "You need to feed," he accused. "You should have told me."

"You weren't exactly in the best of moods last night, Highness. I could wait."

"Don't," Gabe said firmly. "Tell me next time."

"Fine, fine," Soren grumbled. "Do we even have time?" He lifted his head to glance at Gabe's phone.

"Yeah. I set my alarm a little early." Gabe didn't feel the need to share the fact that he'd been setting his alarm earlier every day to sneak extra time with Soren before his shifts.

"All right." Soren stretched languidly, reminding Gabe once again of a contented house cat. The next moment, Gabe's breath left him in a huff as Soren abruptly flipped him onto his back, straddling him smoothly in the same movement.

"I want your neck again," Soren demanded, pale eyes glinting.

"Yeah, um." Gabe tried to focus on Soren, and not on the way that statement made his cock swell, for some reason. "Where else would you do it?"

"Oh, there are all sorts of places I can drink from you," Soren purred, walking his fingers along Gabe's chest, a wide grin crossing his lips. "A plethora to choose from."

Gabe swallowed hard, his mouth dry. There were so many versions of Soren. The sweet one from last night. The teasing, sultry one from the club. The vulnerable, prickly one afraid to ask for help. And then this one. The side of him that might have terrified Gabe just a year before. Hungry and wicked and...fucking *sexy*.

Gabe couldn't help but grab onto the vampire's hips, holding him in place. "I'm sure we'll try them all."

Soren grinned wider, his eyes darkening to black, his fangs peeking out from behind pink lips. "We will," he promised hoarsely.

Gabe held his breath as Soren leaned over him, moving so slowly Gabe was sure it was deliberate.

So dramatic, his vampire.

Finally, Soren pounced. Gabe winced at the flash of pain, but almost immediately, that...*tingling* sensation started. The one he'd felt when Soren fed from him at the club. It began at the bite, traveling down his spine, all the way to...

Gabe groaned as his cock filled rapidly. "Fuck," he breathed.

Soren growled in response, his strong, delicate hands digging into Gabe's shoulders.

Gabe groaned again. Why did this feel so fucking good?

He had needed to hold himself back in the club, not wanting to go too far in a public place, but they were alone now. He moved his hands from Soren's hips to the vampire's ass, grinding against him. Soren was just as hard as he was.

It wasn't enough.

Gabe frantically pushed his underwear down, groaning in relief as his erection was freed, all the while listening to Soren gulp greedily. He grabbed at the vampire's silken pajama pants, tugging them down, freeing Soren's cock as well.

"Fuck, baby." Gabe lined them up and used his hold on Soren's ass to grind their bare cocks together, Soren's copious amounts of precum helping ease the glide. His vampire was making feral little sounds as he drank. Gabe had no idea why those sounds were so fucking hot. They just…were.

Eventually Soren released Gabe's neck and rose, black eyes gazing down at Gabe. Even like this, Soren's vampire side front and forward, he was so fucking beautiful.

"Kiss me," Gabe begged.

Soren grinned down at him, slowly licking the trickles of Gabe's blood from his lips. "You sure, Highness?"

Gabe took one hand off Soren's ass, grabbing the back of his vampire's head, pulling him close and kissing him hungrily. There was a faint metallic edge to it, but Gabe couldn't find it in himself to care that he was tasting traces of his own blood. Not when he felt like he would die if he had to wait another second to have Soren's mouth on his.

"So needy, Highness," Soren whispered against his lips.

"Can't help it," Gabe panted. "Feels so fucking good."

"Mm," Soren hummed his agreement, rocking against Gabe, his movements bringing them both to release in moments. Gabe held him tight as they both shuddered through their orgasms.

"Fuck," Gabe sighed, their mingled cum cooling on his stomach. "That's really something. The whole biting thing."

Soren leaned over him, giving small, kittenish licks to the bite on his neck. "Stay still. I need to close this properly."

"Magic saliva," Gabe murmured, maybe a trifle delirious from the combination of blood loss and mind-melting orgasm.

"Yes, exactly. Magic," Soren agreed.

Gabe wasn't so out of it that he didn't catch the irony in Soren's tone, and he thought back on what he'd told the vampire the night before. It was true Gabe had never been a fantasy-prone kid. He'd liked what was right in front of him. His family. His friends. Sports. He'd taken comfort in the simplicity of the world around him, in things making sense. He hadn't seen the appeal of adding a bunch of illogical bullshit to an already confusing world.

But it turned out all that was a lie anyway. Even without magic, life was unpredictable. His father's life had been taken away in one freak accident. His mother had forgotten Gabe's existence in a few years. And magic had appeared in Gabe's world after all, for better or worse. His brother was a vampire, for fuck's sake. And Gabe had another one in his bed right now.

And it was the best thing that had happened to him in years.

So maybe Gabe should stop reaching for a normal life that didn't even really exist and accept the one he'd fallen into, fangs and all.

Soren finished his ministrations, lifting himself off Gabe and flouncing onto his back. "Rinse off, Highness. I'll let the mutt out. Then we need to get you some food and water. Can't have you woozy on your last shift of the week." He gave Gabe a wicked look. "Maybe we can get Jay to make you something."

"Don't even— Oh fuck, do you think he heard that? Vamp hearing and all?" Gabe had forgotten about their vampire guest. It was way too easy for him to focus in on Soren and only Soren.

"I didn't hear anything!" Jay's voice sounded from across the hall.

"Fuck." Gabe ran a hand over his face, laughing in spite of himself. Fucking vampires everywhere.

He took a lightning-quick shower before handing the bathroom over to Soren and bounding down the stairs. Gabe still had a good amount of time before work—maybe he could fit in a short run?

Hydration first.

He was interrupted on his way to the kitchen by the sound of knocking on the front door. Gabe hesitated. Should he wait for one of the vampires? But Soren was in the shower, Jay still in the guest room presumably. And there hadn't been any sign of trouble since Soren had fought Hendrick off.

Gabe peered through the peephole. "Oh fuck."

Danny had warned him Ferdy could jump the backyard fence. Gabe had been skeptical, given the puppy's smaller size, but still, he should have told the others not to leave him out back unsupervised.

He opened the door quickly. The man holding Ferdy by the collar smiled ruefully at him. "This one yours?"

He was big and broad, with blond hair and dark eyes peeking out from under a trucker hat, looking like a local in flannel and faded jeans.

"Oh yeah." Gabe reached a hand out for Ferdy. "I'm sorry, man. He must've gotten out of the backyard somehow."

"Must have." The guy smiled at him, still holding on to the puppy. "Nice place you've got here."

"Thanks." Gabe could have told the guy it was his brother's place, but he didn't see the point. It wasn't any of this stranger's business. And Gabe just...didn't like the guy's vibe. There was something off about him.

Or maybe living with vampires had made him paranoid.

"I can take him," Gabe said pointedly, grabbing Ferdy's collar. There was a tense moment where Gabe thought, for whatever reason, this guy wasn't going to let go of the dog.

But then the moment was over, the stranger tipping his hat like some sort of parody of a country yokel. "I'll be on my way, then."

"Um, all right. Thanks."

Gabe locked the door behind him.

"Your stalker is back."

"Excuse me?" Gabe looked up from the vending machine selections he'd been studying, trying to decide whether bringing Soren home some candy would be a nice gesture or an incredibly stupid one.

He wanted to give the vampire...something. For listening the other night. For making it feel less terrible to come to work. For making Gabe feel like life was full of more possibility than he'd let himself believe.

Candy was probably a stupid way to do that. But Soren liked...sweets. And pretty things. And Gabe, for some reason.

Should Gabe be buying him jewelry or something?

Chloe cleared her throat, and Gabe brought his focus back to the moment. Danny's friend was leaning against the wall next to the vending machine, nursing a giant coffee. "Who is he?" she asked. "The little dark-haired kid who's been coming to work with you, hanging around the cafeteria."

She meant Jay. "Oh yeah." Gabe ran a hand through his hair. "He's, um, a friend of Soren's."

Chloe raised a dark brow at him. "Danny and Roman's roommate? Why is his friend coming to work with *you*?"

Well, fuck. Gabe had been hoping no one would notice that he and Jay had been arriving and leaving together. It wasn't exactly normal to bring random friends to the hospital for an entire shift. Or technically allowed, for that matter.

"Um." Gabe searched for an excuse. "He's new in town. Doesn't know anybody yet."

Chloe laughed in disbelief. "And you thought he'd make friends in the hospital cafeteria? In the middle of the night?"

"What? No. He's new, but he's got...family. Sick family. Family he's been visiting. I've just been giving him a ride?" Fuck. Apparently Gabe was a terrible liar. He hadn't had that much experience with it. He'd never even realized it was a weakness.

Chloe looked skeptical but made a sympathetic noise anyway. "Aw. Poor guy. He seems like such a sweetheart too. He's been charming the cafeteria staff. I overheard him calling them 'culinary geniuses.'"

Fucking hell. Gabe bit back laughter. "He is," he grunted. "Total sweetheart."

Chloe took another sip of her coffee. "You excited to be almost done with dog duty? Danny's back in a few days, right?"

"Oh. Yeah." Gabe's stomach sank at the thought. He wanted to see his brother, sure, but it would also be the end of his temporary living situation. A situation he'd gotten very...fond of.

"You never texted me for doggie walks," Chloe pointed out. "You managing by yourself?"

"Nah, Soren's been helping me."

"Huh." Chloe gave him an inscrutable look. "Didn't take that one for the pet-loving type."

"Uh-huh. Well." Gabe turned his attention back to the candy in front of him, ready to be done with this conversation. He didn't want Danny's best friend finding out something was going on between him and Soren before Danny found out himself.

Gabe chose three different options at random, bending low to fish them out of the machine. "Anyway. See ya."

"Catch ya later." Chloe waved him off, more than used to his antisocial nature at work.

Gabe tried to corral his thoughts as he made his way over to the cafeteria. Right. Danny and Roman would be home soon. Which meant there would be no reason for Gabe and Soren to keep living in the same place. They had decided not to hide this thing between them from his brother but hadn't defined what this thing *was*.

Gabe sighed. Would Soren want space, now that they weren't required to be near each other? Would he want to...stay with Gabe instead? Would that be crazy? To ask the vampire to move in after just a few weeks? But the thought of sleeping without Soren in his arms made Gabe's chest tighten. He'd gotten used to having the vampire around all the time. He didn't want to go back to the way things had been before.

Danny and Roman had just *chosen* each other. After barely any time together at all. Gabe wanted *that*. He wanted to choose Soren. He wanted Soren to choose him back.

Would Soren choose him back?

He found Jay at one of the cafeteria tables, exactly where Gabe had left him the night before. The little vampire smiled widely at him, pointing to his plate. "Look, Gabe. It's an omelet."

Gabe laughed. "So it is."

"This tastes...very different from what I made." Jay narrowed his eyes at his food, as if willing it to divulge its secrets.

"Don't you get bored, sitting here for twelve hours?"

Jay shrugged. "Time passes a little differently when you've been alive as long as I have. I don't mind it. I eat. I watch people. I've never gotten to see so many humans in my life. Not like this. Everyone smells so good. Well"—he wrinkled his nose—"mostly everyone."

Gabe raised an eyebrow. "You know you can't feed on anyone here."

Jay huffed. "I know that. I also read." He held up his phone. "Vee helped me set up books on this thing years ago." He leaned forward, whispering like it was a secret, "I like *romance*."

Gabe nodded, not sure what to say to that.

He let Jay finish his omelet, and they headed for home. Jay's eyes had widened in delight at the candy, so Gabe had given him a bag of Skittles, too embarrassed to tell the vampire it was all intended for Soren.

They drove the short drive to Danny's house in silence, Jay too busy popping candy into his mouth to talk much. At least until they pulled into the driveway.

"You should just tell him how you feel."

"What?" Gabe blinked in surprise, turning to the vampire next to him. Where the hell had that come from?

"Soren," Jay said casually, as if they were continuing a conversation and he wasn't just blurting non sequiturs out of the blue. "He's not going to make the first move. Hendrick really messed him up, you know. Emotionally. *Major* trust issues."

Gabe didn't know where Jay had gotten the idea that this was something they needed to discuss. But Gabe didn't really have anyone else to talk to about it with, so...

"You think he'd be, um, into that? Me telling him...feelings stuff?" Jesus. If this was the best Gabe could do, a conversation about feelings with Soren wasn't going to go very well. "L-Love stuff?" he corrected hesitantly.

"Oh sure." Jay popped the last of his Skittles into his mouth. "You guys are mates. It's totally obvious."

Was it though?

"Have you met a mated pair before?" Gabe asked.

Jay nodded enthusiastically. "Just one. They came to the den to stay for a little while, before they realized how toxic it was there. I liked...watching them." He glanced over, flushing immediately at the look on Gabe's face. "Not, like, in bed. Just in general. They were so sweet with each other. Tuned into each other's emotions. It was like magic." Jay sighed dreamily.

"Well...it *is* magic, right? The whole fated mates thing."

Jay looked delighted at the thought, his gray eyes sparkling. "You're right. It *is* magic. Isn't that cool?"

It was definitely something.

Gabe eyed the little vampire next to him. "Soren said you were pretty sheltered. But you don't sound nearly as archaic as Roman. Is that all the reading?"

"And I watch a lot of TV," Jay said proudly. "Like, *a lot*."

Gabe should keep that in mind, if he decided to join the vampire club. Watch a lot of TV, don't sound like an ancient, out-of-touch geezer.

If he was *invited* to the vampire club, that was. First he had to tell Soren...love things.

Climbing out of the car, blinking at the bright morning sun, Gabe thought maybe having the whole "I think I'm in love with you, do you want to move in with me?" conversation wouldn't be so bad. Apparently he had Jay's vote of confidence, even if he hardly knew the admittedly strange vampire.

That counted for something, right?

And he and Soren didn't even have to discuss the mates thing yet. There was no rush on that. They had plenty of time.

That was what Gabe was thinking, right up to the point where the big blond man from the day before stepped out of the shadows and snapped Jay's neck.

Seventeen

Soren

Soren paused midstitch, crochet in hand, listening closely. Ferdy was normally a quiet dog. Soren had hardly ever heard the little mutt bark, other than that one time Ferdy had seen a squirrel on one of their forest runs.

But now the puppy was barking up a storm.

"Ferdy!" Soren yelled, projecting his voice to carry through the bedroom door. "Hush!"

The frantic barking continued.

Soren sighed, stretching his neck to glance at his phone on the bedside table. It was close to seven in the morning. Gabe was due to be home. But Ferdy didn't bark in alarm every time Gabe got back from work.

Something else was going on.

Soren climbed off the bed, tossing a shirt over his bare chest. He'd been *lounging*, damn it. "Hush, puppy!" he yelled out once more. It had zero effect.

Soren was down the stairs and at the front door in an instant, shepherding a barking Ferdy off and shutting him into the living room on the way, just in case. He opened the door, ready to laugh at his own paranoia once he saw it was just some forest critter or stray cat sending the dumb dog into a frenzy.

What Soren saw instead made his blood run cold.

Hendrick was standing there, a bruised and bleeding Gabe held in front of him.

Literally *held*.

Gabe was dangling almost a foot off the ground, Hendrick keeping him in the air with one hand on the back of his neck. Soren's vamp was out and taking control in an instant, its eyes zeroing in on every detail.

There was Jay, his crumpled form sprawled to the side of the porch.

Snapped neck, most likely. It was one of the quickest ways to incapacitate one of their kind for a short period of time, especially if one could take them by surprise.

Gabe was...not *unharmed* but alive. There was blood, yes, but most of it seemed to be coming from his nose. Broken, maybe.

Soren scanned his human quickly. No obvious bite marks, no severed arteries. But his right leg was twisted at an odd angle, and his eyes were open at half-mast, the glazed look in them suggesting he was in a high level of pain.

Soren struggled to keep himself calm. He hated seeing Gabe looking so helpless. Hated it with a passion that had his blood boiling.

His human was *strong*. He was brave, no matter what his insecurities said to the contrary. Hendrick didn't have the right to even look in Gabe's direction, let alone harm a single hair on his head.

The vampire in Soren wanted to tear, wanted to maim, wanted to rip Hendrick's head off for hurting his mate.

But he couldn't. Not yet. Gabe was alive. He was more or less whole. But he wasn't anywhere near out of danger yet.

Hendrick himself barely looked rumpled. No surprise there. One human wouldn't be enough to slow him down, not with Jay out of the way. And judging from his position, Jay hadn't been able to put up much of a fight before going down.

Soren turned his focus to the enemy. Hendrick's broad face held a smile, but his dark eyes were flat. Cold. A snake's eyes. He was dressed out of character, in flannel and denim. Clearly an effort to blend in.

It shouldn't have been enough. Soren should have been able to track his scent, if Hendrick had stayed in town. He should have been able to find him before now.

"Apologies," Hendrick said, not sounding sorry at all. "I roughed up your friend a bit here. He doesn't seem to like me very much." He gave Gabe a little shake in emphasis, his body swaying in Hendrick's hold.

"Fucking asshole," Gabe mumbled, his speech coming out slurred. Soren wondered if his mate had a concussion. Heat flushed through his body at the thought.

Soren watched closely as Hendrick's knuckles whitened, the larger vampire's grip tightening on Gabe's neck. Hendrick could snap that neck with just that one hand, if he wanted to. Humans were fragile. So fucking fragile.

And Soren's human was being held by a monster.

Soren made a choice. "Gabe," he said sharply. "Shut up."

Soren ignored the hurt in Gabe's eyes at his words, focusing on Hendrick instead. Hurt feelings could heal. A broken neck could not.

Not for a human, at least.

Soren could feel his body trembling and could only hope it was subtle enough Hendrick wouldn't notice.

Soren should have *known* better.

He'd been going out every night Gabe was at work, allowing himself to be seen about town, hoping to draw Hendrick out again. He'd thought the lack of response meant Hendrick had moved on. Figured out Soren was more trouble than he was worth.

Clearly Soren had been wrong. Hendrick had instead found Soren's weakness, his one *fucking* weakness, and he was holding it in one palm, ready to crush it at a moment's notice.

Soren took a deep breath, pushing his vampire back. Brute force wouldn't help him now, not with Hendrick so much stronger than he was. Soren needed to think. To plan.

He felt his fangs recede, knew his eyes were returning to their natural pale blue. He tried to keep his expression neutral, but Hendrick's smile widened anyway, the cretin clearly pleased at whatever he saw in Soren's face.

"I've been thinking," Hendrick said slyly. "I don't like how our last little talk went. Clearly, I've been keeping you on too long a leash. You've gotten...confused. Forgotten who you belong to."

I don't belong to anyone. The words were on the tip of Soren's tongue. But he took one look at Gabe's golden eyes, wide now with fear and frustration, and he held them back. To anger Hendrick would be to risk the one thing Soren cared about more than his own sorry hide.

"What do you want, Hendrick?" Soren asked instead. "You want to hurt me? Pay it back? I'm right here."

Hendrick shook his head, tutting softly. "No, angel. I simply want to...reconnect. I've missed you, you know."

Soren's stomach turned as a million different memories fought to push to the front of his mind. Memories of Hendrick's hands on him. Memories of pain and humiliation and his choice being taken away from him.

Soren wanted to tell Hendrick he'd rather die than have those slimy paws touch him ever again, but he needed to get out of this situation. Soren needed Gabe to be safe. He'd worry about the consequences after.

"Shall we go inside?" Hendrick suggested, moving to push Gabe forward, into the house.

"No." Soren crossed his arms, not budging from his position in the doorway. "No need. I'm bored of this town. Drop the human. Let's go."

Hendrick didn't release Gabe. "You'll go with me?" he asked, clearly skeptical of Soren's capitulation.

"I'll go," Soren agreed. "Put the human down."

"This human..."

"Was a distraction." Soren didn't look at Gabe, keeping his eyes on Hendrick's. "A *pet*. I'm bored of him now. But it would cause...problems...with Roman and his vampire mate, if you were to kill him. They might follow us."

It wouldn't be enough to convince Hendrick Gabe meant nothing to Soren. Even if he could pull it off, the other vampire wasn't above killing Gabe just for sport. As a punishment. Soren needed the bastard to realize Gabe's death would be more trouble than it was worth.

"It's not worth it," Soren said. "Let's go."

"You don't need to pack?" Hendrick taunted, not making a move to release Gabe.

"There's nothing here I want."

Hendrick didn't move.

Soren's gut clenched as he realized...he needed to bend. To make a concrete gesture that he was choosing Hendrick. He stepped forward out of the doorway, leaning over Gabe like the human wasn't even there.

He pressed his lips to Hendrick's. Lightly, keeping his mouth closed. But his stomach churned at even that much. Hendrick swiped his tongue against Soren's closed lips, laughing at Soren's shudder. That was the thing with Hendrick. Soren didn't have to pretend to enjoy it. Hendrick preferred it when he didn't.

Soren leaned back before Hendrick could attempt to deepen the kiss any further. "You ready?" he asked. His voice came out surprisingly steady. That was good.

He could do this.

Hendrick finally—*finally*—released Gabe, tossing Soren's human to the ground like a sack of garbage. Soren didn't look to see him land. He was afraid, if he did, his inner vamp would insist on killing Hendrick right then and there.

And then they would all die.

He grabbed Hendrick's hand and pulled him to a busted-looking Jeep in the driveway. "This your car?" Soren asked, pulling open the driver's side before Hendrick could answer.

"So eager," Hendrick tutted. "You'll drive, angel."

Behind them, Soren could hear Gabe pleading in a wrecked voice. "Soren, please. Don't do this. Don't go."

But his human didn't come after them. How could he? With his bent, most likely broken leg. Soren's breath caught in his throat, the keys Hendrick had handed him poised at the ignition.

He didn't have a choice. He had to go.

Hendrick made his way into the passenger seat, and Soren started the car. He didn't want Hendrick to see him falter.

"That human seemed awfully attached to you," Hendrick mused, sharp eyes on Soren's profile.

"Humans are stupid that way," Soren muttered. He drove them away, taking deep, steady breaths as he made his way out of the neighborhood.

Soren was in the situation he'd feared for so long. He was back in Hendrick's clutches. He waited for the dread, the fear, the familiar feelings of worthlessness. But all he could manage was an immense relief, tinged with a sadness so deep Soren wondered if maybe somehow he was bleeding internally.

They were moving away from Gabe. Soren's human would be safe. His *mate* would be safe.

That was all that mattered.

And under the relief, under the sadness, there was the *rage*. How dare Hendrick do this? How fucking *dare* he? To come back into Soren's life. To try to take away one of the only good, true things to ever happen to him.

Hendrick didn't have his old friends to back him up anymore. Soren didn't have to play nice. Soren *wouldn't* play nice. He just had to get them far enough away.

"Where to?" Soren asked, keeping his voice as neutral as he could.

"There's a place I've been staying. It will do for now," Hendrick answered. "So we can have a little...privacy. Just the two of us."

Merging onto the freeway, Soren considered driving through the median, into oncoming traffic. Maybe he could cause some sort of explosion, like the movies. Hendrick would perish.

The world would be a better fucking place; that was for sure. But there was no guarantee in that. Either or both of them could survive a crash. Innocents could die. The odds just weren't good enough.

Hendrick had touched Gabe. He'd *hurt* him. He would pay for it. Soren would make sure of it. He'd pay for all of it.

Soren just wished he'd been better prepared. This motherfucker deserved a slow, painful death. But that might not be possible at this point.

Soren knew one thing though.

Only one of them was getting out of this situation alive.

Eighteen

Gabe

Gabe had felt helpless before. He'd lost people he'd cared about. But he'd never felt this pure fury, this all-consuming frustration.

Hendrick had *taken* Soren.

Soren, who was just learning to open up again. Soren, who made Gabe feel safe and comforted for the first time since his childhood. Soren, who had stayed in this town, after over a century of running, just to remain close to him.

Hendrick had taken him.

And Gabe hadn't been able to do a single thing about it. Had been taken out of the running in an instant, Hendrick overpowering him without so much as a misplaced hair for his effort. The vampire had snapped Jay's neck, and before Gabe could even process that, his leg had been bent, his face smashed. It was like Lucien's attack all over again.

Except this time, Soren hadn't been able to swoop in and save him.

Soren had been taken instead.

Gabe panted from his prone position on Danny's porch. Fuck. He needed to get up. He didn't know if walking was possible, with whatever Hendrick had done to his leg. But he could at least sit upright.

He pulled himself up into a seated position, his right leg stretched out as best he could in front of him. It hurt. Everything hurt. But it was nothing compared to the pain he'd felt at seeing Soren walk away. Like having his heart ripped out of his chest. It was exactly what Gabe had been fearing these past three weeks. Soren leaving. Soren leaving *him*.

And Gabe realized he might have been able to handle it, under any other circumstances. If Soren had left because he'd realized he'd needed more, realized Hyde Park wasn't enough—realized *Gabe* wasn't enough—Gabe could have survived that. Could have watched Soren go back to his globetrotting and club-hopping and lived to see another day.

It would have hurt, yes. It would have broken Gabe's heart. But he could have handled it, for Soren. He could handle Soren leaving if it was what Soren needed. But this. Soren going with that piece of shit slimeball, putting himself into that psycho's hands...

Gabe hadn't been fooled by any of the bullshit Soren had spouted at Hendrick. Soren's words about Gabe being a pet, an easy distraction. Gabe knew better. Soren had been protecting him. His vampire had thought he'd had to go with that fucking monster to protect Gabe.

Well, fuck that.

Gabe hadn't been able to stop his dad from dying. He couldn't prevent his mother's dementia from progressing. He couldn't keep Danny from turning against his will.

But he could sure as shit do something about this.

So he hadn't been able to protect Soren because he was human—fragile, weak, mortal. Well, then he wouldn't *be* human anymore.

He couldn't stop life from changing. He clearly couldn't keep bad things from happening. But he could choose what in life he wanted to focus on. He could choose what to strive *for* rather than against.

Gabe wanted love. He wanted belonging. He wanted to be understood.

And Soren—weird, unhinged, fantastical Soren—understood him. He let Gabe be the real version of himself, not just the superficial golden boy.

Gabe would fight for that.

"Jay," he called, shocked by how hoarse his voice came out. "Jay!" No answer. Gabe tried to move over to the vampire, to bend his right leg, but gasped when the sharp pain hit him.

Right, no moving. He had to be patient, even if it felt like he was ready to crawl out of his skin. The little vampire wouldn't stay down. Soren had said only beheading or fire could kill them.

Gabe could scream—it was so frustrating, that none of his extensive medical knowledge was any fucking use in determining the time it takes for a vampire to heal from a broken neck. But surely it wouldn't take long, right? Considering how quickly Soren's broken ribs had healed. So Gabe sat on the porch in the weak morning sun, waiting for Jay to wake up.

Gabe's phone was broken, smashed by Hendrick in the shuffle, so he couldn't see how much time was passing. He briefly regretted not being able to call Danny. Or even Roman. But what good would that do anyway? They were due home the next day, but even if they moved their flight forward, left Bali that instant, they were still a full day away—who could say they'd get there in time to help?

So Gabe sat and waited, and tried not to think about the gutted look on Soren's face when he'd opened the door to find Hendrick holding Gabe on the porch. Or the sight of Soren kissing that slimy douchebag. He marveled briefly that his anxiety wasn't taking over. But this was kind of like what happened during codes at the hospital. Gabe could be calm in an emergency. He could put his emotions on the back burner to save a life.

And he *would* save Soren's life.

Gabe brought his mind away from the trauma of the past half hour. He tried to remember only the good. How beautiful Soren had looked at the club, dancing freely under the flashing lights. How peaceful it felt to be held by Soren on the couch. In Soren's bed. He tried to channel the inner calm he felt when he had Soren in his arms. He didn't come close to it, but it helped, if only a little.

When Jay finally stirred, after what felt like an eternity, Gabe at last felt like he could take a full breath. Beyond the frustration of waiting helplessly, he'd been terrified one of the neighbors would walk by, or someone would call the police. Gabe couldn't have any outside interference, not now. It would only slow him down.

Plus, how the fuck did you explain when the dead body with a broken neck suddenly revived itself?

It seemed to take Jay a minute to orient himself, and then he was up, leaning over Gabe in an instant. "Gabe! Are you okay? What happened? Where's Soren?"

"I'm fine." Gabe wasn't, but he would be. "You were ambushed by Hendrick. Soren's gone."

"Oh God." Jay looked around them frantically, as if Gabe was pulling a prank and Soren was just hiding in the bushes. "I'm sorry!" the little vampire wailed when he couldn't find anything. "I'm so sorry!"

"It wasn't your fault." Gabe tried to comfort him. "He attacked you from behind."

"Your leg," Jay said, reaching toward Gabe's bent extremity, stopping just before he touched it.

"Listen, Jay," Gabe said, not wanting to waste any more time. "I need you to do something for me."

Jay stopped his flailing, peering at Gabe with anxious eyes. "Do what?"

Gabe took a deep breath. "I need you to turn me."

"And you're sure about this." Jay wrung his hands, brows furrowed. It might have been adorable, if Gabe weren't so fucking impatient to get this show on the road.

"I'm sure," he answered from his spot on the couch. He'd had Jay drag him in here—almost passing out from the pain—not wanting to push their luck any further than they already had by lying out on the porch for everyone to see.

They'd found Ferdy locked in the living room, barking frantically. They'd taken him to Soren's bedroom for now. Gabe could only hope none of the neighbors called the cops on the loud puppy, but he didn't want him in here when whatever had to happen...happened.

"I'm not leaving him to do this on his own."

Jay didn't look reassured. "But I've seen it take days for someone to turn. You might— You might be too late."

"Do you think Hendrick will kill him?" Gabe didn't want to think of that possibility, couldn't bear it, but he needed to know.

That made Jay pause. He shook his head reluctantly. "Unlikely. And I think he would want to...draw it out, even if he did."

Fuck. Gabe couldn't let himself dwell on the thought. Soren would be okay. He had to be.

"I could go after them," Jay offered.

"And how will you find them?" Gabe countered.

"Um..."

"When my brother turned, he said he could...*feel* Roman. Mates can sense each other's emotions. They have a bond. A palpable bond. I know I can find him. I just need you to turn me."

Jay's gray eyes bore into him. "It's permanent, Gabe. Forever. You'll never be human again."

For the first time since they'd met, Gabe could feel Jay's age. There was regret there, underlying Jay's statement—had this vampire been given any more choice in his transition than Soren had?

Gabe tried to put all his sincerity into his words. "I would do it anyway. To be with him. I wasn't sure before, but...I know that now. I would. So just do it."

He'd let fear and resentment hamper him all his adult life, and what had it gotten him? It had almost ruined his relationship with Danny permanently. It had taken away time with his mother he'd never get back. It had made him a...well, just a worse person overall.

But Soren. Soren had made Gabe *better*. More open, less fearful. Gabe could accept magic in his life, if Soren came with it.

"Soren's gonna kill me," Jay protested. But the hand-wringing had stopped. He seemed to be getting used to the idea.

"I'll take all the blame," Gabe reassured him.

Jay took a deep breath, clearly bolstering himself. Gabe tried not to scream in frustration. He'd made his choice. He wouldn't regret it. He wanted this conversation over and done with.

He held up a hand when Jay finally leaned over him. "Not the neck."

Jay blushed. "Oh. Um. Sorry. Of course." He gently picked up Gabe's right wrist. "Is this okay?"

Gabe nodded. "That's fine."

He watched the dark head bend over his wrist. A sharp flick of pain, a surge of that now-familiar pleasure, and then a strange...lightheadedness. Gabe realized now how little Soren had taken from him, those two times, compared to the speed with which Jay was draining him now. He could feel himself slipping quickly into unconsciousness, only vaguely aware when liquid started dribbling into his mouth. Jay's blood? And then...

Pain. Fire. *Burning.*

Gabe heard screaming. He was pretty sure it was him, but he was too delirious with pain to register the source. He coughed, choked, screamed some more.

Who knew dying would be so painful?

And then only darkness.

Gabe woke up quickly—apparently much more quickly than Jay had anticipated, judging by the little vampire's startled, wide eyes.

The pain was gone. Like it had never happened at all. Maybe Gabe had dreamed it.

"I—I've never seen it happen so fast," Jay stammered. "It's only been a few hours."

Gabe didn't have time to wonder over it all. He'd woken with a hole in his chest. An ache. A pull.

Soren.

His mate was in trouble. Gabe felt a pulsing under his skin, a drive to find him, to help him.

Soren had been taken. Taken from Gabe.

Rage and anger rose quickly. "Going now," he growled. Jay protested. Gabe cut him off. "I wouldn't try to stop me."

"What if you kill someone?"

Gabe scoffed. "Hendrick? He'd deserve it."

Jay gave him a strange look. "No — I— Aren't you...hungry?"

Hungry? Oh, for blood.

Feeding was the farthest thing from Gabe's mind. "I don't want blood. I want *Soren*."

That was the only thing Gabe was craving—to touch his mate. To hold him. There was a new beast inside him, and it needed soothing.

He needed his mate.

Nineteen

Soren

"Turn here."

Soren obeyed the order, guiding the car through a busted, wide-open iron gate, onto a long gravel drive. They passed through practically a mile of scrubby pine forest before arriving at what Soren presumed must be their destination.

It looked like someone's summer hunting cabin. A depressing wooden structure with a vague air of abandonment. Soren could just make out the banks of what appeared to be a small lake behind it. He parked the car, the quiet of undisturbed nature enveloping them. Hendrick didn't seem to be in any hurry to break Soren's silence.

To be fair, he generally preferred it when Soren kept his mouth shut.

Soren surveyed the cabin skeptically as they made their way inside. Hendrick must have really been hurting to find a hideout quickly—this place wasn't nearly as grand and fine as his usual haunts. The living area was poorly furnished, a sprinkling of dust coating every surface. The room's one redeeming feature was a massive fireplace, almost big enough for someone to roast a whole deer in there, if that was their thing.

Hendrick stopped in the doorway to the living room, gesturing for Soren to enter ahead of him. Soren walked toward the back window closest to the fireplace, affecting an interest in taking a better view of the lake, in reality happy to get as far away from his captor as this horrid cabin would allow.

He stopped in his tracks before he could get there, held in place by a form on the threadbare couch, initially hidden from view by the angles of the room. Soren rolled his eyes.

There was a dead body in this cabin. Not exactly a fresh one either.

He was an older man, probably somewhere in his sixties, waxen face covered with a shaggy beard. The cabin's owner, Soren assumed. He looked at Hendrick, disgust curling his lip. "Christ, Hendrick! You didn't bother to clean up after yourself?"

The bigger vampire looked characteristically unrepentant. "I needed him."

Why the fuck would Hendrick need an accessible corpse? Unless...

Understanding dawned. Every living creature had a distinct scent. At least, Soren had found that to be the case since the day he turned, and his enhanced senses had kicked in. Modern toiletries mucked it up a bit—fruity body washes, floral conditioners—as did feeding. For a brief while after drinking from a human, a vampire could take on subtle notes of their scent.

Soren took it all in. Hendrick's out-of-character flannel outfit. The days-old corpse in front of them. Was this really how Hendrick had been evading Soren's notice in town? He'd been masking his scent since their fight, spying on Soren without leaving a trail. Soren might even be impressed if his hatred could allow for it. His ex had never been quite so devious before.

That corpse looked awfully stiff though. "Have you been drinking from a dead man, Hendrick?"

Soren shuddered at the thought. Blood from the dead was...*dead*, for lack of a better word. Sluggish. Cold. Unfulfilling. It was taboo among their kind. Considered disgusting and gauche. How far gone was Hendrick, to cross that line over and over, just to lurk in the shadows and spy on his old possession?

"Gross," Soren said out loud, unable to keep it to himself.

"Clean it up for me," Hendrick ordered, seating himself on the ratty armchair opposite the cabin's dead owner.

Soren sniffed. "And do you have tools I can use, or will I be digging in the hard ground with my bare hands like some kind of caveman?"

"Just dump it in the lake," Hendrick suggested airily.

"And have it float right back up in half a day?"

"What do we care? We'll be long gone by then."

So Hendrick didn't intend to stay, then. Good. They weren't nearly far enough from Hyde Park. They'd barely been driving for a full hour, following winding side roads up north. What was the point of even stopping here?

Hendrick answered that question for Soren with his next statement. "And don't even think about running off, or I'll drive right back to your little human. Have myself a fresh meal."

Soren stiffened. So that was it? Stay in close proximity to Gabe as a threat, making sure Soren remained...docile? It only made sense in the short-term. What was Hendrick planning once they left? Soren thought of the stairs they'd passed on their way to the living room. The bedrooms must be on the second floor. He supposed Hendrick didn't need very long to get what he came for.

Soren didn't want to think too hard about that.

"Got it," he said, walking over to the body. He had to pass the armchair on the way, and he was stopped by a sudden, bruising grip on his arm. It took everything in him to suppress a shudder.

Soren hated this slimy cretin's touch. He hated even breathing the same air. He hated more than anything that he'd had to touch his fucking mouth to Hendrick's, and that Gabe had been forced to witness it.

Hendrick pulled Soren toward him until their faces were inches apart. "So pretty, my angel," he cooed, his voice full of false affection. "I've missed looking at you." He brushed his fingers along Soren's face.

The beast inside Soren wanted nothing more than to rip this vampire's fingers right off, maybe his entire arm for good measure. But Soren was at a disadvantage. Hendrick was stronger than him, when it came to brute force. And he was surely looking for a reaction, an excuse to put Soren in his place.

But for once, Soren could be patient. He could be patient for Gabe.

"I'm not touching you with this filthy thing in here," he said, pushing his bottom lip out slightly. Any defiance was a risk, but Hendrick didn't usually mind whining or even a little pouting. It was signs of strength he couldn't stand.

Hendrick stared hard for a moment, then relaxed his hold, seeming to concede to the point. "Hurry up, then."

Soren tugged his arm out of the other vampire's grip, then stepped to the couch, heaving the hideous corpse over his shoulder easily. He headed out the back, walking the body over to the lake, scouting the area as he went. He didn't see any visible neighbors, no roads other than the one they'd arrived on. The only other building was a rundown shed to the side of the cabin.

It was a ghost wood. Abandoned.

Outside, away from Hendrick's suffocating presence, Soren did his best not to fall into despair. He tried not to think of the look on Gabe's face when Soren had told him to shut up, the sound of Gabe's voice as he'd pleaded for Soren not to leave. Soren had been so stupid to think he'd get a happy ending. To think that his past mistakes wouldn't catch up to him. Gabe's twisted leg...

This was the second time Gabe had a broken bone because of Soren. It was two times too many.

Soren contemplated his next steps while searching the area for rocks to put in the poor corpse's pockets. The easiest plan would be to let Hendrick take what he wanted. Lure him into a false sense of security, then...attack? Better yet...run. Run and don't look back. Let Gabe live his normal human life, away from all of Soren's supernatural bullshit.

Never mind that Gabe already had a supernatural brother and brother-in-law. This was Soren's pity party; he could be in denial if he wanted to.

So let Hendrick have Soren. Touch him. Hurt him. It was what Soren would have done in the past. Take the smaller loss of his dignity, of his bodily autonomy, in exchange for his eventual freedom.

But he didn't want to do it that way anymore. He didn't want to sully the memory of Gabe's touch with Hendrick's slimy fucking paws. Even more so if he never got to feel the touch of his human again. He wanted to hold on to those memories.

Gabe's strong hands. The way he let Soren lead. The way he looked at Soren like he was something precious.

Once the body was laden down with rocks, Soren tossed him unceremoniously into the shallow lake. It wouldn't hide a corpse for long, but oh well. Soren had bigger things to worry about. He hesitated in returning to the cabin. He wondered what Gabe was doing now. Soren hoped he wasn't in pain. He hoped Jay had woken up quickly and taken Soren's human to the hospital.

Soren ran a hand through his hair, unconsciously copying Gabe's mannerisms. He realized his hands were shaking.

Gabe hurt. Gabe suffering.

He couldn't take it. It was *wrong* that Soren wasn't there. His mate was in pain. His mate *needed* him.

Fuck running away. Soren *belonged* in Hyde Park.

And he would do anything to get back where he belonged.

Soren came back into the cabin to find Hendrick laying a fire in the massive fireplace. For what possible purpose, Soren hadn't the foggiest clue. They sure as hell didn't need the warmth.

The bastard probably just wanted to create the proper dramatic atmosphere. Because that was what Hendrick was, when it came down to it: a pathetic drama queen with no purpose of his own, who had to feel ownership over another person to feel like he was worth anything at all.

"You didn't run off," Hendrick commented, eyes on the fire, oblivious to Soren's unspoken scathing evaluation.

Soren resisted the urge to answer with the deserved, "Well, obviously the fuck not, if I'm standing here." That was the kind of answer that would end with Soren broken and bleeding and unable to run. Which was exactly why Hendrick was *the worst*.

Why state the obvious if he didn't want sarcastic answers in return?

"Come closer." Hendrick beckoned with one hand, still not deigning to meet Soren's gaze. "Let me look at you."

"I'm okay over here."

"Soren..." Soren hated that chiding, warning tone, like Hendrick was talking to a stubborn child. "It's enough to make me think you don't like me."

"I *don't* like you." Whoops, he wasn't supposed to say that part out loud.

Hendrick gave him a hard look.

Soren used to be so much better at being cautious around this bastard, but he was having such a hard time working up the old fear. He wanted to be done with this charade. He wanted to get back to Gabe.

"Why do you want me?" he found himself asking.

"You belong—"

"Yeah, I know. I 'belong' to you. But why do you *want* me. You don't even *like* me. Is it really worth all this? The stalking, the hiding out in this dusty cabin with a smelly dead body, for someone you don't even *like*?"

Hendrick's gaze finally met his, eyes cold and hard as ever. "Perhaps you're all I have left."

Soren pondered that. It was maybe true. Hendrick's friends were gone, the den he'd been a part of for his whole vampire existence falling apart. Soren wondered how the other vampire hadn't gone feral yet. He probably wasn't far from it. Maybe that was why he was trying so hard to take Soren back again. Maybe he thought it would delay things—that a familiar face would tether him, even if Soren's soul couldn't officially do the job.

Soren wished he could find it in himself to feel sorry for Hendrick, but he just...couldn't. This bastard had taken too much from him already. He didn't deserve Soren's pity too. Still, Soren wasn't above trying to reason with him, if it meant not getting the shit kicked out of him in a fight.

"You should start over, Hendrick," Soren said, keeping his voice soft, nonconfrontational. "This is a chance for you. Find someone you fit with. Someone whose very existence doesn't make you want to beat the life out of them."

Hendrick tilted his head, studying Soren with a strange smirk on his face. "You think I haven't had other pets?"

Soren blinked, taken aback.

Hendrick laughed, poking again at the fire. "I've had others, angel. Other pretty treasures. How else do you think I wiled away the time all those years you ran from me? None managed to keep my interest for long."

"Where are they now?" Soren was afraid he knew the answer already, but he had to ask.

Hendrick's grin widened. "Where do you think? Disposed of properly. Like I should perhaps have done with you. You make me sentimental, I think. You were my first...*possession*. The first vampire I made just for me." He ran his gaze over Soren, heavy as a physical touch. "And still the most beautiful."

Soren tried to process the words he was hearing. How many people had Hendrick killed, in his long lifetime? Trying different partners out for size and murdering them when they didn't match his needs.

This was why Soren couldn't find any pity for the other vampire. Because Hendrick was a cruel, vicious bully. One who treated other living creatures like nothing more than toys to play with and trash at will.

His very existence was a waste of space. A waste of Soren's time.

Soren could feel the swirl of emotions he felt toward Hendrick...amplifying. His bitterness at everything Hendrick had subjected him to in the past. His fury in being taken away from the human he belonged with. His complete and utter rage that this sad-sack, poor excuse for a man could continue to cause him so much pain for no real reason other than selfish desire and boredom.

Okay, maybe Soren didn't have a swirl of emotions. Maybe he was just fucking *pissed*.

"You're incapable of love, aren't you?" Soren asked, his voice trembling with anger.

Hendrick finally dropped the stick he'd been using to stoke the fire, turning his full attention to Soren. "*Love?*" he asked, voice dripping with disdain. "Is that what you think you've found for yourself? With the little human?"

Soren didn't know why he was taken aback by the question, but he was. He flinched, unable to school his reaction properly.

Hendrick started laughing again. "You think you've found a kindred soul?" he taunted. "Who would want you, angel? You're good for one thing. That pretty face. And you ruin even that with your mouth every. Fucking. Time."

Soren's temper flared. "At least I've never had to abuse or coerce others just to get someone to share my bed." So much for reasoning with his captor. Hendrick's smirk fell from his face in an instant, his features twisting with fury. His eyes darkened, his fangs dropped, and he rose from his crouch in one swift movement.

That was the thing about manipulative assholes. They really hated being called out on their own bullshit.

Without another word, Hendrick charged Soren, a blinding blur of muscle. Soren darted back easily. He may not have had the advantage over the other vampire when it came to brute force, but he *did* have speed. He was out the front door in a flash, reaching out a hand to grab the shotgun he'd stashed on the porch.

Turned out the shed had some useful tools in it after all.

Soren briefly gave thanks for *Deliverance*-core, backwoods cabin owners and the firearms they kept. It wouldn't be enough to kill a vampire, but it would be enough to slow one down.

Soren aimed a blast at Hendrick, the charging vampire's eyes widening in the split second he had to register the weapon.

One shot in the chest was enough to push Hendrick back a few feet, but not for long. He kept coming. The next shot did some nice damage to his left arm.

Okay, Soren's aim was...not great. But Hendrick was doing him a major solid by continuing to run straight for him.

Not just a manipulative asshole. A *stubborn* manipulative asshole.

Finally Soren hit Hendrick straight in the face with his third shot. The vampire's charge stopped in an instant, his body slumping over onto the porch.

Soren's triumph was quickly waylaid by disgust.

"Fucking *gross*." Soren held a hand to his mouth, almost wanting to retch, not sure if a vampire body was even capable of it. He was all for blood, but brain matter flying everywhere was just...nasty.

He took a minute to collect himself, keeping his eyes off the massacred body in front of him. Hendrick may have been a horrible, murderous dick, but Soren still didn't relish the sight of his wasted body.

He sat down on the porch, as far from the mess as he could. He'd expected more...relief. But Soren could still feel rage and fear and worry swirling in his stomach. Maybe it would take some time to process his victory over his longtime tormentor.

He lost himself in thought, reflecting on everything that had brought him and Hendrick to this point. Could Soren have done anything different, to avoid this gruesome outcome?

He wasn't sure how long it had been when he finally stirred from his seated position, but the sun was substantially higher in the sky. Soren needed to make a decision. He had options now.

He could leave Hendrick here, allow the other vampire to heal over time. Hendrick's head was mangled, but it wasn't completely severed from his body; he *would* heal, eventually. Soren could leave him to it and hope that this fight would be the one to teach Hendrick to stay away for good.

Soren could run again.

He laughed to himself, the sound tinged with hysteria. Who was he kidding? He wasn't going to run. He didn't *want* to leave. Part of Soren's soul was still in Hyde Park. The best part of his soul. And if he was going back... Soren didn't want to look over his shoulder for the rest of his very long existence.

And then there was the other side of things: how many others would die, if Hendrick was left to live?

So it was time to dispose of Hendrick. The world would be better off without him. Soren wondered if perhaps Hendrick had *wanted* to end his own existence. If that was part of why he'd continued to pursue Soren even without the threat of his den of vampire friends to keep him safe.

Soren found he didn't care much either way.

He lugged Hendrick's body to the fireplace, avoiding looking too closely at his mangled head. Soren tossed him in just as unceremoniously as he had the cabin's owner into the lake.

He watched long enough to ensure the body caught fire, then went back out to the dilapidated shed, where he was sure he'd spotted some gasoline cans. He supposed he could have saved himself some time and poured those on Hendrick first thing, catching him by surprise after disposing of the cabin's owner, but Soren had wanted... He wasn't sure what.

He'd wanted closure, he supposed, as stupid as that made him feel in hindsight. He'd wanted to give Hendrick a chance to do the right thing.

So much for that.

Soren was exiting the shed when he caught sight of a familiar form on the porch.

Gabe. Still in the clothes Soren had last seen him in, looking rumpled and torn and definitely the worse for wear. But his human was standing tall—both legs straight and strong—not a wound to be found on him.

Soren took that in.

Huh. His human wasn't...*human* anymore.

And Soren understood suddenly, that wave of emotion he'd felt back in the cabin, confronting Hendrick. The mate bond. Soren had been feeling Gabe's feelings on top of his own. Their rage combined. Just as he could feel Gabe's relief now. His confusion. His love. Soren stood frozen, the can of gasoline clutched in front of him.

"I came to rescue you," Gabe said sheepishly from his place on the porch, not making any move to get closer.

"I'm burning a body," Soren explained, voice dull. He didn't know what to think. He didn't know how to feel.

Gabe sighed, running a hand through his hair. He looked at Soren with hopeful eyes. "Can I help?"

Twenty

Gabe

Gabe had driven fast—faster than he ever had in his life—feeling that pull toward his person guiding him, directing him. He'd been ready to fight. To rip skin and break bones. To use the new strength he could feel coursing through his veins.

And then he was there. A weird, abandoned-looking cabin with smoke coming out of the chimney. He could smell his mate even over the stench of burning flesh. And there was Soren—blood-spattered clothes, soot smudging his skin—having already fought his own battle. Not in trouble at all.

For all the urge to run toward him, Gabe found himself suddenly...nervous. Soren had just been through an ordeal. Had been recaptured by the same person who'd tortured him on and off for centuries. And Gabe had been no help at all. Had been used as bait, in fact. And was now here too late to do anything but help clean up the mess.

Soren looked at him strangely, his eyes uncharacteristically dull, holding on to what looked like a rusted gas can. "You're unsettled," he said, after a long silence. "I can feel it. Nervous about being bonded to a murderer?"

"What? No." Gabe took a step forward. Paused. The new presence inside him was restless, unsure. It wanted their mate where they could feel him, touch him. But Gabe wasn't sure Soren would want that.

"I would have killed him for you," Gabe offered lamely.

Soren arched a blond brow at him. "Upset I did it myself?"

Gabe's mate was feeling prickly. Defensive. Gabe could hear it in his words and also...*feel* it. A current of emotions running from Soren to Gabe. It was hard to pick everything out—Gabe was barely used to labeling his *own* emotions, let alone someone else's—but little bits of clarity came through.

Guilt. Apprehension. *Hope.*

Gabe fought to find words, wrestling with his very human concern and his new, less-than-human instincts. "No, I didn't— I don't—" He stopped, unable to finish the thought. He found there was only one thing to ask. "Can I hold you?"

Soren's face softened, almost imperceptibly, as he nodded, setting the gas can onto the ground. Gabe rushed forward, wrapping Soren up in his arms, tucking his vampire's head under his chin.

Fuck. That was so much better.

They should just...always be touching. The knots in Gabe's stomach untied themselves. The beast inside him settled. He breathed in deeply, inhaling Soren's clean, cold scent.

Soren was stiff at first, unyielding. But slowly the tension in his body eased. After a long moment without speaking, all of Gabe's attention on the feel of the small, warm body in his arms, Soren giggled—that familiar, delightful sound. "You, uh, really like touching me, don't you, Highness? I can feel it."

"What?" Gabe asked, confused. He wasn't hard. He'd been too keyed up to feel anything but relief to have Soren in his arms again.

Soren giggled again. So lovely. "*Inside*," he clarified. "I can it feel through the bond."

"Oh. Well..." Gabe was glad Soren couldn't see his blush from his position under his chin. Gabe had just been learning to share his feelings, and now he didn't even have to. Soren would be able to sense them, whether Gabe intended him to or not. Gabe found he didn't mind it nearly as much as he might have in the past. He couldn't think of anyone else he'd want inside his brain like that, but Soren...

Soren was different.

"I was supposed to tell you love stuff," Gabe found himself blurting out.

"Love stuff?" Gabe couldn't see Soren's face, but a rush of fond amusement came through the bond.

"Yeah...like...I love you?" It was easier than he would have thought to say the words with Soren in his arms, keeping him grounded, but it still came out like a question.

Something stronger than fondness leaked through the bond this time. Gabe cherished the feeling. Soren rubbed his head into Gabe's chest, speaking his next words into Gabe's shirt. "You turned for me."

"Yes," Gabe answered simply.

"I killed him." There was no regret in Soren's voice, or through the bond. A statement of fact only. A request for understanding.

Gabe responded with equal frankness. "I know. I can smell the burning."

Soren sighed, his breath warm against Gabe's collarbone. "It wasn't very nice of me."

Gabe hugged his vampire tighter. "You did what you had to do to protect yourself."

"I think I felt you," Soren said, turning his head to the side so his words came out clearer. "My anger at Hendrick, it was like—like it multiplied. Intensified. I think that must have been when you turned."

"Mm." Gabe had definitely been angry, to say the least. Had wanted to gut Soren's stalker like a fish. He'd never known he could feel rage like that before.

"You and I could be very dangerous together," Soren said, pressing a kiss to Gabe's chest.

Gabe wasn't sure he cared. If it was evil assholes like Hendrick that took the brunt of their combined anger, he could live with that. Easily. "I guess we should hope no one pisses us off, then," he said mildly.

Soren hummed in acknowledgment.

They ended up burning the whole damn cabin down to the ground. It was strangely satisfying, watching it all go aflame. Maybe Gabe had the makings of an arsonist.

They sat in silence together on the forest floor, within view of the flaming building but a healthy distance from the heat, until it was nothing but smoldering ashes.

Gabe, lost in thought, startled when he felt Soren's delicate hand curl into his. Huh. It was usually Gabe initiating the hand-holding.

"I love you too," Soren said softly, eyes on the smoking rubble in front of them.

Gabe grinned smugly. "I know. I can feel it."

Soren huffed at him. "You're going to be insufferable with this bond, aren't you?"

"Probably."

They sat in silence again. Eventually Soren turned to face him, and Gabe was surprised to see pain etched on his vampire's features.

"I didn't mean what I said. Any of it," Soren said, pale eyes pleading.

"Baby." Gabe wrapped an arm around Soren's shoulders, tugging his small frame against himself. "I know you didn't. You were protecting me."

"You turned for me," Soren said for the second time, voice breaking on the words.

They were already touching, shoulder to shoulder and hip to hip, but Gabe reached out a hand, wanting even more contact. He traced a finger along Soren's cheek. "I did."

Soren grabbed onto his finger, halting its progress. "To help me fight Hendrick."

"Yes."

"But you didn't— He was already—" Soren gave him a helpless look. "Do you regret it?"

Gabe smiled softly, plucking his finger out of Soren's grasp and resuming its tracing, etching the shape of Soren's face. "Not a bit."

Soren glared at him. "Why not?"

"I want to be with you. Always. Forever. I want to be your *mate*." He pressed a brief kiss to Soren's lips, fighting to ignore the beast inside him that wanted him to deepen it, demanding he take more.

He could wait. He *would* wait. They had time...

Soren flushed. "How did you even know? I never said..."

Gabe laughed. "As much as you love to call me one, I'm not *actually* an idiot. I guessed we were mates." He paused, removing his hand from Soren's face, suddenly uncertain. "Is it okay that I did it?"

Maybe Soren hadn't actually wanted to be stuck with Gabe for a whole eternity.

"Of course it is," Soren huffed, pressing his face back into Gabe's palm. "Idiot."

Gabe smiled, warmth blooming in his chest. "Glad you feel that way."

"Speaking of feelings..." Soren gave him a sly look, swiping his tongue over pink lips. "I can feel how much you want me. You're practically bursting with it. Why aren't you making a move?"

It was true. Gabe knew he should be in a somber mood, what with the murder-covering arson they were committing, but all he could think about was how much he wanted to touch Soren...

All of Soren.

This new energy inside him wanted to claim their mate more than anything. Wanted to touch and lick and fuck him into oblivion.

Gabe shifted uncomfortably. "It's just...you've been through something. With someone who has a history of...taking without consent. I can wait."

Soren stared at him. Gabe flushed at the scrutiny.

"You really would," Soren said, long seconds later, awe in his voice. "Newly turned, the baby vampire inside you raging for its mate, and you would...*wait* for me. To be ready."

Gabe wondered if he should be offended at the surprise Soren felt at that, but one second of reflecting on Soren's past and he couldn't blame his mate for any amazement he might feel at others' restraint.

He shrugged, refusing to take credit for common human—common *vampire*, he corrected himself—decency. "You've been waiting for me a whole lot longer. I can hang on."

Soren kissed him then, soft and sweet, in a way he rarely did. He licked gently at Gabe's lips, coaxing them open, slipping his tongue into Gabe's mouth. Gabe groaned, leaning into the kiss, unable to keep himself this time from deepening it, licking into Soren's mouth.

Soren released the kiss first, leaning back with a wicked smile on his face. "You need me to make the first move, Highness?"

Heat burst along Gabe's skin. It was a form of torture, not reaching out to touch his mate. But he wanted to let Soren lead.

Soren leaned in closer again, his lips a breath away from Gabe's. "Let me tell you a secret." Soren lowered his voice to a whisper. "I trust you."

Gabe let out a slow breath, his whole body tense with the effort to remain still. Soren's smile softened at the edges, but heat blazed in his eyes. "I trust you to touch me," he continued. "I trust you to fuck me. I trust you to love me. I know you won't use your strength against me."

Gabe was trembling. The power this vampire had over him. "Can I...?"

"Not here." Soren grabbed his hand, dragging Gabe upright in an instant. "I want to be away from this fucking place."

"Away from this place" didn't mean as far away as Gabe had thought. Soren was only moving them to the other side of the lake. They sprinted toward their destination, Soren keeping his hold on Gabe's hand. The tension in Gabe eased as they ran, his hand in Soren's, and he couldn't help but laugh in delight.

It felt amazing to move like this. They were so fucking *fast*. Gabe had always used running as an outlet, but he'd never exactly been a speed demon. Now though...

They reached the other side of the lake in mere seconds. It was amazing.

Soren stopped by one of the pine trees on the edge of the shore, pressing Gabe back against the trunk with one hand to his chest. "You should feel very special right now," he purred, leaning in and licking a stripe along Gabe's neck. "I don't usually abide sex in *nature.*" He lifted his head and wrinkled his nose in distaste. "But I'll make an exception for you."

"We don't have to," Gabe managed, ignoring the way his hard cock was aching behind his zipper. He'd been fully erect since the moment Soren had kissed him. His new state apparently made him easy as hell. "We could find a motel or something. I can wait."

Soren smiled at him, the love in his eyes so palpable it took Gabe's breath away. "I know you can, Highness," he said. "But your vamp isn't the only one dying to get its hands on its mate."

Soren kissed him again. There was no gentleness in it this time. Soren plundered. He claimed. He *took*. He sucked Gabe's tongue, bit at his lips. Gabe groaned, palming Soren's ass with needy hands.

Soren broke the kiss. "Take these filthy clothes off me," he ordered breathlessly.

Gabe complied, hastily undressing first his mate, then himself. Soren attacked his lips again the moment they were both naked.

Gabe's hands traveled from Soren's pert ass down to the backs of his thighs. He lifted him easily, wrapping those slender legs around his own hips, reversing them so it was Soren's back against the tree.

The new presence inside Gabe was vibrating with satisfaction. *This* was what they needed. Soren, in their arms, wrapped around them. Skin on skin. Touching and being touched.

The smell of smoke and ash was still in the air, but underneath that was Soren's cool, soothing scent. Gabe breathed it in as best he could without taking his lips off Soren's, his hard cock rubbing against his mate's, precum leaking over them both.

Gabe groaned, his hands moving back over Soren's ass, his fingers dancing along his cleft.

Wait. Fuck.

Gabe released Soren's mouth, dodging back when Soren tried to reclaim his lips immediately. They were missing some essential items.

"We don't have any, um. Fuck, we can just—" Gabe looked around them, as if maybe a local lube peddler would pop out from behind one of the trees.

"No," Soren cut him off with another kiss. "You *will* fuck me, Highness. I need you inside me. Now. Immediately. Fucking *yesterday*."

"I don't want to hurt you," Gabe said helplessly.

"I can take it," Soren promised. He tugged at Gabe's right arm, leaving Gabe to hold him up with one hand. Gabe was strong enough now that it wasn't even a strain. Soren took Gabe's index finger into his mouth, hollowing his cheeks and sucking hard, laving at Gabe's digit with his tongue.

"Fuck," Gabe hissed, his cock jerking.

Once Gabe's finger was properly soaked with spit, Soren guided Gabe's hand back to his ass. "Open me up, Highness."

Gabe moaned, pressing his finger against Soren's hole, rubbing and circling gently, his breath catching as his digit slipped inside. He took his time with it, watching the different expressions flit across his mate's beautiful face. Gabe could feel the urgency humming underneath his own skin—the need to claim, to get his cock where it belonged—but it was easy enough to ignore, with Soren looking so damn enticing, rocking against Gabe's finger.

Soon enough he had two fingers scissoring, and Soren was panting. "Enough," he ordered breathlessly.

Gabe shook his head. "Not yet. You're not ready, baby." He withdrew his fingers, ignoring Soren's whine of protest. He wrapped the same hand around Soren's leaking cock, gathering the precum and mixing it with his spit, easing three fingers slowly back into his mate.

Soren keened, pushing back against Gabe's hand. "If you don't fuck me soon..."

Gabe kissed him to silence the threat.

Impatient, impulsive vampire.

He waited until his three fingers were going in easy, and Soren was cursing his name with every other breath. That was it. Perfect. Fucking perfect.

He'd waited long enough.

Gabe slicked his cock up with more of Soren's precum, pushing the head against Soren's entrance. "Is this what you want, brat?"

"Fucking finally," Soren breathed.

Gabe slid inside his mate slowly. *Excruciatingly* slowly. He groaned as the heat enveloped him. "So fucking tight, brat." He gave Soren a minute to adjust, his muscles trembling with the effort to stay still, then started fucking his vampire in slow, even thrusts.

"Harder," Soren panted, fingers sinking into Gabe's curls.

"Your back," Gabe protested. Soren's bare, silky skin was pressing against the tree.

Soren shook his head, tightening his grip in Gabe's hair. "I can take it. I'm not fragile. Fuck me harder."

So Gabe did. He set a brutal pace, giving in to the beast inside him, thrusting into his mate with abandon. Soren moaned long and low, encouraging his ferocity. He tugged at Gabe's hair, tucking his head into Gabe's shoulder, groaning and whimpering and whining in that delicious way he did.

Gabe gasped as sharp teeth bit into his neck.

Soren was drinking from him. Vampire to vampire.

"Fuck, baby," Gabe groaned, pounding furiously into Soren. It felt so *fucking* good. It wasn't the same tingle of pleasure-laced venom he'd felt as a human, but instead a deep, primal satisfaction at having his mate claim him this way. The beast inside him roared in delight.

Gabe was too lost in pleasure to know how it happened, but he...*changed*. His fangs dropped, his vision sharpened. The moment Soren lifted his head, Gabe reciprocated, biting into his vampire's neck with a growl.

Fucking *hell*. Soren's hot blood filled Gabe's mouth, and it tasted just as good as Soren smelled. Pleasure raced down his spine, and he lost it in an instant, flooding Soren with his cum, his hips stuttering, his vision whiting out as he rode the waves of his orgasm.

He barely registered Soren bucking into him, the wetness of Soren's release covering his stomach.

Heaven. This was heaven.

He only allowed himself a few gulps of Soren's blood, not knowing yet how much was too much, but that seemed to be more than enough to appease the beast. They had claimed their mate. It was content for the moment.

Gabe kissed and licked along Soren's neck as they both came down from their merging, Soren's fingers combing gently now through his curls. He kept Soren there against the tree, not willing to take his cock out of Soren's warmth yet. The trauma of the day was catching up with him, and he needed this connection. Needed to know Soren was still here. With him.

Forever.

Soren was scratching along Gabe's scalp, humming in delight every time Gabe shivered. "You turned for me," Soren said, now for the third time.

Gabe paused his kissing. "I did. But also for—for me too though."

Soren leaned back against the tree to meet Gabe's eyes. Gabe felt a wave of self-consciousness rush through him. But this was Soren. Nothing bad had ever come from Gabe being vulnerable with him.

"I've let fear rule so much of my life." He brushed a piece of Soren's golden hair out of his eyes. "I wanted to know what it felt like to make a choice based on something a little more...hopeful."

Soren sniffed, clearing his throat. "You can't take it back, you know."

"I know. Maybe I'm a little more open to magic in my life now." Gabe grinned. "Plus, I'm like, super strong. I bet I could run an ultramarathon no problem, right?"

Soren's brows lowered, the other vampire scowling at him. Gabe laughed, wincing when the action jostled Soren on Gabe's over-sensitive cock. "Maybe we shouldn't have this conversation with my dick still inside you."

He withdrew his softened cock slowly, easing Soren gently to the ground. Soren looked up at him, still flushed and nude and so unbearably beautiful. "I just don't want you to regret it. Regret me."

Gabe reached for his hand. "I couldn't. I *won't.*"

Soren arched a brow. "What about feeding? You think you can drink human blood?"

Gabe shrugged. "You can teach me. Maybe we could go dancing one night, find a pretty thing to share together?"

Soren did his best to keep his expression blank, but Gabe could feel the rush of want through the bond. Gabe grinned. He'd had a feeling ever since their night out together that Soren might like something like that. Not an actual threesome—they were both too possessive for that, apparently—but some flirting, a little innocent touching, a pleasure-filled feeding. That would be...exciting. For both of them.

Soren looked to their pile of clothes skeptically. "We should probably rinse these off in the lake. And then..." He smiled at Gabe, that gloriously manic grin Gabe had learned to love. "Take me home?"

Twenty-One

Soren

"We going inside?"

Soren didn't answer. For once, he was the one keeping them in the car. He stared at the little yellow house—his home for the past year. Soren had thought just that morning that he'd never see it again.

But did you really?

Soren shook his head, annoyed at his own denial. He'd lied to himself, when he'd left with Hendrick. He'd told himself he was resigned to leave Gabe for good, but there was part of him—that inner, mindless, core part of him—that knew he'd never willingly leave his mate. Not for long. Even if it had been for Gabe's own good. Even if Gabe really *had* decided he wanted a normal human life, Soren wasn't sure he'd have been able to be that selfless as to let him go.

He looked to Gabe in the driver's seat—they'd taken Gabe's car back, leaving Hendrick's stolen vehicle a smoldering wreck to go along with the cabin—who was looking at him with furrowed brows.

"I'm not a good person," Soren told him, not for the first time.

Gabe shrugged easily. "I'm not so sure I am either."

Soren narrowed his eyes at his mate. "You're awfully chill about all this. Did turning into a vampire take away the anxiety corner of your brain?"

Gabe relaxed back into his seat, the picture of easy unconcern. "It's a relief in some ways. Letting go. Letting it in. You're a vampire. So's my brother. Now I am too. One big happy monster family.

So the world is more magical and confusing than I gave it credit for...so what?"

"I can't tell if I'm annoyed or turned on by this change in attitude."

Gabe grinned at him. "Knowing you, it's both."

Soren scowled. Ugh. His mate was so fucking handsome when he was happy.

They'd dipped into the lake after their forest dalliance, trying to rinse off the smells of smoke and sex, and Gabe's curls had dried into a dark disarray, his golden-brown eyes practically shining as he smiled at Soren.

Soren couldn't help it. He leaned in for a kiss. He wanted to touch all that golden beauty. Gabe met him halfway, opening easily to Soren, letting him explore his mouth with tongue and teeth.

Soren hummed into the kiss and considered climbing over the center console and into Gabe's lap, but Gabe pulled away before he could, ending it all much too soon. He placed a finishing peck on Soren's lips. "We should go in," he said. "They're here."

Soren sighed, glancing out the car window. That was the other reason for Soren's hesitation to enter the house. A familiar car in the driveway.

Danny and Roman were home.

Soren huffed. "So annoying. How are we going to explain all this?" He gestured vaguely at Gabe, trying to encompass their relationship and his former human's change in mortality. "They leave for three weeks and now you're a vampire."

Gabe shrugged again. If he kept doing that, Soren might have to smack him. "We were going to tell them we're together anyway. Now we just have a little...bonus detail to add."

Soren huffed again. "So. Fucking. Chill."

Gabe laughed, placing another kiss on Soren's lips. "I'm sure I won't always be. I haven't had a personality transplant. I'm just relieved as hell." He cupped Soren's face in his broad hands. "You're *here*. You're unharmed. I didn't lose you. Anything else we can handle together."

Well, goddamn. What was Soren supposed to do with sweet words like that? His mate was going to make him melt into a puddle like some sort of sentimental...something.

Soren had a feeling his entire reputation for who-gives-a-fuck badassery was about to take a deep dive.

He got out of the car. Dealing with Danny's and Roman's anger would probably be easier than dealing with all this mushy love stuff. Gabe was two steps behind him as they walked through the front door. They didn't have to search the house for anyone. Everyone was in the hall already.

"Fuck," Gabe swore softly.

"Fuck," Soren agreed.

Roman, fangs out, was holding Jay up against the wall by his neck. The little vampire's gray eyes were wide, his face turning an interesting purple. Danny had a hand on Roman's arm, as if in the middle of trying to calm his hotheaded mate.

Roman growled at their entrance but didn't look over, keeping his eyes on the perceived threat—he was clearly in protector mode.

Danny, on the other hand, turned to them, still holding on to Roman's arm and smiling sheepishly. "Oh, you're home! Maybe you can explain, um... Do you know this guy? Roman's feeling a little 'grr' about walking into a stranger here."

Soren sighed, waving a hand airily. "Rome, meet Jay. Jay, the guy currently trying to crush your windpipe is Roman. He lives here. That's Danny, his mate."

Jay did his best to smile, garbling out something that sounded an awful lot like, "Nice to meet you," because of course he did.

Roman finally turned his black eyes to Soren. "You know this one?"

Soren crossed his arms, arching a brow at his overprotective friend. "Duh. I just said that. Try to pay attention if you're going to accost people. He's my friend. He's harmless."

Soren would usually feel a little bad calling another vampire harmless—it would be a blow to any predator's pride—but Jay just nodded as best he could in Roman's tight grip. Roman growled again in warning before loosening his hold with obvious reluctance, allowing the smaller vampire to slide down the wall to his feet.

Jay cleared his throat, rubbing a hand on his neck, his normally soft voice coming out hoarse. "Sorry to surprise you. You have a lovely home."

Danny smiled easily at the little vampire, stepping in between him and Roman. "Thank you. Any friend of Soren's is welcome here."

Such a sweetheart, that one. He and Jay would get along just fine.

Danny looked back to his mate, laughing ruefully. "Well! Glad we cleared—" He paused midsentence. Inhaled deeply. Turned his big brown eyes to Gabe. "You smell...*different.*"

Uh-oh. Gabe smiled nervously at his brother, running a hand through his hair. "Uh. Well. The thing is..."

Danny inhaled again, taking a step toward his brother. "You— You're—"

Roman, unhelpful brute that he was, broke in. "He's a vampire," he said flatly.

It was a rare sight, to see pure rage take over Danny's sweet features. Soren might have enjoyed witnessing it, if that anger weren't 100 percent directed at himself.

"What. The fuck. Did you do. To my *brother*?" Danny ground out, stalking closer.

"Who? Me?" Soren asked innocently, stepping backward, almost bumping into Gabe.

"Danny...," Gabe started. He moved to Soren's side.

"Actually, it was me who turned him," Jay offered up.

Well, Christ. There was Roman holding Jay up by the neck again. This was an absolute clusterfuck. Would it be bad if Soren started laughing? Probably. No one here seemed to have a sense of humor at the moment.

He opened his mouth to explain. "We're fucking."

That...wasn't what he'd intended to come out.

Next to him, Gabe sighed. "Jesus, Soren."

"I don't care what your *dicks* are up to," Danny growled. "Why did your little crony turn my brother?"

And...that was it. The thought of Jay as some sort of wicked "crony" of Soren's was just too much. Soren finally did start laughing.

"Soren..." Roman growled out a warning.

"Mates!" Gabe blurted out to his brother. "We're mates. I'm his mate. We're...together." He reached for Soren's hand, possibly wanting to demonstrate their togetherness, possibly just looking for comfort. "You can chill, Danny," he continued. "I *asked* Jay to turn me."

"*Chill?*" Danny asked, staring at their joined hands in disbelief. "Gabe 'vampires are gross' Kingman, what the fuck happened while I was gone?"

Gabe glanced apologetically at Soren. "I never said vampires are gross."

Danny threw his hands into the air. "You most certainly fucking did!"

Roman, who'd once again released Jay, sighed deeply, clearly done with all of them. "Perhaps we should all sit down for a proper discussion," he suggested. "We have apparently missed much while we were away." He turned soft eyes to Danny. "Perhaps some tea, mon amour."

"You and your fucking tea," Danny grumbled, but he turned and walked toward the kitchen. Roman followed, giving Soren a vicious glare on his way out.

Okay, so maybe "taking care of things while Roman was away" wasn't supposed to include letting strange vampires into the house and allowing Gabe to give away his humanity without his brother's knowledge.

Lesson learned.

The three remaining vampires stood in silence, until Jay cleared his throat once more. "So," he said sincerely, his voice already coming out clearer, "your friends are super nice."

They clustered in the kitchen, a cooled mug of mostly untouched tea in front of each of them. Soren started from the beginning. The *very* beginning. How he'd been turned. His time at the den. His many years running, being caught, running again. His pull to Gabe. Their...courtship.

Skipping over the juicier details of that particular chapter, of course.

It was strange, after so many decades of keeping secrets. Letting it all out. Trusting the people he cared about with his past. His present. His hopeful future.

Gabe held his hand through it all.

"I never knew," Roman said softly, his bright-blue eyes trained on Soren. "I guessed you had...trauma in your past. But I never knew the extent."

"I'm sorry, Rome." It was true. He wished he'd had the chance to place his trust in his friend sooner. To tell him on his own terms, rather than in the aftermath.

Danny cleared his throat. "And, Gabe, you're...um...."

Gabe seemed to know what his brother was trying to say. "I'm happy with my decision," he said, squeezing Soren's hand. "I love Soren. I want to be with him." Warmth bloomed in Soren's chest at Gabe's easy declaration.

Danny smiled wide. "Well that's...that's *awesome*," he said, seemingly genuine. "We're both vampires now. I won't lose you. We could even all live together." His eyes widened. "Ohhh! We'll be our *own* den. A not-shitty one. We'll live and work when we want, and when it's too obvious we're not aging, we'll find somewhere new to call home."

Oh, Danny. He was a fucking treasure, embracing this major change with the same ease and enthusiasm with which he'd accepted the existence of vampires in the first place. Soren could feel Gabe's pleasure at Danny's words, but his mate stayed silent. Soren sensed he was a little overwhelmed by his brother's acceptance.

Danny's smile dropped, a thoughtful frown taking over. "Um, that is...if you want to? Or maybe you two want to go off on your own?" He looked over to Roman for reassurance, clearly no longer sure of himself.

Soren glanced at Gabe, who was looking back at him. Soren squeezed his mate's hand, a wordless message. "We'll stay," Gabe said firmly. "I want to stay. We're a family. Right?"

"Right." Danny nodded sharply, then smiled happily, first at his brother, then at Roman, surreptitiously brushing tears from his eyes that everyone pretended not to notice.

The joy Danny clearly felt at having his brother for an eternity seemed to do wonders to soften Roman's anger at Soren. His friend relaxed for the first time since their return, running a hand along his mate's back.

Gabe coughed. "Um. I'm kind of...kind of hungry?"

Oh. Duh. It was astonishing actually, that Gabe hadn't fed yet, hadn't been driven mindless with the need for blood. But Soren remembered something like this with Danny. It seemed like vampires who turned with a mate bond already forming were a different breed—less ruled by a thirst for blood, more driven by the bond itself. It lent them a...*stability* new vampires usually lacked.

Danny sighed ruefully. "I guess it's time for some more hospital theft."

Danny had started with blood bags when he turned, to ensure he didn't go overboard drinking too much from any human victim in his newbie-vampire zeal. It may have been an unnecessary precaution, but clearly he wasn't willing to take the risk with Gabe either.

Danny looked to Gabe. "We could go to the hospital together? I can help with any compulsion we might need."

Gabe nodded, but his hand tightened around Soren's. His mate was feeling a little nervous to be alone with his brother. Soren understood. Their relationship was a complicated one, both strong and fragile at the same time. Their love for each other was undeniable, but past hurts and misunderstandings left them occasionally ill at ease with each other.

But the two of them had time—endless time, now—to figure it out. Soren squeezed Gabe's hand in reassurance. "Go," he told him. "I'll be waiting here."

He watched his mate leave with his brother.

And then it was Soren, Roman, and Jay. And an awkward silence, broken only by Ferdy sniffing around under the kitchen table. Jay looked down, smiling at the puppy. "Hello, dog," he said. "Would you like me to take you out?"

Jay clearly hadn't learned to talk to pets any more normally in the past week.

Roman glared at him, Jay blanching at the look. "Um...if that's okay with you?" he asked timidly.

Roman eyed him warily, taking in the way Ferdy was gazing up at the little vampire in adoration, tail thumping.

"He's taken him out before," Soren reassured his friend. "Ferdy likes him. Your dog's a bit of a slut, honestly."

Roman turned his glare to Soren. So *touchy*. And okay, yeah, maybe he hadn't fully forgiven Soren; that much was clear.

Jay fetched Ferdy's leash, more than happy to leave the tense atmosphere of the kitchen.

And then there were two.

Soren and Roman sat in silence for a long moment. Soren took a sip of his cold tea, slurping obnoxiously, wondering if he could antagonize Roman out of his silence without saying the first words.

It worked beautifully. "You should have told me," Roman accused, those bright-blue eyes locked unwaveringly on Soren's.

The guy was not one to shy away from eye contact; that was for sure.

"It was *my* past," Soren said mildly. "My decision."

"Did you not trust me to help you?" Roman asked, more sadness than anger in his tone. "I trusted you to help *me*. Many times."

Soren ran a finger along the rim of his mug. "It wasn't like that."

"Explain."

"Rome. What happened to you with Luc was...painful. I know that. I'm not minimizing it. But what happened to me was different. I was treated like—like *property*. For centuries. It messes with your sense of self. To be told you exist at someone else's pleasure. A plaything."

Roman frowned but nodded at him to continue.

"I didn't want you to get hurt helping me. Hendrick had...people. Other vampires who could have killed you. *Would* have killed you.

And I thought it was— I don't know. I thought it was okay. To suffer periodically. If it meant living life the way I wanted. I thought I could wash away the bad with enough pleasure. With enough fun. I didn't think I was worth taking a stand for."

"Ah. Mon ami. No," Roman protested. "You are worth—"

Soren held up a hand. "I know *logically* that was wrong. But it took something...big to wake me up to it."

Roman raised a dark brow. "The brother."

"I know you hold a grudge against him because of your precious Danny..."

"I do not think Gabe is a bad person," Roman protested. "Just...stubborn. Pigheaded, if you will. But he has changed for you. Quite literally."

Soren tried not to look smug. He really did.

Roman smiled sadly at him. "I am sorry I could not help you before. When you needed it."

"Yeah, well." Soren shrugged. "I just don't want you thinking any differently about me. That I'm not a badass."

"But I never thought you were a bad ass." Roman said it like two distinct words.

"Liar! I'm intimidating as hell."

Roman grinned, white teeth flashing. "You are." He raised his mug, his grin dropping. "I do not think less of you. We are more than our pasts, yes?"

Soren raised his own mug, and they toasted with their cold, nasty tea. "To being more than our pasts."

They sipped in unison. "I killed him," Soren found himself saying, an echo of his earlier words to Gabe.

Roman nodded, expression neutral. "You did."

Soren fiddled with his mug. "You spared Luc."

"I did." Roman tilted his head, studying Soren. "Not everyone is redeemable, mon ami. We both know that."

Soren felt something release in his chest. Gabe's acceptance of it was one thing, but Soren's mate was seeing the whole situation through love-colored glasses. Roman's easy understanding went a long way toward assuaging Soren's guilt.

"I am happy for you, you know," Roman said. "You found your person. Even if it is a bit...incestuous?"

Soren glared. "He's not *my* brother."

Roman laughed. He did that a lot more these days, now that he had Danny. Soren refused to be charmed by it. He threw the wrapper from his packet of tea at the other vampire.

Insufferable creature.

But it felt good, having Roman and Danny back. Soren was home. With his friends.

With his *family*.

Twenty-Two

Gabe

Gabe eyed the blood bag in his hands, cool to the touch and almost frosty on the outside from the blood bank's refrigerators. He'd seen an untold number of these bags in his career in medicine—had ordered them for patients time and again—but he'd never in his life expected to be *drinking* from one.

Danny was eyeing him sympathetically from his spot in the driver's seat. "Kind of weird, huh?"

Gabe's brother had fetched three blood bags in total, leaving Gabe to sit in the parking lot while he did it ("What if you get all hangry and bitey?"). He'd caught the blood bank workers at shift change, only needing to compel one person to look the other way while he pilfered their loot.

Now they were pulled into the parking lot of a small park near Danny's house, well away from the streetlights. Gabe sighed, running his fingers along the edges of the bag. "'Weird' is putting it lightly."

"We could go back to the house," Danny offered. "Heat it up. It'll taste better that way."

Gabe shook his head. "No. I, uh, want to get it over with." He also didn't want to hurt Soren's feelings if he ended up gagging over the taste. Drinking from Soren had been one thing. Gabe had been lost to lust and pleasure, to the need to claim his mate.

Drinking blood from some random person felt a little different. Gabe was committed to the whole vampire-for-eternity deal, no doubts about it, but he just needed to...sit with it for a minute. The whole blood-drinking thing.

When a minute had turned into five, he glanced at Danny, his younger brother still waiting patiently. "How do I...?"

He hadn't been making a conscious decision of it before, back in the forest.

Danny looked confused before realizing what it was Gabe was asking. "Ohh. Let your demon out? Just...um, I don't know...relax? It *wants* to come out. You just have to let it."

Relaxing. Cool. Totally Gabe's strong suit.

He took a deep breath before letting it out slowly. He focused on the buzzing sensation that had been building under his skin since their return to Danny's house. It wasn't the gut-wrenching need from when he first turned, when Soren had been missing, but it was still a form of...*craving*. A kind of hunger Gabe had never felt before, bone-deep and distracting as hell.

He could feel the change as it happened, subtle but unmistakable. His vision sharpened, details in the dark car becoming clear as day. His incisors lengthened. Gabe ran his tongue along each one carefully.

He didn't look at his brother. He wasn't ready to see Danny's reaction to Gabe's second face. Instead he tore a hole through the blood-filled pouch, taking a small sip.

A noise came out of him, some sort of weird growl. Danny was right—it probably would have been better warm—but it wasn't the worst thing Gabe had tasted in his life. It fulfilled some deep need. Soothed that itchy craving. Gabe finished the bag in a few greedy gulps. The buzzing under his skin dampened with each swallow, until it was gone, along with the blood.

"You want more?" Danny asked, holding up a second blood bag.

Gabe shook his head. One had been enough. He wanted to go home.

He wanted Soren.

Gabe...*pushed* the vampire back inside. He wasn't sure how he even did it, but it retreated easily enough, satisfied with the blood he'd given it. He could feel its eagerness to return to Soren as well.

"Okay," Danny said easily, placing the bag back into the mini cooler he'd brought. "We'll have it in the fridge just in case. And really, you should be okay feeding regularly, if it's anything like it was for me. Just make sure Soren's with you your first time."

"To stop me from going too far?"

"That and, uh..." Danny blushed, shifting in his seat. "Just in case you get...worked up."

Gabe coughed. "*Oh.* Um, okay." One of the downsides of becoming part of the vampire world was turning out to be all the intimate details he was learning about his brother's sex life.

Danny laughed awkwardly, then cleared his throat, his eyes on the steering wheel, where he was drawing little invisible patterns. "So you and Soren, huh?"

Gabe sighed happily. "Yeah."

"I guess it makes sense," Danny offered up.

Gabe's brows rose. "It does?" He knew it made sense to *him*, but he was surprised Danny saw it that way.

"Mm-hmm." Danny looked up from his invisible drawing. "I've never seen you so easily intimidated by someone. I should have realized it was attraction. I just thought you thought he was...creepy."

Gabe laughed. "Well, I did. Sort of." He ran a hand over his face, trying to fight back his smile. "But I also thought he was so beautiful it *hurt.*"

Danny's dark eyes were searching. "And you're happy? You didn't feel pushed into this?" At Gabe's frown, he rushed on. "I just need to hear it from you, okay? When it's just us. It was a shock. You have to see that."

Gabe nodded slowly. He did see. "I mean, circumstances might have pushed me into it, but I would have done it anyway. Eventually. I want him. I want to be with him."

Danny made a sound of acknowledgment. "You've just been so...hesitant...about vampires is all."

Jesus, Gabe really had been a jerk.

"Well, yeah. I mean, it's weird as hell. My own body doesn't make sense to me anymore." He gave Danny a tentative smile. "There's something special about you, Danny. That you accepted it so easily. But *life* is weird. And scary. And unexpected. I feel like I've had the rug pulled out from under me repeatedly since I was a teen. At least this was my choice. *He* was my choice."

Danny smiled at that. "Well...wow."

"I'm happy with him." Gabe shrugged. "He...soothes me."

"Soothes you?" Danny gave him a questioning look.

Gabe ran a hand through his hair. "Yeah. All that jagged anxiety, that nervousness, that fear... It eases up when I'm with him."

Danny's face fell in an instant. "Anxiety? Gabe, you never told me..."

Of course Gabe hadn't. He'd somehow gone through his whole adult life thinking feelings were meant for shoving under the rug. Not for sharing or processing or any of those other supposedly healthy things.

He tried to find the words to explain it. "I just— I thought...I thought *I* was supposed to be the one looking out for *you*. The older brother. I didn't want to worry you; I wanted to take care of you." He sighed, leaning back against the headrest. "But I fucked that up too."

Danny hummed, nodding. "Yes, you did."

Gabe stared at his brother in disbelief. "Asshole," he accused, voice full of affection.

Danny smiled at him, then gave a little sigh, looking out the car window. "We don't know each other very well, do we? As adults."

"Not in some ways, I guess," Gabe agreed. "That's my fault too."

"Well, we've got time now," Danny said. He laughed then, clear and bright. "We've got so much fucking time."

"Yeah." It was a nice thought. More than nice.

"I want to tell Mom about Soren." Gabe surprised himself with his own words.

"You do?" The hope and happiness in Danny's eyes were like a knife to the gut. Gabe had been so resistant to anything involving their mother for so long.

"Yeah." Gabe nodded. "I know she might not— I know it might not mean anything to her. But it feels...important. To tell her."

"She'd have liked Soren," Danny said earnestly. "I mean...before. He would have made her laugh."

"She might have been confused by it. I never got to tell her I was bi. I don't know why I waited."

Danny shrugged. "She wouldn't have minded. She would have wanted you happy."

Happiness. It had become such a foreign concept over the years.

"Should we go home to our guys?" Danny asked.

Their guys. Gabe grinned at the thought.

Happiness didn't feel like such a foreign concept anymore.

Gabe stood in the doorway of his one-bedroom apartment, watching Soren closely as he took it all in for the first time. He'd been intending to stay in Soren's room again, but Soren had warned him that it could get...uncomfortable.

("You might find there are drawbacks that come with the combination of excellent vampire hearing and sharing a house with your brother and his insatiable husband.")

They'd left Danny's quickly after, promising to come to brunch that weekend. When Gabe had pondered aloud why they were having brunch when now literally none of them needed food to live, Soren had elbowed him in the ribs and told him to hush.

And now Gabe had Soren here. In his home. For the very first time.

Looking around with new eyes at the blank walls and cheap Ikea furniture, Gabe realized it wasn't much of a home at all. There was no character to it. No sense of comfort. No style. No *life*.

"Uh-uh," Soren said from his spot in the living room, crossing his arms. "No way."

Despite the fact that he'd been thinking literally the same thing, Gabe went on the defensive. "It's not *that* bad."

Soren widened his eyes, waving a hand around himself in demonstration. "It's tasteless. A ridiculous bachelor pad." He pointed to the TV area. "You have an Xbox, but you don't have a single *rug*."

Gabe shrugged. Who needed rugs? "My living area wasn't really a priority before. I worked and worked out and tried not to be here more than necessary." He walked into the living room, tugging Soren closer when he reached him. "We'll get a house."

Soren arched a blond brow. "I choose."

Gabe wrapped his arms around his mate, pressing a kiss to his neck. "You choose. I'll get you any house you want." Gabe could *sort of* afford it. He was still paying off the massive student loans he'd accrued in med school, but...well, he'd make it work.

Soren shot him a haughty look. "Oh, Highness. No, no, no. *I'm* the rich one in this relationship. *I'm* the vampire sugar daddy."

Gabe's brow furrowed. "Vampire sugar daddy?"

Soren giggled to himself. "Inside joke. Point is, I pick the house. I *buy* the house. You just sit there and look pretty."

Gabe's frown deepened. "I'm a *doctor*."

Soren shrugged. "Be a doctor and look pretty, then."

Well, Gabe already had that covered, more or less. If Soren wanted to be the big spender in their relationship, Gabe had no qualms about that. He pressed another kiss to Soren's neck, unable to help himself. "Want me to give you a tour?"

Soren gave a theatrical shudder. "No need. I'm nervous to even see your bedroom. It's going to be double-digit thread-count sheets and crusty tissues everywhere."

Gabe sighed. "Once again, I'm a *doctor*, not a frat boy."

Soren seemed unconcerned with the distinction. "Just point me to the bathroom. We both need a shower."

"We bathed in the lake."

Soren gave him a horrified look. "Good lord, frat boy. That doesn't count as *bathing*."

Just when Gabe had finally gotten used to "Highness."

"I refuse to let 'frat boy' be my new nickname," Gabe insisted, not proud of the petulance in his voice.

"Like you have a choice." Soren wiggled out of his hold, tugging on his arm. "Shower now."

They did, giving each other lazy hand jobs under the hot spray, Gabe reveling in the sensation of giving pleasure to his partner and *feeling* that pleasure through the bond, his mate's satisfaction enhancing his own. No wonder their sex in the woods had been so explosive. It was a whole new level of intimacy.

Soren snarked at him for his scratchy, mismatched towels, but there was little bite to it—Gabe's vampire was too blissed out postorgasm. Soren was always softest after sex.

They lay on Gabe's stiff, unyielding sofa afterward, Soren on Gabe's chest, Gabe running his fingers along every reachable inch of Soren's soft skin, just to feel it.

"You never wanted anything homier?" Soren asked drowsily.

"I didn't see the point. It was just me." Gabe tilted his chin down to look at Soren. "What kind of places did you like to stay in, over the years?"

Soren pursed his lips. "Lavish hotel rooms mostly. I didn't stay in any one place long enough to want a proper house. Never had roommates either, until here."

Gabe smirked down at him. "I think you like it. Otherwise, you would have found your own place by now."

"Finding my own place would have meant acknowledging I didn't intend to leave," Soren said seriously.

Gabe was so glad Soren had stayed. He told him so for good measure.

"What do you want now?" Gabe asked. "A mansion?" He could see Soren in some massive old Victorian, waltzing down the stairs in a silk robe and fur overcoat.

Soren looked at him like he was insane. "That would be tacky, in a town like this." He ducked his head into Gabe's chest then, a habit he had when he was about to say something he would consider "mushy." "We could find someplace close to Danny's," he muttered. "That might be nice."

Gabe decided wisely not to tease him about it. "Yeah," he said simply. "That might be."

His own apartment was on the other side of town from his brother's. When he'd moved back to Hyde Park, it hadn't seemed like a priority to be physically close to his brother's place. Now he recognized it as just another one of his subconscious avoidance tactics.

Soren hummed in thought. "A little nicer than Danny's though."

"Hey," Gabe protested. "That's my childhood home."

Soren giggled. "And your childhood home is little. And quaint."

"*You're* little and quaint" was Gabe's super mature response. Take that, vampire.

"I'm little. I'm not *quaint*," Soren said indignantly. "I'm gorgeous and chic and way too good for this town."

Gabe couldn't argue with that. He pressed a kiss to Soren's head. "You are."

Soren settled down at his easy agreement, burrowing even closer into Gabe's body. Gabe almost wanted to tease him about being so snuggly, but he didn't want to give Soren any reason to stop.

Eventually Soren broke the silence. "I never thought I'd let myself belong to anyone again." He said the words softly, almost as if to himself.

Gabe frowned, his fingers pausing their dance along Soren's skin. "You don't *belong* to me."

Soren shrugged one delicate shoulder. "You know what I mean."

Gabe did know. But still...

"If it makes you feel better, tell yourself I belong to *you*. I don't mind that."

He watched in delight as the tips of Soren's ears reddened. "I guess we can both belong to each other," Soren said eventually, mumbling the words into Gabe's chest again.

Gabe could definitely live with that.

He rubbed his nose into Soren's soft hair, breathing him in. And then, because he could, he said, "I love you, brat."

"Ditto."

"Did you just *Ghost* me?"

Soren giggled. "Such a good movie."

Much later in the night, a whispered "I love you too" came from Gabe's chest region.

Yeah, happiness was definitely not a foreign concept anymore.

Epilogue

Soren

Soren leaned against the parked car, face turned to the sun, his eyes shut behind his sunglasses. They were well into autumn, and the days were starting to cool down again—not that anyone in his social circle was bothered by cold weather—but there wasn't a cloud in the sky.

An excess of sunny days was one point he could award Hyde Park.

The Kingman family was another.

He wondered if anyone watching him would be fooled into thinking he was as chill as he looked. Really, what Soren wanted more than anything was to bite at his nails right now, but he was trying to force himself into a relaxed state, to keep any of his worry from seeping across the bond.

It was Gabe's first time using his own compulsion to visit his mother, and he'd told Soren he wanted to be alone for it. It wasn't that Soren didn't believe he could handle it, just...

Soren sighed to himself. He supposed he'd gotten used to being in each other's pockets all the time.

Truly tragic, how dependent he'd become. It was hard to mind it, though, when life was so very sweet. Overall, Soren was surprised how easily Gabe had adjusted to being a vampire these past six months.

His mate was much more adaptable than he gave himself credit for.

Soren opened his eyes at the sound of Gabe's steps as he exited the front of the care home, turning his head to watch him approach. And what a lovely sight to see.

So fucking handsome, his mate.

Gabe had let his curls grow a little longer than before, almost down to his chin, and he was holding them back with one of those soccer-player headbands Soren was getting a real kink for.

Soren grinned at him, the picture of easy unconcern. "Hello, handsome."

Gabe gave a snort as he walked over. "I could feel your worry through the bond, brat. You can't fool me."

Soren shrugged. Super chill—that was him. "All the more reason to tell me. How did it go?" He had a general sense, given he hadn't felt any negative emotions from Gabe's side of the bond, but he still wanted the verbal reassurance his mate was okay.

Gabe's answer was to wrap his arms around Soren the moment he was in reach. He rubbed his chin over the top of Soren's head, breathing him in with deep inhales. Needy mate.

Soren struggled half-heartedly against his grip. "Hey! I did my hair today."

"I like it better messy anyway." Soren could hear the grin in Gabe's voice.

"You just like it when I have sex hair," Soren protested.

Gabe hummed. "I *do* like it when you have sex hair. Can I give you some now?"

Soren kicked his shin. "Focus, you big lug."

Gabe sighed, his breath ruffling Soren's strands. "It went fine. I was her brother again today. She seems to stay regressed to her younger years lately...but I was able to keep her calm and content."

Soren finally relaxed fully into Gabe's hold. He'd known his mate could do it, but he was still relieved to hear it had gone well. Gabe pressed a kiss to the side of his head. "I told her how you were doing as well."

Soren tilted his head up to look at him. "But she doesn't know who I am."

Gabe shrugged. "No, but she doesn't seem to mind the updates anyway."

"You've been telling her I'm...what, exactly?"

"My boyfriend."

"And she thinks you're her brother?" He could feel Gabe nodding against his head. Soren was dumbstruck. "You've been posthumously outing your dead uncle?"

Gabe leaned back to grin down mischievously at him. "She said it wasn't all that surprising. Apparently there was some neighborhood boy she always thought he had a crush on."

Unbelievable.

It struck Soren, not for the first time, the change in his mate. Six months ago, Gabe would never have been able to joke about this. Soren was so goddamn proud of him.

"I told her we were getting married," Gabe added.

Soren arched a brow. "Are we, now? If this is your idea of a proposal, then hell no. I want flowers. Candles. A chocolate fountain."

Gabe smirked at him. "How cliché."

"Is it cliché or is it classic?"

Gabe shook his head, hugging Soren tighter. "This isn't me proposing. I will though."

This idiot. "You're not supposed to tell me *beforehand.*"

"We're mated for all eternity, and me wanting to marry you is supposed to be a surprise? Roman and Danny are married."

Soren scoffed. "You want to marry me to copy your brother?"

Gabe reached a hand up, running a finger along Soren's cheek. "I want to marry you because we belong to each other, and I want everyone to know it. I want a ring on your finger. I want a ring on *my* finger."

Oh. *Well.*

Soren wouldn't mind that part. The one downside of a happy, emotionally healthy Gabe was that he was now ten times more appealing. Ten times more...*golden.* People on the street eyed him like he was a big stack of chocolate-chip pancakes. And he was. But he was *Soren's* big stack of chocolate-chip pancakes.

Everyone else needed to back the fuck off.

Soren still gave a huff for good measure. "I don't want a courthouse wedding like those two did. So absolutely boring."

Gabe shot him a teasing look. "We could get married in the woods. Out in *nature*."

"I'm divorcing you just for saying that."

"We're not married yet."

"Preemptive divorce, then."

Gabe kissed him, the jerk. "Come on, brat. Let's go home. You can sit on my lap while I drive."

They'd found a place close to Danny's after all, a tasteful Victorian Gabe had given Soren free rein to decorate as he chose. Soren—absolute saint that he was—had even offered a room up to Jay, but his friend had chosen to try living on his own for the first time in his multiple centuries of existence, renting out an adorable apartment closer to downtown.

Soren shook his head as he opened the passenger side door. "For the thousandth time, I'm not doing that. I refuse to get pulled over by the cops because you can't handle not being cuddled for five whole minutes."

Gabe's turning into a vampire had done absolutely nothing to curb his touch-prone behavior. If anything, it had gotten worse. Soren supposed it was his cross to bear, being mated to a cuddle slut.

He could think of worse things.

Soren led Gabe to sit at the edge of their bed (their much-improved bed, now that they'd moved into a proper house and Soren had gotten his say in the decorating). "Stay in here. Get naked. Close your eyes."

Gabe smirked at him. "I already know what's coming. I'm the one that asked for it."

"Well then, now you know what it felt like to be told ahead of time that you were going to propose to me. No surprises for either of us today."

Gabe rolled his eyes, only to obediently close them immediately after.

They were celebrating Gabe's "six-month vampiversary" with a gift of his choosing. (When Soren had told his mate in no uncertain terms that there was no such thing, Gabe had shrugged and said there was now and that he already knew what he wanted for his big day. And Soren had given in immediately, lovesick fool that he was.)

Soren undressed quickly in the bathroom, taking a brief moment to admire himself in the mirror once he added the key...accessory. He slipped back out into their bedroom—opulent yet tasteful, *much* improved from the one in Gabe's old, horrid apartment—and struck a pose. "You can open your eyes now, Highness."

Gabe did, immediately flushing as his gaze landed on Soren. He swallowed hard, seemingly at a loss for words, his thick cock swelling in front of Soren's eyes. Soren smirked back at him, hands on his hips, enjoying his mate's undivided attention.

Even if it *was* a silly idea, he knew he looked amazing.

Soren was wearing his brown fur coat. The same one he'd worn when he'd first arrived in Hyde Park what felt like an eternity ago. The one Gabe remembered so clearly—apparently with much more fondness than Soren would have imagined—seeing as how, for his *vampiversary*, Gabe had requested Soren wear the coat.

Requested that he wear *only* the coat.

Soren watched as Gabe's eyes traveled slowly over him, taking in every bare inch. He could feel his mate's desire pulsing through their bond. "Like what you see?" he purred, running a hand over his chest.

Okay, it may have been ridiculous, but Soren was rolling with the whole thing.

Go big or go the fuck home.

Gabe licked his lips, his eyes locked on Soren's bare legs. "So fucking beautiful, baby." He let out a slow breath. "I thought that the first time I saw you. That you were the most beautiful person I'd ever seen. It terrified me, the attraction I felt toward you."

Soren hummed, stalking closer, his own erection bobbing in front of him, pink and flushed. Gabe slipped his hands under the coat to palm Soren's bare ass as soon as he was in reach, before hauling him forward onto his lap, Soren's legs straddling his hips.

"Thank you for my gift," he murmured, leaning in to capture Soren's mouth before Soren had a chance to tell him again how ridiculous he was.

Soren made up for the lost opportunity by plundering his mate's mouth, licking into it with abandon while grinding his ass against Gabe's cock. The thick head teased at his hole, notching against it and then sliding away with his next movement.

Gabe ended the kiss well before Soren was ready, ignoring Soren's whine of protest.

"No, baby. Not like this." He flipped them, dropping Soren onto his back on the bed, Gabe's muscular body hovering over him. "It's my day. I get to be sweet with you."

Soren smirked up at him. He supposed he could handle that. It was easy, with Gabe, to let himself give in to sweetness. Soren's mate had shown him over and over again that he loved all sides of him. Bratty. Wild. Domestic. Sweet. Gabe liked it all and didn't value Soren any less for any of it.

So if he wanted to worship Soren for his special day, then Soren would allow it.

Soren expected Gabe to remove the coat, but Gabe only pushed it open further, exposing more of Soren's body to his heated gaze. He then proceeded to kiss and lick every inch of skin he could find, sucking gently on Soren's nipples, tracing his ribs with his tongue. Every touch sent licks of pleasure dancing up Soren's spine. He was embarrassed to be panting and trembling in less than a minute, his hard cock aching, flushed and leaking over his stomach.

It didn't help that Gabe kept calling him beautiful. Gorgeous. Perfect. Over and over again, murmuring his sweet nonsense words. He lingered over the insides of Soren's thighs, licking and sucking marks that faded in an instant.

"I fucking love your skin here," Gabe murmured. "Like the finest silk."

Soren's only answer was a stuttered moan. This was becoming torture, this slow seduction. He wanted Gabe's mouth on his cock. Or *his* mouth on Gabe's cock. Or Gabe's cock inside him.

Any or all of the above would do.

Instead, Gabe used both hands to push Soren's thighs back, pressing them against his chest. "Hold these for me, brat."

Soren gripped his own thighs and gasped, pleasure swirling in his stomach, as Gabe's warm tongue probed at his hole. His toes curled as Gabe licked a circle around his entrance, bringing a whine out of Soren he couldn't even begin to hold back. "Like that, baby?"

Soren lifted his head to scowl down at him. What a silly question. Gabe already knew he did.

Gabe only smirked at him, leaning back down to lick and suck mercilessly at Soren's entrance, eating him out with ferocious enthusiasm. Soren gave up any pretense of holding his own against his mate's seduction. He threw his head back onto the pillows, panting and whining and writhing like a little hussy. He was barely aware of Gabe grabbing the lube, but soon enough he could feel the blunt head of his mate's cock pushing against his hole.

Perfect.

Soren whimpered as Gabe slid into him in one steady thrust. So fucking *full*. Gabe smiled down at him tenderly—flushed and trembling and no more immune to his own seduction than Soren was—leaning in to press his lips against Soren's.

"Fuck, baby," he moaned against Soren's mouth. "So fucking perfect."

Soren could feel that it was. Gabe's pleasure was dancing against Soren's through the bond, raising Soren's desire to an almost unbearable pitch.

Gabe slid out slowly, pressing back in at a smooth, steady angle that hit Soren's little bundle of nerves perfectly. Soren keened, desperate. He could have come just like this, with Gabe giving him kiss after sweet, lazy kiss, his powerful hips making Soren see stars.

But Gabe clearly had other ideas. He rolled them over in one smooth motion, his cock never leaving Soren's body. He grinned up at Soren from this new position. "Ride me, brat."

Soren was struck still for a moment by the sight of him, golden and glowing with pleasure. So fucking *handsome*.

He placed his hands on Gabe's chest, rolling his hips in the way he knew drove him crazy. Gabe groaned in response, his fingers tightening on Soren's hips, desire flowing through the bond. Soren smirked down at him. He knew how to drive his mate wild.

The fur coat slipped down his shoulders as he bounced on Gabe's cock. Soren let it drop.

Gabe was looking up at him in awe, mouth slack, eyes glazed, low groans leaving his lips with every swirl of Soren's hips.

He looked at Soren like he was royalty. A deity.

It was that look as much as anything that had Soren spiraling over that edge, his release spurting over Gabe's chest. Gabe followed not long after, his hips stuttering up into Soren, his face tight with ecstasy.

He pulled Soren down onto his chest afterward. "Thank you, baby. A perfect present."

Soren hummed his agreement.

They cuddled afterward, Soren sprawled over Gabe's chest, talking about everything and nothing. Soren's crochet projects. Jay's continued atrocious attempts at cooking. Gabe's work.

He was still at the hospital, where he was determined to stay until their merry band's lack of aging became too apparent. Then they would relocate. Perhaps all together. Or perhaps the couples would separate for a while. But Soren had no doubt even if they did, they'd find their way back together again.

Gabe had been right, before. They'd made their own den. And it was one full of love. Loyalty. Friendship. The kind of community Soren had never thought he'd get to have.

Soren looked forward to the day he could travel again. When he could finally show Gabe all the world had to offer. But for now, he was happy where he was, in a way he never thought he would be.

Gabe brushed a hand down Soren's spine. "Penny for your thoughts, brat?"

"I love you." Soren spoke the words into Gabe's chest.

Gabe smiled softly down at him, golden eyes shining. "I love it when you tell me that."

Soren poked his ribs. "Say it back."

"I love you, brat. I'm so happy you came to Hyde Park. So happy you stayed."

So was Soren.

Staying was the best decision he'd ever made.

The End

Author's Note

Thank you so much for reading book two! I hope you enjoyed Gabe and Soren's snarky little love story as much I enjoyed writing it.

These two were such a delightful challenge for me. They both have their defenses way up (Gabe from fear, Soren from past trauma), drawn to each other but both reluctant to let the other in. Given how prickly they can be, I was honestly surprised by how sweet their romance came out. There was so much trust and understanding waiting just under the surface, and I absolutely love the way they softened each other's edges. They each make the other feel so safe and cared for.

My babies!

What's Next?

Book three will be Lucien! Our not-so-little troublemaker. I'm finishing up his story now, and I'm absolutely smitten with both him and the human he falls for. His book will be out November 3rd.

As for book four... I'm thinking Jay might need his own love story as well :)

If you want to stay in the know, you can sign up for my newsletter for updates and news on upcoming releases. And I can always be reached by email if you just want to say howdy. I love, love, love hearing from my readers!

graebryanauthor@gmail.com

If you enjoyed Soren, please consider leaving a review on Amazon or Goodreads. I'd love to know what you thought, and as an indie author, reviews are just so incredibly helpful in getting these stories in front of more readers.

Thank you and happy reading!

About the Author

Grae Bryan has been reading romance since she was far too young to know any better. Her love for love stories spans all genres, and while her current series is of the paranormal variety, she knows she'll be exploring other worlds further down the line.

She lives in Arizona with her husband, who graciously shares space with all the imaginary men in her head. When not writing, she can generally be found reading more than is healthy, walking her monster-dog, or cuddling her demon-cat.

Find her online: graebryan.com
Facebook: @GraeBryanAuthor
Instagram: @authorgraebryan
Sign up for her newsletter: graebryan.com/contact/

Made in the USA
Columbia, SC
15 April 2025

56648829R00136